The Six Boat

A Novel of the Wartime Coast Guard and the Normandy Invasion

By: Stephen J. Tresidder

Upper Lakes Publishing
Alanson, Michigan 49706

BACK COVER: Two U S Coast Guard 83 foot cutters of Rescue Flotilla One speed to the rescue on D-Day, June 6, 1944. The cutters of Rescue Flotilla One saved hundreds of lives in the icy waters of the English Channel off the coast of France. The little cutters maintained unceasing patrols off the invasion coast. Photographer Unknown.

FRONT COVER: Omaha Beach on the morning of June 6, 1944, D-Day for the invasion of France during World War Two. Photo By: Chief Photographer's Mate Robert F. Sargent, USCGR.

DISCLAIMER: These photos are republished from the U S Coast Guard Collection and are in the public domain. Their appearance does not imply or constitute any form of endorsement of this publication by the U S Coast Guard, the U S Department of Homeland Security, or the U S Department of Defense.

Dedication

This novel is dedicated to the men and women of the United States Coast Guard who served bravely in World War Two. Their service should not be forgotten or overlooked through the passing of time. Their sacrifice and accomplishments are a guide to the present. Semper Paratus.

Author's Note

This is a historical novel set during the Second World War. Like the other branches of the United States armed forces, the Coast Guard grew dramatically during the war and took on many roles. It maintained its traditional role of search and rescue from its many stations around the United States. It assumed new duties calling for it to escort merchant ships through waters infested with enemy submarines. Coast Guard crews were required to operate landing craft at invasion beaches in the European and Pacific Theaters of war. The Coast Guard also assembled Rescue Flotilla One. Sixty of its wooden 83 foot long patrol boats were sent to Poole, England to support the Normandy invasion of France on June 6, 1944.

The Normandy Invasion saw the largest seaborne invasion force ever assembled. The Normandy beaches were divided into five sectors. Gold, Juno and Sword Beaches were to be assaulted by British and Canadian forces. Omaha and Utah beaches were to be attacked by American forces. Thousands of ships were involved. Ten of thousands of men were to fight their way ashore. The invasion force was assembled in southern England, and then under cover of night, sailed to France.

This is the story of three people whose destiny brought them together as a result of the creation of Rescue Flotilla One. While the characters and their experiences in this story are all fictional, and not intended to reflect the life or actions of actual persons, the historical background of the mission and the Normandy Invasion is based in fact. The description of the various Coast Guard assets is also factual. For instance, there was a Coast Guard lifeboat station at the north end of the Portage Ship Canal on the Keweenaw Peninsula of Michigan. Also, there was a Secretary Class cutter named the USCGC Campbell that performed convoy duty in the North Atlantic. Finally, the sixty wooden patrol boats that formed Rescue Flotilla One, and their crews, served bravely off the coast of France from June to December of 1944.

While the characters in this story are fictional, there are brief references to President Franklin Roosevelt, British Prime Minister Winston Churchill, Admiral Ernst J. King USN and Admiral Russel Waesche USCG, all of whom played a part in the formation of the

Rescue Flotilla. There was concern at the highest levels that the Normandy Invasion fleet could suffer losses to its ships thus requiring a water borne rescue force. The Coast Guard, in its traditional role, was given the job. The Flotilla rescued 1,438 men with the loss of only two patrol boats.

This story also makes reference to the two Mulberry Harbors that were portable docks and protective break walls developed by the British and towed to France. Their placement and construction began as soon as the invasion beaches were secured on June 6, 1944. One was located off Omaha Beach in the American sector. The other was located off Gold Beach in the British sector. These were designed to rapidly resupply the invasion armies until French ports could be captured and brought on line. The Mulberry off Omaha Beach was destroyed by a severe storm on June 19, 1944. This storm also resulted in the loss of the two Coast Guard patrol boats that were part of the Flotilla. The Mulberry at Gold Beach served for 10 months.

The reader who has read my earlier novel, Vermilion Point, will once again meet Jack Trevenen who is older now and nearing retirement from active duty in the Coast Guard. He is still haunted by the death of his young wife Catherine many years earlier, and has never remarried. Jack will go down the road toward love again once he arrives at Poole Harbor.

Stephen Tresidder

1941

CHAPTER ONE
SAILINGS

Captain McKeil stood on the bridge wing of his ship, the *SS Inland Mariner*, and looked up at the massive wooden timbers that formed the iron ore dock at Superior, Wisconsin. Ore was loaded into the dock from railroad cars shunted on to its top. The railroad cars then dumped the ore into huge bins in its center. The bins were emptied into the ship by chutes located on the side of the dock that were lowered into position allowing the ore to spill out. Even though the *SS Inland Mariner* had three large holds, the deck openings or hatches as they were known, were more numerous and there were several for each hold. This allowed bulk cargo to be distributed throughout each hold.

The loading of the ship was routine and handled by the First Mate, even though Captain McKeil kept a close eye on all the activity. McKeil stepped back into the bridge and met the First Mate looking at an outline of the ship's hull mounted on the bulkhead. It had a series of lights displayed on it reflecting the trim of the ship as the cargo went in. The cargo had to be distributed in such a way as to allow the ship to ride properly. As Great Lakes ships had increased in length they could "hog" or "sag" in bad weather making for a worrisome ride.

McKeil looked at the Mate and growled: "I don't want any wiggle in her, I don't give a damn what the loading manual says. That was written by a bunch of piss ant engineers who have never been to sea. All they are interested in is protecting the owners from liability. We have to get the cargo hauled and know best how these ships ride."

The First Mate was in his late forties and had been sailing on Great Lakes ships for over twenty years. Most of them had been like this one; long and low, steam driven, with deck houses fore and aft.

The long expanse of hatches down the center of the ship could make for a dangerous walk when going fore and aft in rough weather. The *SS Inland Mariner* was an older ship but had been cut in two during layup the previous winter and lengthened by forty feet. She was now almost six hundred feet long. This loading process was no different than dozens of others he had done, but the Captain always seemed to have a comment. It was late October and all the shipping companies were pushing their Captains to get in all the loads possible before the winter ice closed the lakes to navigation.

The First Mate looked away from the light board and said: "Don't worry Captain, I'll get the ore loaded in Number One and Number Three holds just the way you like 'em. No wiggle."

McKeil grunted his assent and added: "Don't be afraid to put a little extra ore in those holds. Load limits be damned. I want a very full ship."

Captain McKeil was in his fifties and looked the part of a ship captain. He was tall and had grey hair and a trimmed grey beard. His face showed the years of sun and wind all sailors experience. Originally from Pennsylvania, he had been a sailor all his life. He had gone sailing on a Great Lakes schooner with his uncle at sixteen. After spending a few years on the lakes he shipped out of Boston and stayed on the salt water. After being shipwrecked off the coast of France he eventually returned to working on Great Lakes ships and had worked his way up to holding a master's license. He was a hard driving captain and liked by the ship owners for staying on schedule and always delivering the cargo. He paid little attention to weather forecasts and put his ships and crews through many a storm. He was known as a "heavy weather sailor".

By nine o'clock on this late October morning the loading was complete and the hatch covers put in place. The *SS Inland Mariner* had the older style telescoping steel hatch covers. They could be slid together to facilitate opening and closing the hatches. To keep water out of the holds in heavy seas each hatch cover had to be securely covered with a tarpaulin which was then battened down. Otherwise, the telescoping design could allow waves sweeping over them to leak water into the hold. Putting the tarps on was a laborious and time consuming job ignored by most ship captains who were used to running on the lakes in good weather. McKeil was of a like mind and didn't order any tarps to be put in place. He wanted nothing to delay their departure.

Several thousand tons of iron ore was in the holds bound for a Lake Erie port. The *SS Inland Mariner* headed out onto Lake Superior. Aside from the crew of thirty there were three women on board; two were guests of the owners and the third was the wife of the steward.

As he headed out into Lake Superior Captain McKeil noted the weather station had storm warning flags flying. The lake looked choppy. But he dismissed the mild concern these raised. He considered the *SS Inland Mariner* capable of weathering whatever blow might come up----if it even did. The ship had ridden well throughout the summer regardless of weather and the increased length simply made them more profitable. He interpreted his duty as requiring him to make the best time possible. A ship sitting tied up at a dock was losing money.

The course McKeil laid out took him north of the Apostle Islands. He would go sixty-nine miles to Devil's Island Light and then would change course for the eleven miles over to Outer Island Light. From there he was slightly less than half way to the Portage Ship Canal which cut through the center of the Keweenaw Peninsula. Following this route he avoided the exposed waters of central Lake Superior. It gave him a chance to duck behind one of the Apostle Islands if the weather got too bad before he reached the refuge of the Portage Ship Canal. He had made this trip many times and knew the route as well as the street where he lived.

With these thoughts in mind Captain McKeil stood on the bridge of the *SS Inland Mariner* as it headed out of the channel and entered the open waters of Lake Superior. He studied the open lake and horizon. The sky was overcast to the east, but darkening and lowering to the west. The lake was grey and showed white caps in all directions. McKeil gave the course to Devil's Island Light to the wheelsman. He felt the ship rise slightly to each wave. She was riding well. With a nod to the Mate on watch he left the bridge and went below for his breakfast.

Senior Chief Boatswain's Mate Jack Trevenen stood in the three bay boat house at the Portage Ship Canal Coast Guard Station. Despite many years of active duty he looked fit and wore his uniform well. His hair had just a touch of grey at the temples. His smooth shaven face and fair complexion made him look younger than his actual years.

Jack studied the 36 foot long motor lifeboat sitting inside the boat house on its cradle. The boat was in perfect condition, something that Jack was strict about as the Officer-in-Charge of this station. The cradle had steel wheels under it that were part of a marine railway system that brought the boat in and out of the water. This was the life boat that responded to open lake assistance calls. There was also a 26 foot long motor surfboat in the boathouse in its cradle. They used this to answer calls in the Portage Ship Canal or Portage Lake. It was also used to tend the pier head lights at the end of the break walls that extended in an inverted "V" from the shore of Lake Superior. The boat house had a third cradle that had an old 26 foot surfboat sitting in it. This boat had no engine, but was designed to be rowed to vessels in distress. It was excess property the District offices in Cleveland had yet to tell Jack what to do with.

This was the third lifesaving station constructed at the north end of the Portage Canal, the first being built in 1885. This "Marquette" style station was put in its present location after the ship canal and its entrance were widened in 1935. Since the United States Lighthouse Service merged into the U.S. Coast Guard in 1939 the station picked up responsibility for the pier head lights at the end of each break wall and a radio beacon. Any other aids to navigation in the canal and the Lower Entrance Light were maintained by a separate station at the south end of the canal.

Even though the canal facilitated east or west crossings of Lake Superior, the canal cut through the peninsula at a diagonal, north to south. Most vessels came in the Lower Entrance and stopped midway at Houghton or Hancock to pick up copper that was being mined in the area. The war in Europe had increased this trade. However, the north end had vessel traffic from east bound ships looking to take a safer route across Lake Superior, especially in bad weather. The station had a larger crew than many as it had responsibility for the pier head lights, radio beacon, and had two boats.

Jack looked up at the gunwale of the 36 foot motor life boat and saw Jimmy Spencer polishing some brass in the well behind the forward cabin. Spenser was young, had blond hair and a round face that smiled easily. Spencer had recently advanced from Seaman to a Third Class Boatswain's Mate. Jack was pleased about this. Spencer was a hard worker, had a good attitude, and doted over the 36 footer as if it were his own.

Jack asked: "Spencer, are you about done up there?"

Spencer looked over the side at Jack and said: "Yes Chief. I'll be down in a moment"

Jack said: "Good. The weather looks like it is turning sour on us. This late in October we could get snow out of this. It certainly has been a cold and wet fall. This front is diving down from Canada and will have some cold air behind it. It is going to run in to some warmer air to the southeast of us and that spells trouble when those two air masses clash. I want everything ready if we have to go out."

Spencer nodded his understanding. He had yet to experience the fury of Lake Superior during a late season assistance case. Pointing in the direction of the old 26 foot surf boat, Spencer asked: "Is it true you were in the U.S. Life Saving Service and rowed one of those on rescues?"

Jack thought before he answered. He didn't like talking about himself. He especially didn't like talking about the season he spent at Vermilion Point Station—two years before the Coast Guard was created. But he was pleased with Spencer's enthusiasm for the service so thought he should know a little history.

Jack looked out the open doors of the boat house and seemed for a moment to float in time. Then he answered: "Yes Spencer, I spent a season at Vermilion Point Station when it was part of the US Life Saving Service. I rowed one like that in good weather and bad. Motorized life boats were just coming into use and our station was small and only had the one surf boat. There were only eight in the crew and we lost some good men one very bad night when the boat capsized coming back from a rescue."

Jack couldn't speak for a moment. He continued staring out the boat house doors. That terrible night and the bone chilling cold of being tossed into the water as the surf boat capsized came flooding back. The water was so cold he couldn't catch his breath and that same feeling came over him now. Anxiety grabbed at him and wanted to pull him down.

Spencer could tell the Chief was lost in his memories and quietly asked: "Chief, are you okay?"

That seemed to break the spell. Jack said: "Yes, I'm okay. In those days the Number One Surfman I worked for claimed a strong back and a stout oar were more reliable than an engine. He was glad we didn't have to depend on a motor to bring us home safely."

Jack put his hand on the side of the 36 footer. He looked directly at Spencer and said: "Don't worry son. This Sterling Petrel engine is reliable and this boat is seaworthy in the worst of conditions. It's frames are close together and it has extra longitudinals. The wood planking in her hull is an inch thick. It will bring us home safely. Now get everything properly stowed and check all the gear. Just in case we have a call."

"Aye, aye Chief. I have the duty tonight so if we have a case it looks like I'll be on the trip!"

Jack slowly walked down the sidewalk toward the main station building. It was a fair distance since the station had over twenty acres of property. The main building had berthing for the single crewmen on the second floor. On the first floor was the radio room, Chief's office, galley and crew's common area. It was a very comfortable station. A far cry from the early Life Saving Service Stations.

Jack paused and looked out over Lake Superior. It felt like the breeze was picking up. The overcast covered the entire sky. It fit his mood. He didn't like being reminded of the season he spent at Vermilion Point. That was the year of the Big Storm that swept all the lakes, sank many ships and drowned hundreds of sailors. He had been in a surf boat in that storm and knew the rage of Lake Superior.

That was the year he had met his wife, Catherine. At the end of Jack's assignment at Vermilion they had returned to his hometown of Hancock, Michigan and married. She had died tragically while attending a Christmas party on the second floor of the Italian Hall in Calumet. When someone falsely yelled "Fire" there was a mad rush to get down the staircase, and many, including her, had been crushed. Catherine was pregnant at the time. Jack would not let himself remember finding Catherine's crushed and distended body that night. It was too painful.

That all happened twenty-eight years ago, in 1913. Jack had never remarried. He never even had another serious relationship with a woman, even though many women found him handsome. He carried his years well. The events of 1913 had robbed Jack of his sense of expectation--something most men share in their youth. The idea there is much to look forward to, live for, or share seemed to have left Jack.

After spending two years with his father in Hancock, and working at the Quincy Mine, he joined the newly formed United States Coast Guard. It had been created by merging the U.S. Revenue Cutter Service with the U.S. Life Saving Service. This offered Jack the chance to go to sea on the cutters that had come over with the Revenue Cutter Service. He was not anxious to go back to a life boat station. He served on various small ships doing law enforcement and rescue work in the near shore waters off the southeastern United States. Some of the Coast Guard's larger ships manned ocean stations and did ice patrol work in northern waters, but Jack was never assigned to one of them. The Coast Guard supported the U.S. Navy in World War One but all that passed Jack by. His ship did coastal duties in the Gulf of Mexico.

The service was glad to have Jack. It liked prior service men who had seamanship skills. Jack was a good sailor and rose through the ranks. Eventually his background got him assigned to life boat stations. His first was on the Outer Banks of North Carolina and later ones had been on the Great Lakes. This was the second station he had been in charge of and it would be his last. Jack was almost fifty years old and was counting the weeks to his retirement in late December.

Jack turned his gaze away from Lake Superior, shook off the chill of the October weather and continued on his way to the main station building. The lake was calm inside the break walls but looked choppy beyond. A fish tug was coming in through the opening in the break walls and heading for its dock further down the canal. Jack wanted to check the station's weather instruments and see who had the duty tonight. If necessary, Jack would help crew the motor lifeboat. He wouldn't put his men in danger unless he was there with them.

Diana Winter sat nervously at a small table in the tea room of the main railway station in Birmingham, England. It was busy and seats were limited. She was concerned a stranger might ask to sit with her and disrupt her planned meeting. Her journey had been long and she was anxious for it to end.

Diana left Germany three weeks ago, crossed Occupied France, crossed Spain and entered Portugal. Until she entered Portugal she had been traveling under her real name and on her German passport. Upon entry to Portugal she went directly to the German Embassy in Lisbon. There staff provided her with a British passport and a new name, Diana Winter. The Embassy also provided her with other necessary travel documents. From Portugal she traveled by ship to Belfast, Ireland. She then took a ferry from Belfast to Heysham on the coast of England. Diana had then boarded a train to Liverpool and stayed two nights in a hotel. On the second day she had a telephone call directing her to take a train to Birmingham to meet with her contact in this tearoom. All this was done under the explicit direction of German Intelligence.

A man suddenly walked up to her table and extending his hand said: "Diana, how good to see you again!"

Unsure of what to do Diana stood and extended her hand in return. The man looked to be in his forties, was of average height, had a trimmed moustache, and rimless spectacles. He wore a tweed overcoat and narrow brimmed hat. He carried a small leather case tucked under his arm. He looked a perfect Englishman.

Diana struggled to remember her code words. Then they came clearly: "How is cousin Anna?"

The man replied: "I'm sorry to say she is under the weather."

Their identities now assured to each other he studied her. She was in her thirties but had a beautiful complexion. Her raven colored hair was shoulder length but held up in a twist at the back of her head. She had dark brown eyes and high cheek bones. Her slender figure was accented by her shapely breasts. She was a strikingly attractive woman. Perhaps too attractive for this job.

Conscious of the close surroundings and other customers in the tea room the man said: "Shall we go out on the platform? It is a nice

October day and we can get away from the cigarette smoke and crush of other customers."

Diana replied: "Of course."

Once outside they strolled down the platform and found a bench off to themselves. Diana started the conversation saying: "What is your name?"

He answered: "That is not important. I'm here to instruct you on the next leg of your journey. You are to take a series of trains to Poole on the English Channel. Once in Poole you will take a room and find employment. You need to develop information about shipping, coastal defenses, and troop movements. Poole is an important and busy seaport."

Diana was flustered. She had understood she was to be given assistance to gain employment at one of the war material manufacturers in Manchester or Birmingham. She wasn't sure what she should say to this unnamed stranger.

She started by saying: "This is a change from what I understood I would be doing. I thought the cross-channel invasion of England was postponed indefinitely last year. The focus is now on defeating Germany's true enemies, the Communists in Russia."

He quickly responded: "Such issues are not my concern. I am here to simply get you on your way. I don't know who makes these decisions What the High Command does with what you report I do not know."

Diana didn't know what to say. She had never been sent on a mission to collect intelligence in an enemy country. She felt she had to trust this man. He spoke perfect English, but so did she. She should not be suspicious of that. While born in Germany, Diana moved to England at a very young age with her father. Her mother's sudden death had prompted the move. Her father was a mathematics professor and she grew up in England while he taught at various schools. They returned to Germany in the late 1930's as her father believed in the rise of National Socialism and wanted to support the rebirth of Germany.

Diana looked at him intently and said: "I will do as you direct. Do I report to you in the future?"

He smiled. "No, you will be given a new contact in Bournemouth. When I get up to leave you should remain seated. I will leave my

9

case on the bench next to you. After a few minutes pick it up and take it with you. It contains some additional funds and railway tickets. When you arrive in Poole you are to telephone your contact. Use the code words we have used. The telephone number is 013 2562 35. Now repeat the number back to me"

Diana nodded her understanding and said: "013 2562 35."

The man said: "Good." Then he leaned closer to her and lowered his voice: "I am curious though. Why do you do this? Is there no man who would keep you in Germany?"

Diana gave him a tight-lipped look with steel in her eyes: "My husband died in 1940 over southern England when his bomber was shot down by a flight of Spitfires."

With that, the man rose and said: "I will give cousin Anna your best. I'm sure your good wishes will cheer her." He then turned and walked briskly down the platform disappearing among the other passengers.

CHAPTER TWO
ASSISTANCE

Jack Trevenen sat in his arm chair trying to read a book in the glow of an oil lamp while the storm beat against the walls of his house. The storm had knocked out the electricity, but the station had a diesel generator to keep it powered. Jack turned his lights off to conserve power as he wanted to keep the radio beacon and radios working. Besides, the oil lamp reminded Jack of his youth and was comforting. Jack was living in a two- story two family frame residence. It was designed for the Officer-in-Charge to live on one side, and the senior petty officer who served as second in command, to live on the other. It was a substantial building and it had survived many storms. It was being tested tonight as the wind moaned around it. Jack didn't really need all the living space as he had no family. First Class Boatswain Mate Blackmore who lived on the other side was married and had two young children.

Jack just couldn't concentrate on his book tonight. The storm had intensified throughout the evening and Jack hoped they would not get an assistance call. This late in the season there were no recreational boats out and the fishing boats would have seen this coming in the afternoon and run for shore. The night should be uneventful.

No, what was preoccupying Jack was his coming retirement and discharge from active duty. He wondered what he would do with himself? He had some savings, and would get a retirement check from the government. It wouldn't be enough to live well on, especially if he lived into his seventies. Jack had to have meaningful work and what he would do, and where he would do it, was unclear and weighing on him.

This last assignment at Station Portage had essentially sent him home. The Coast Guard had a way of doing that with final duty stations. Jack was only a few miles from Hancock where he was raised and went to high school. When he first got the orders for Station Portage he was not happy. The Keweenaw did not hold good memories for him. He had been somewhat estranged from his father during much of the time he was in the service. His cutter was on patrol in the Gulf of Mexico when his father died and he could not attend the burial service in Hancock. He later made arrangements for a headstone while on leave. His wife had died in Calumet, but he had buried her at Vermilion on the shore of Lake Superior where they had met and fallen in love. He couldn't tend her grave from the Keweenaw as Vermilion was almost two hundred miles to the east.

When he retired from the service Jack didn't want to go work in the copper mines in the area. All he could think to do was go to sea on a merchant ship either on the lakes or the oceans. Having been to sea and lived on a ship, the shipboard routine and isolation seemed like a very lonely existence. Jack realized he had lived more than half his life, maybe much more than half. Death was definable for him. While he didn't fear it, he felt he owed himself some contentment, some pleasure before he passed. Jack sighed out loud. He had to stop thinking about it. It just made him irritable and sometimes that showed in his dealings with the crew.

Suddenly, there was a loud knock on the front door that startled Jack and ended his thoughts about life after retirement. Jack quickly got up and crossed the room. He opened the door to Spencer who stepped inside along with a rush of snow and cold wind. Jack noted the wet snow was more intense than when he last was out. The back and shoulders of Spencer's peacoat were covered with snow from his trip to the residence from the main station building.

Spencer pulled off his wool watch cap. He was breathless since he had run most of the way. He spoke up between breaths: "Chief, Blackmore wants you over at the radio room right away. Sparks is working a merchant ship west of here that is struggling in the weather and high seas. Sounds like it might be an assistance case for us. The ship is quite a way out."

Jack could tell Spencer was anxious about what the potential assistance case might require of them. Jack looked at him calmly and replied: "Don't worry son. Everything will be fine. Tell Blackmore I'm on my way."

Spencer turned, pulled on his watch cap, and said: "Right away, Chief!" With a blast of snow and cold air he went back out into the stormy night.

As Jack put on his foul weather gear and oilskins his stomach also churned a little from anxiety. He muttered to himself: "Son of a bitch. Tonight of all nights. So much for getting through the shipping season without an incident."

As Jack turned down the oil lamp, opened the door and pushed out into the storm he thought: "We may still get lucky. We haven't heard an SOS so I may still get a good night's sleep."

Jack stood in the center of the main station building shaking the melting snow off his oil skins. The wind was fierce and had to be a steady 40 or 45 knots with higher gusts. Every now and then a window pane rattled from the wind. First Class Boatswain Mate John Blackmore walked out of the communications room and grinned at Jack saying: "We might have some business tonight, Chief."

Jack looked at Blackmore. He was younger than Jack but had flecks of grey in his black hair and full moustache. He was a good boat handler and tonight he was in charge of the watch. Jack liked him and enjoyed his young children. Blackmore had been at Station Portage for longer than Jack and was close to making Chief, something Jack endorsed. He would be a good candidate for a station of his own.

Jack smiled back at him and asked: "What have we got?"

Blackmore said: "Come in the radio room and Mulvaney can tell you firsthand about the radio traffic."

Jack and Blackmore walked into the small room that had the radios and telephone. It also had other weather instruments and instruments related to the radio beacon. A large chart of the western end of Lake Superior, including the Keweenaw Peninsula, hung on the wall. All the log books for the station were kept here. There was a small desk in front of the radio equipment where Radioman Third Class Sam Mulvaney sat. Mulvaney was young and a very talented man when it came to the communications equipment. He looked like the young Irishman he was with his red hair.

Mulvaney had a headset on and his face reflected his concentration. Jack put his hand on Mulvaney's shoulder and asked: "Who is in trouble?"

Mulvaney, slightly startled, turned, took off his head set and said: "It's a freighter called the *SS Inland Mariner*. She is about six hundred feet long based on what I can tell from our directory of Great Lakes ships. They loaded iron ore in Superior early this morning and are heading for us."

Jack turned and looked at the chart on the wall. Doing some rough calculations in his head Jack traced a line with his finger from Superior, north of the Apostle Islands. Without turning Jack asked: "Has she given you a recent position?"

"She is a couple of hours east of Outer Island Light. It sounds like they are in some heavy seas with higher wind gusts than we have."

Jack turned and said to no one in particular: "Why doesn't she turn and take shelter behind one of the Apostle Islands?"

Blackmore spoke up: "If the Inland Mariner is in eighteen or twenty foot seas with wind gusts 55 to 60 knots it may not be safe to turn around and head for shelter. Like most of these lake ships she is probably under powered, particularly fully loaded."

Jack nodded his agreement. He turned and asked Mulvaney: "What does she want from us?"

Mulvaney said: "She claims to be holding her own but wanted to make sure our pierhead lights and radio beacon were on."

Jack looked at Blackmore and asked: "They are, aren't they?"

Blackmore nodded yes and added: "The waves are breaking over the north break wall fairly regularly. With the pierhead lights on acetylene they should be alright—as long as the waves don't get water in the light fixtures themselves. The radio beacon is on the generator and that is running fine. The Inland Mariner should be able to pick that up and ride it right in."

Mulvaney added: "Chief, based on the radio calls I don't think they know exactly where they are due to bad weather. But the Inland Mariner is more than halfway here so she just has to ride out the weather and will probably show up here tomorrow morning."

Jack said: "Is the telephone working? I want to go into my office and call Operations in the District offices and let them know what is up. They have that lighthouse tender over in Duluth they could send out if the Inland Mariner sends out a call for assistance. I'm not sure we could do much with the 36 footer in this weather."

Mulvaney shook his head: "The phone went down with the electricity. With all this wet snow there are probably trees down on the lines."

Jack decided there was nothing else to do but wait and see what developed. He found a comfortable chair in the crew's common area, lit his pipe and sat down to await the nights events. A few of the crew who were not on duty and sleeping upstairs had been awakened by the wind. They came down to see what was going on but soon returned to bed.

Captain McKeil stood in the pilothouse of the *SS Inland Mariner* bracing himself against the chart table to keep his balance against the huge seas battering his ship. He had not been to bed all night and now it was 4am. It would be daylight in three hours and he badly wanted to see the light and hopefully an easing in the storm conditions.

After the departure from Superior Wisconsin, the weather deteriorated rapidly. McKeil kept remembering the storm flags flying straight out in the wind as he left Superior's harbor. He mused to himself that for once the weather forecasters had gotten it right. The barometer dropped rapidly and the northeast wind backed northwest and steadily increased. While the western end of Lake Superior is more sheltered than the open stretches of lake to the east, the seas still have many miles over which to build. By late afternoon there were sixteen to eighteen foot waves. Wind speeds exceeded 50 knots. Snow squalls obscured the visibility. McKeil was worried about being driven aground in the Apostle Islands so he had made his course more northerly to give the ship more sea room. But as the winds backed northwest and then west north west, it gave the ship a heavy following sea and it did not handle well. The wind and waves increased. Every so often a huge sea would bear down on the ship and sweep the entire length of the deck.

By late evening they had been able to contact the Coast Guard Station at the Portage Ship Canal and was assured its radio beacon and pier head lights were working. That gave McKeil some comfort, but he was a long way from the Portage Ship Canal and those aids to navigation were not yet able to help. The snow had been wet and heavy and he had not been able to get a fix on Devil's Island Light or Outer Island Light. He was dead reckoning and thought he was east of the Apostle Islands and more than halfway to the Portage Canal. At darkness he and the Chief Engineer agreed to check down the speed to help with steerageway. They also had started the bilge pumps. Hours would be added to what was normally a simple run.

The wind shrieked and moaned around the pilothouse. The ship creaked and groaned as the steel hull worked against the waves. McKeil looked aft through the rear windows in the pilot house. He looked down the long expanse of spar deck. In gaps in the snow the lights on the after deckhouse shown bright but the deck lights running down each side of the spar deck were damaged and many were not showing. The waves now had to be twenty feet or more. There was solid water over the deck quite regularly as the waves rolled over the ship. The water struck the back of the forward deck house and briefly piled up before spilling into the lake. When this occurred it felt like a giant hand was pushing the forward part of the ship downward. The ship was handling poorly and seemed to have a slight list.

The First Mate was off watch in his cabin. He was trying to sleep despite the rolling of the ship and the sound of the waves slamming against it. He could tell the storm had gotten worse.

McKeil decided he wanted to sound the ship. McKeil picked up the bridge phone and rang the First Mate's cabin. When he heard the receiver being picked up McKeil shouted over the storm: "Get up here. I want you to inspect the ship."

As the First Mate stepped out into the passageway the motion of the ship caused him to have to brace himself carefully as he walked. He could hear the waves booming against the hull. Despite the difficulty in moving about and climbing the ladders from his cabin to the pilot house, he quickly appeared before McKeil. It was the first time they had talked since late afternoon. At that time the First Mate had tried to convince McKeil to seek shelter in the Apostle Islands.

McKeil was angry and would have none of it. He did not want to fall behind schedule.

McKeil looked at the First Mate. Raising his voice over the sound of the wind he said: "I want you to get into Number One hold and see if you can see any damage. Our rails are down in places and some of the deck lights are out. I want to know where we are taking on water. The ship is sluggish." Pointing to the inclinometer on the pilot house wall McKeil said: "The past couple of hours we picked up a list to port. Sound the bilges forward if you can. I don't think you need to get into Number Two or Three holds, but use your own judgment."

The First Mate nodded his assent. He was still mesmerized by the weather outside the pilot house. In the exterior lights of the pilot house he could see the swirling snow, which at times even obscured the steering pole on the bow of the ship. When there was a gap in the snow he could see the huge black waves with foaming tops in the reflection of the lights. The wave tops were being torn away by the wind. That combined with the laboring movement of the ship was ominous to him. Much more so than when he was trying to sleep in his cabin. Suddenly, he realized the importance of his task and quickly went below.

McKeil waited impatiently for the First Mate to return. It seemed like it took forever. Finally, he came back. His clothes were wet and covered in ore dust. McKeil was testy and said: "What took you so long!"

The First Mate ignored the attitude and reported: "It is not good Captain. The bilges are flooded. With a full cargo on board the intake screens for the pumps are probably partially blocked by the ore and don't get good suction. We have two vents down and are taking some water through them. But there are more serious problems. With no tarps on the hatch covers, and the waves sweeping the deck, the telescoping hatch covers are leaking. The narrow gap between the leaves allows water into the holds every time we take a big sea on deck."

McKeil cursed: "God dammit why weren't those hatch covers tarped."

The First Mate was not going to accept blame. Standing toe to toe with a determined look he said firmly: "Captain, you didn't want our departure delayed by the extra work. It takes time and lots of effort to tarp all those hatches. You were willing to chance October weather."

McKeil stared back at him and then turned away. He thought there is nothing for it but to ride it out and wait for daylight.

The First Mate kept going and said: "Captain, I don't think the waves are getting bigger. I think we are getting lower in the water. I got on top of the cargo in Number One and could see the port side hull plates—the ones that showed above the cargo. At the join, where the 40 feet of additional hull was added, I saw popped rivets."

The First Mate let this news sink in. McKeil said nothing but turned to look aft through the pilot house windows. The wheelsman and the Third Mate on watch looked at each other solemnly.

McKeil shook his head as if to make the news go away. Then he said to all in hearing: "We still have steerageway. It will be daylight in a couple of hours. I've been through worse than this. Just keep your wits about you." Looking at the First Mate McKeil said: "Go below. I want you to take the watch just after daybreak."

The First Mate said "Aye, aye Captain" and started his trip back down to his cabin.

Jack Trevenen woke up with a start. For a moment he didn't know where he was. Then he realized he had fallen asleep in a chair in the main station building while awaiting developments with the *SS Inland Mariner*. Someone had thrown a blanket over him. Jack tossed it aside, stood up, stretched and looked at the clock. It was about 5:30 am. Mulvaney was sitting in the radio room with his feet up reading a book. No one else was to be seen. Jack stuck his head in the radio room and said: "Where is Blackmore?"

Mulvaney looked up: "He is in the galley making some coffee."

Jack asked: "Did you hear anything from the Inland Mariner?"

Mulvaney answered: "Nothing, Chief."

Blackmore walked up to Jack and handed him a cup of coffee. Then he said: "Chief, where do you think the Inland Mariner should be by now?"

Jack walked over to the chart on the wall and looked at the distance between the Apostle Islands and their station at the entrance to the Portage Canal. Doing some rough figuring Jack said: "In good weather it should be here by now. They would be slowed some by the storm. I think they should show up a couple of hours after daybreak."

This conversation caused Jack to look out at the storm and check the barometer. In the darkness Jack could see the storm was letting up. Then he asked: "Are we off the generator?"

Blackmore said: "We are. Lights and telephone came on an hour ago. Radio beacon and pier head lights all working."

Jack nodded his approval. Then he said to Mulvaney: "Get on the radio to the Inland Mariner. Find out their status and position. They should be picking up our radio beacon by now. I'm going to change and shave and I'll be right back"

Mulvaney said: "Aye, aye Chief" and turned to his set.

When Jack came back a short time later Mulvaney was looking troubled. Jack said: "Well, what did the Inland Mariner report?"

Mulvaney looked at his notes from the transmissions, then said: "They claim they have a slight list and are taking on water. Both pumps are running, but they don't want assistance at this time. They have our radio beacon and think they are about 18 miles out, maybe less. They claim the waves are about 12 to 14 feet, but the wind is dropping to 35 to 45 knots. The snow has let up and they are down to occasional squalls. They are checked down and won't get here before mid-morning."

Jack could see why his radioman was worried. The *SS Inland Mariner* might be in worse shape than the Captain wanted to report. Jack said to Blackmore: "You are on duty until 8 am. We are going to need to get underway. I'd rather you and I take the 36 footer out even if you work a long day."

Blackmore nodded his agreement.

Jack continued: "Get Spencer up and the duty engineman. Get the boat out of the boat house and warm the engine up. I don't want to take any chances. We could meet her and follow her in. I want to make sure it has enough steerageway to clear the entrance between the break walls in this weather. This station was put here, in part, because ships had trouble with this entrance."

Daylight on the *SS Inland Mariner* showed a leaden sky and dark grey angry waves at least ten to twelve feet high. The wave tops were breaking and the spray was occasionally being blown off. Streaks of foam snaked down the wave backs. The snow was reduced to an occasional squall and the wind was steady from the northwest at 30 with higher gusts. There was some mild icing on the deckhouse. Captain McKeil was glad of the daylight. It was easier to assess the ship and the weather conditions in the light.

The electric cable bringing power forward to the pilot house from the stern was still intact, but he had lost his telephone line to the stern. The ship was lower in the water but it still had freeboard. The waves no longer regularly swept the deck, only an occasional big sea. The ship was sluggish responding to the helm. The wind still whined in the rigging above the pilot house. But they had a good signal from Station Portage's radio beacon and McKeil was sure it would lead them the last miles to the entrance to the Portage Canal. They expected to be able to see the north pierhead light soon.

The First Mate appeared to take over the watch. McKeil had not slept all night and had remained in the pilot house the entire time. He was exhausted. He looked at the First Mate and said: "I want you to go aft and tell the Chief Engineer I want everyone not on watch to be in their cabin in their life jackets. We lost our phone connection and I want to make sure we are ready in case the old Mariner can't make it. You check and make sure they are in their life jackets and cabins too. I secured the spar deck hours ago but if you time it carefully you can get aft without getting too wet."

The First Mate asked: "Captain, have you radioed anyone for assistance?"

McKeil was tired and irritated by the question. He growled: "What the hell is the matter? Don't you think I can bring her in safely? I spoke to the goddamn Coast Guard and told them we should be there by mid-morning. We got this far, we can get the last few miles. The worrisome Coast Guard just called us and said it's sending the life boat out to meet us. If I can't make the entrance they want me to try to beach the ship south of the entrance. Like hell I will. I'll sail this bastard right into the canal."

The First Mate said nothing and turned to leave to head aft. McKeil watched him dance his way down the deck avoiding the water thrown up by the waves. He disappeared safely into the afterdeck house. He was back in a few minutes. He reported: "Captain, the Chief Engineer has everything under control back there. He is a good sailor and knew what to do hours ago. There is no hot galley and everyone is hungry, but other than that, alright. But the ship is in trouble. You can sense it more on deck and back aft. It is twisting in these seas and I'll bet there are more rivets gone at that join on the port side. Some of the hatch covers really took a beating and some of the leaves are bent upwards."

The First Mate paused. Then he asked: "When will the lifeboat get here?"

McKeil said harshly: "Will you stop worrying about the god damn lifeboat and this ship sinking. The Coasties won't be here for a couple of hours."

The First Mate glumly nodded and turned to relieve the Third Mate who had the watch. He started to tell the wheelsman he had a man coming forward to relieve him when there was a sickening "bang" caused by steel tearing. McKeil and the First Mate instinctively turned toward the sound and looked out the after windows of the pilothouse. There was a crack in the deck between Hatches 4 and 5 and running from the port side three quarters of the way across the width of the ship. The deck forward of that seemed to be lowering and separating.

McKeil turned to order the engines stopped but the Third Mate was already on the Chadburn ringing down "All Stop". The First Mate got to the radio and started rapidly sending: "May Day, May Day" followed by their approximate position. McKeil activated the general alarm to alert the entire ship, but men were already coming out of the afterdeck house going up to the boat deck to uncover the life boats.

What McKeil saw next seemed to be in slow motion. The crack in the deck opened up and the forward part of the ship began to swing to starboard. There was a roar as the cargo spilled out of the ever increasing gap in the side of the ship. The spar deck on the forward part of the ship was awash and the bow began to tilt downward. Even though the engines had stopped there was still way on and the stern section that was still moving forward pushed the forward part of the ship even more to starboard. For a moment it looked like the ship was folded in half with the bow section pointing aft and laying alongside the stern section. Then the two halves slowly separated with the powerful sound of steel plate breaking and being torn apart.

McKeil was frozen in place. Neither could he speak. The Third Mate had grabbed life jackets from the rack overhead and threw one at him yelling: "Captain we have to abandon ship."

The wheelsman and First Mate had quickly pulled on lifejackets, crossed the slanting deck, and were through the pilothouse door on the high side of the ship. They stopped on the wing outside the door and looked down at the deck behind the forward deck house. There was a raft stowed there and two sailors and the two women passengers were struggling to free it. McKeil appeared next to the First Mate and looked down and saw the water rise and wash the helpless individuals and raft away. Suddenly, the forward part of the ship lurched sideways and began to roll over. The First Mate yelled "Jump Captain and swim for it, she is going over"

Right before McKeil jumped he looked over and saw the stern was still upright. In his confused state he mumbled: "She is going to steam off and leave us." Then he felt himself immersed in ice cold water and he could not catch his breath.

After pulling on long underwear and wool clothing Jack Trevenen had grabbed his foul weather gear and headed back to the main station building to do a little calculating of their intended speed, course and distances. Then he went to the boat house at the double quick. When he got there the 36 foot motor life boat had been launched and the engine was warming up while idling smoothly. Blackmore was in the after cockpit at the controls. The duty Engineman Vic Patterson was in the engine compartment and Jimmy Spencer stood in the forward cockpit ready to handle the lines when they left the dock.

The 36 foot motor life boat had an enclosed engine compartment amidships. In front of it was a cockpit to allow survivors in the water to be pulled aboard. Forward of that was a long low cabin with seats inside to get survivors in out of the weather. At the very bow of the boat was what was called the "glory hole". This was a hatch that opened in the passenger cabin roof and allowed a crew member to stand up in the opening and assist with rescue efforts.

The after cockpit was behind the engine compartment and this was where the steering station and engine controls were located. It had a removable canvas cover to protect the coxswain from the weather. The engine compartment was entered from here. Finally, there was another smaller cabin behind the after cockpit that stored line, tools, throwing devices and first aid supplies. The boat was self-righting and self-bailing and in good weather could do 8.5 knots. The boat was rated to rescue up to 30 survivors.

Jack stepped from the dock into the after cockpit. Blackmore looked at him and said: "Chief, you don't have to make this run. Especially with you being so close to retirement. I'm fully qualified to take her out, even in this weather."

Jack grinned and said: "I know you are. I trust you. The Coast Guard owes me one more good ride before I'm done and I think this is it. You'll take the controls and serve as coxswain as though I wasn't here."

Blackmore smiled and said: "Aye, aye Chief." Then he looked at Spencer and said: "Get those lines off Jimmy and let's get underway."

Jack opened the door to the engine compartment and looked at Engineman Patterson: "Vic, everything look good in there?"

Patterson answered: "Fine, Chief. It's ready for a romp."

Jack smiled: "It will get one this morning. If the motion of the boat gets too much for you down there come on up with us."

Patterson said: "Thanks, but I should be alright."

Blackmore maneuvered the boat out of the slip and they headed out the canal. In short order they were between the break walls and headed for the entrance. It was a gloomy overcast morning. There was a good breeze out of the northwest that Jack estimated to be about 25 to 30 knots. It would be blowing harder once they were out in the open lake. Jack was glad it had stopped snowing. The waves looked to be well over 8 feet and every so often one would break against the break wall throwing a blast of white water and spray high up into the air. As they left the calm waters between the break walls and passed between the pierhead lights the boat rose to the waves and pushed out into the lake.

Under the canvas cover in the after cockpit Blackmore and Jack were quite dry and sheltered from the wind. Jack spoke loudly over the sound of the engine, wind and waves: "I did a little estimating before we left the station. I don't think we are going to find the Inland Mariner if we just steer a straight line from our entrance to the last position she gave us. That position is an hour and a half old. In last night's weather they couldn't have gotten a fix on anything or seen the lighthouses in the Apostles. They were probably just dead reckoning and who knows what they allowed for set and drift. Plus, she is still steaming to the east."

Jack pulled a small note book out of his pocket where he had written down some navigational information. He showed a page with their initial course on it to Blackmore. Then he said: "I think the Inland Mariner must be to the south and east of the last position they gave so let's steer this course. I don't want to miss them. In waves this big as we will not be able to see much in any direction when we are down in the wave trough."

Blackmore nodded his agreement. Then he asked: "How long do you think it will take us to get out there?"

Jack said: "We can quarter the waves on our starboard bow and probably get 6 or 7 knots out of her without doing harm to the boat—or ourselves. It shouldn't take more than an hour and a half to two hours."

Just as Jack said this their life boat drove through the crest of a breaking 10 foot tall wave and slid down its back, burying its bow in the wave trough. The boat lifted to meet the next oncoming wave throwing water into the forward cockpit, over the top of the engine compartment and against the windshield in front of Jack and Blackmore. Blackmore held the steering wheel tightly and the boat maintained course. The men looked at each other knowingly. This was how it was going to be for the next few hours.

But once everyone was reminded that the boat was within its capabilities the crew settled down for the trip. Jack decided to get warm in the engine compartment and Spencer stayed in the forward cabin. The cook had sent them sandwiches and a couple of thermoses of hot coffee that were welcomed and shared.

Blackmore had the wheel and Jack was in the engine compartment when Blackmore heard the radio crackle. The transmission was garbled. Blackmore pounded on the engine compartment to get Jack's attention. Jack popped out and said: "What's up?"

Blackmore said: "I just heard a radio transmission. I couldn't make out who sent it but I'm sure I heard a mayday. Then it went silent."

Jack replied: "Let me call the station and see if Mulvaney heard anything."

Just as Jack said that the radio came to life again. This time with: "Coast Guard 36495 this is Station Portage. Over"

Jack immediately answered: "Station Portage this is Coast Guard 36495. Over."

Mulvaney spoke: "Coast Guard 36495 this is Station Portage. Chief, I just picked up a mayday from the Inland Mariner. They gave the same position they gave us earlier and then stopped transmitting. I tried to raise them but I can't get any response. I'll keep trying and let you know if I contact them. Chief, they may be a casualty."

Jack had a grim look on his face after this news. What had started as a precautionary run could now be a rescue of multiple survivors. They were about 3 miles out and there were no other Coast Guard assets nearby so Jack knew this problem would be theirs to solve.

Blackmore looked at Jack. He had been thinking all the same thoughts. Then he said: "What can we do?"

Jack answered: "There is nothing for it but to keep going just as we are. Pray I reasoned right when I estimated where we would find her. Stay on the same course. I need to go forward and tell Jimmy to get ready to take on survivors.

As they went further out in the lake there were snow squalls around but the storm was blowing itself out and the wind slowly started dropping. The waves became lower and further apart. The decks were slippery but there was no serious ice forming on the boat. Blackmore went into the engine compartment to get warm for a spell. Spencer took out a pair of binoculars and scanned the horizon. Jack had the wheel and was glad to be operating a boat again. Then Spencer started pointing to the horizon to the northwest. There was a ship beginning to appear.

Blackmore came out of the engine compartment and seeing the ship got on the radio. Through a series of transmissions they learned the freighter *SS Republic* had heard the mayday and was coming to the position reported by the Inland Mariner. Blackmore told them to keep coming as they were afraid the Inland Mariner was a casualty and they might need help with survivors.

After another hour or so the coast guardsmen were tiring from the rough weather and its effect on the movement of the boat. The constant bracing and balancing needed to stay upright as the boat rose and fell with the waves was wearying. Jack was beginning to doubt his estimations as to where to find the Inland Mariner.

Suddenly, Jimmy Spencer who was still bravely keeping lookout started pointing repeatedly to the northwest. He yelled back to Blackmore and Jack: "I can see a debris field about 100 yards out." Blackmore and Jack cast knowing looks towards each other and Blackmore brought the wheel around to head the boat in the direction Spencer was pointing.

As they came up on the floating debris they saw pieces of wood, two life jackets some pieces of canvas and a white life ring with the words "*SS Inland Mariner*" stenciled on it in black paint. Spencer grabbed one of the life jackets with the boat hook and brought it aboard. It was similarly stenciled. Blackmore got on the radio and told the *SS Republic* of their find and asked them to come to their position.

Blackmore looked at Jack and said: "Do you think we can actually get 30 survivors on board in these waves?"

Staring straight ahead Jack answered: "I don't think we are going to have to. It looks to me like a lot of men drowned here this morning."

Shortly after this exchange Spencer pointed off the port bow and Blackmore throttled back and steered in that direction. There were two bodies floating in the water. One was a woman floating face down in a life jacket only partially fastened. The other was a sailor in a peacoat with a torn life vest. Patterson came out of the engine compartment and he and Spencer got them aboard and covered them with a blanket. Almost at the same time the *SS Republic* radioed they had spotted survivors on an overturned life boat and were proceeding to take them aboard.

As the lifeboat crested a wave they all spotted a life raft to the north and Blackmore steered for it. There were two men and a woman on board. They came alongside the raft and Patterson and Spencer got them in the forward cockpit. The survivors were all suffering from exposure and Spencer wrapped them in blankets. The woman saw the bodies of the two victims on the cockpit deck as she entered the forward cabin. The foot of one of the bodies was sticking out from under the blanket covering her and the woman recognized her friend's shoe. She broke down crying and sobbing and started striking her fists against Spencer's chest as he tried to comfort her.

One of the men spoke through blue lips: "I'm Captain McKeil. This lady is one of our passengers and was traveling with the deceased woman, the one you have there, under the blanket. The deceased man next to her was on watch as our wheelsman. This other crewman with us is an Able Seaman who got the raft free and saved us. I haven't seen any of the others who were on the ship. We broke in two and...." His head sank to his chest and his voice just trailed off. After Spencer got them settled in the cabin, he shared the last of his coffee with them and tried to convince them they were safe.

Jack and his crew continued to search the area well into the afternoon. They only found two more bodies. One looked like he was one of the Inland Mariner's officers given his clothing. McKeil identified him as the First Mate after they brought the bodies on board. The SS Republic radioed she had picked up sixteen survivors, and with no hope of picking up any other survivors, was continuing on her way to Duluth. Jack advised them to report to Coast Guard Station Duluth upon arrival so they could get the details on the survivors and the sinking.

Spencer came back to the after cockpit and said to Jack: "Chief, we need to get the three we rescued to shore and a doctor. The woman keeps vomiting due to the motion of the boat. The crewman just lays there. I think he and the Captain are in shock"

Jack paused for a moment. He looked around at the grey horizon and grey waves that still tossed them around. It struck him this might be the last time he went on a rescue mission given his retirement. He looked at Blackmore and said: "I think we have done all the good we can. If there is anyone else still out there they would have died of hypothermia by now. Let's get back to the station. My legs are about worn through trying to keep my balance on this damn deck."

Blackmore smiled and said: "Aye, aye Chief. I'll have you home in your arm chair before you know it."

CHAPTER THREE
SIGNAL FLAGS

Frank Hawes knew a good thing when he saw it and it was sitting right in front of him. Hawes ran a wholesale tobacco business in Poole and distributed to retailers in Poole and Bournemouth on England's south coast. His business needed a part time bookkeeper and the attractive brunette sitting in front of him seemed right for the job. Her resume claimed she had clerical experience including book-keeping, and she wasn't married.

Hawes was in his fifties, portly and balding. He had a ruddy complexion and glasses which he now looked over the top of to see Diana Winter and ask: "So Diana, what brings you to our part of England?"

Diana sat primly in a wool suit with her hair nicely done and hands folded in her lap. She smiled at Hawes and said: "I've been up in the north of England working but decided to come down here with it being November and the winter coming on. The weather up there can be dreadfully cold and wet and I'm hoping for a better winter down here. I should tell you I have also taken part time employment at the Lion and the Cross down on the quay in Poole. I'm not sure what they want of me-some office work and probably some serving as well. The hours they want from me should not conflict with yours."

Hawes knew the location of the pub and also knew it to be a popular spot right on the harbor. He nodded at Diana and said: "They have good fish and crisps and a nice view of the water. I don't think they are as busy as they were before the war, but that can't be helped. I have my woes too as tobacco has to be imported and the ships are not getting through like they used to. Damn U-Boats."

Diana was proud of the fact her smile directed at Hawes had not changed a bit when he made reference to the toll German submarines were taking on Atlantic convoys bringing supplies to England. Diana asked: "When would you like me to start?"

Hawes said: "Tomorrow if that is possible. I'll have our route manager take you around the country to some of our better customers so you can meet them and get to know our business. I hope we have a mild winter for all our sakes and those damn German bombers stay away from Poole."

Diana rose, extended her hand, and said: "Thank you very much. I will see you tomorrow."

As she turned and went out the door to his office Hawes studied her legs and the curve of her behind. Her skirt fitted snugly and showed a very nice figure. Her breasts were perfect. Yes, Frank Hawes thought, I'm going to enjoy that view all winter long.

Diana went out onto the street and walked the few blocks to the flat she had rented. It had been a successful few weeks. She had two jobs and a place to live. Diana had already begun to take walks, or ride her bicycle, out into the country to study coastal defenses and military camps. There was a Royal Marine base not too far away she intended to monitor. Poole's harbor had a fishing fleet, several small coastal freighters, and visits from ocean going cargo ships and Royal Navy vessels. It was a fine natural harbor. The job at the Lion and Cross on the quay would allow her to watch the harbor and hear the sailors talk as they ate or drank. The tobacconist job offered the potential to pick up military news from a wide area that might be of interest to her.

Diana had contacted the handler German Intelligence had assigned her. It was a woman. She was in Bournemouth. They spoke by telephone and used coded phrases. The woman was curt on the telephone. She had given Diana instructions on how to report and what telephone number or addresses to use. Diana was to report by mail for routine matters. For information of particular interest Diana could use a public call box. A meeting would be arranged soon.

When she first arrived in England Diana had been very nervous. She was convinced everyone was watching her and knew she was an enemy agent. Every unexpected sound made her jump. She had a continuous dull headache and very little appetite. But that was passing. The English coastal countryside was beautiful, even with the late fall weather. Since she had lived in England for most of her life she was becoming very comfortable here.

A friend of her father, a Colonel in the German army, was the reason she was a spy. After her husband died in the air war over England in 1940 she was filled with rage and sought revenge. The Colonel saw a way to channel that for the benefit of the Fatherland. Thus, she was trained as an agent to return to England. Her father's last teaching position in England was far away from Poole. She saw little chance she would run into old acquaintances who knew they had returned to Germany in the 1930's. Even if she did meet someone from the past, she would simply say she had returned to England to escape National Socialism. Her new name would be a problem, but she would use the excuse she had to change it to escape Germany while protecting her father's identity.

As Diana lay in bed that night sleep did not come easily. Despite her success in establishing herself in Poole there remained an empty feeling of estrangement from all around her. She was sure she would never know love again, neither physical or spiritual. She pulled up her night gown and ran her fingers through the triangle of silken hair between her legs. She gently slid her finger over her outer lips and then into her cleft. But it brought no arousal. No feeling of sexual urgency. She could remember the feel of her husband's strong erection entering her and brining her to climax. But that could never happen again.

Diana's training had encouraged her to use her sexuality to obtain information, including intercourse. Diana had no particular feeling about that one way or the other. She would use her body if necessary. But given her assignment that seemed unlikely. Basically, she was just a set of eyes and ears to report information to others. Frank Hawes had studied her figure and she was sure that is why he offered her the position without checking her experience or skills. He had to be kept at arms length to keep her employment.

Diana finally settled on the remembrance of her handsome husband in his dress grey Luftwaffe uniform. She would honor the dead. Sleep took her away.

Jack Trevenen sat at his desk in his office in the main station building. It was November now and he had less than two months left before he retired. The question of what he would do with himself once he left the service still had not been answered. The winter was arriving in true form and the snows were accumulating. The boats were all up in the boat house, but there still wasn't much ice forming. That allowed the motor surf boat to go out and do winter maintenance on the aids to navigation. But the station was settling in for the long northern Michigan winter. Jack thought maybe he would just stay on the Keewenaw for the winter and then ship out on one of the lake ships next spring. At the moment he was filling out more paperwork to be sent to his detailer in Headquarters to document his departure from active duty.

Jack had received word that Chief Michael Duggan would be replacing him. Jack wanted as much time as possible with him before he left to acquaint Duggan with station operations. The plan was for Duggan to get there by December first. That gave Jack close to three weeks with him. Jack had leave coming and could retire at the end of November but he had decided to stay on. He had no place particular to go and was in no hurry to get there. Jack had served with Duggan on a 125 foot cutter when they were both younger. Jack thought he would be good for this job if he hadn't changed from when Jack knew him. Duggan had a wife and three children so the living quarters would be lively.

Jack had these thoughts running through his mind when he became conscious of someone standing in the doorway to his office. He turned and saw Captain McKeil standing there. McKeil had become something of a problem child. When they got back to the station after the assistance call to the *SS Inland Mariner* the Able Seaman and the woman passenger they had picked up were taken to the local hospital in Hancock. McKeil had insisted he was fine and was given some dry clothes and a bunk in the crew quarters. At first he was grateful and was cooperative. He telephoned and wired a report to his owners and they in turn wired him some money. At that point Jack had expected him to leave, but he stayed on. Jack required him to contribute to the mess fund and had told him he could stay until the Coast Guard investigators had interviewed him regarding the loss of his ship. After that he had to find other accommodations.

In the interim McKeil had become loud and argumentative. He started drinking throughout the day. Many of his rants were against his now drowned First Mate who he blamed for the sinking. When not complaining about the Mate he challenged the quality of the work done by the shipyard claiming its carelessness caused his ship to break apart. He was becoming an irritant to the crew.

Jack turned to McKeil and said: "Good morning, Captain. I have a letter from the Coast Guard offices in Duluth saying as part of our investigation of the sinking they are sending Lieutenant Griffin to interview you tomorrow. He should be here after lunch. Please be here. I'll have you use this office."

McKeil looked at Jack with a scowl on his face and said: "God dammit. They are going to keel haul me and put me on the beach over this. I haven't heard a single word from the owners about a new position. Now your people will want to charge me and take my license."

Jack looked at him evenly and said: "You don't know whether anyone is going to charge you. You can't expect a ship to sink with a significant loss of life and not have the Coast Guard investigate the circumstances. I understand the passenger we brought back and your Able Seaman have already been interviewed. They are recovering and have returned to family. So you are being treated no differently. No Captain is perfect. In hind sight we can all say we should have done things differently. But that doesn't make you derelict in your duty."

That seemed to calm McKeil and he sat down heavily. He stared at the floor in silence then pulled an open pint of whiskey from his back pocket. He took a deep swig and put the bottle back in his pocket.

Jack bristled and with an edge in his voice said: "McKeil, I've allowed you some slack due to the loss of your ship. It hurts any of us to see a vessel go down. But I've told you before there is no drinking on this station. If you want to drink you go into town."

McKeil looked up at Jack and said: "The Chief Engineer was a good man. I'd sailed with him for years. We lost almost all the black gang. They went down with her." Mckeil looked down again and shook his head. There was silence between them.

Jack said: "Look, I don't know what is going to happen as a result of our investigation. But I do know they take time. The shipping season is almost over on the lakes with the coming winter and ice setting in. You sailed the oceans. Go out to the east coast and ship out as an ordinary seaman if necessary. President Roosevelt's Lend Lease program has put new life in the Atlantic shipping trade. All the supplies we are sending to Great Britain requires merchant ships and men. The newspapers say the German submarines aren't sinking American ships as the Germans don't want us in the war."

McKeil didn't respond. He just sat for several minutes and then stood up and said: "God damn all of you. God damn you." Then he turned to leave.

Jack stopped him before he could go out the door. "Captain. Be here at 1 pm tomorrow. And leave the bottle here."

McKeil looked at Jack, snorted and handed him the pint of whiskey. Then he said: "You bastards even take a man's drink." Then he turned on his heel and went out the front door of the station into the cold and snow.

The next day Jack sat in his office looking up at the clock. It was nearly the end of the noon meal hour and McKeil hadn't returned to the station after leaving yesterday. Jack stood up and went out to the entry way and looked out the window. It was snowing lightly. He saw a government owned sedan pull up and park in front of the station. A Coast Guard officer got out and opened the trunk to take out a large brief case. Jack quickly pulled on his coat and hat and went out to greet their guest. As the Lieutenant came up the walk Jack snapped off a crisp salute that was promptly returned. Jack extended his hand and said: "Welcome to Station Portage. I'm Chief Trevenen."

The Lieutenant shook his hand and said: "I'm Lieutenant Griffin. Good to meet you Senior Chief. I think you've been expecting me?"

Jack said: "I have. Glad you got here before the weather worsens. Come in and get warm. I can get the cook to put up some lunch for you."

They went inside and after the Lieutenant had a quick meal he and Jack went into Jack's office for a talk. Jack took stock of the young man sitting in front of him. He had sandy colored hair and some freckles. He smiled easily and unlike some officers didn't seem pretentious at all. Jack was impressed with his youth and rank.

Jack started the conversation: "I don't know where McKeil is. He has been going downhill since we first brought him in following the sinking. I think he has some considerable guilt and remorse over the loss of his vessel. Unfortunately, he started drinking several days ago and I had to step in and stop that—at least when he is on the station. I told him yesterday to be here at 1 o'clock. We'll have to wait and see if he shows. He didn't stay aboard last night."

Griffin looked troubled but didn't respond. He just took some materials from his brief case and then turned to Jack and said: "I understand Chief. I have some things I want to review so that will take a little time. I have your report and don't have any questions about it. Just go about you day and if he arrives let me know."

Jack rose and said: "Yes sir. I'll let you know right away."

About an hour later Captain McKeil arrived. Jack met him at the front door and with a stern look said: "It is about time you showed."

McKeil said: "I needed to talk to a sea lawyer or two about all this before I answered any questions." Jack detected a slight odor of alcohol.

Jack escorted McKeil to his office and introduced him to Lieutenant Griffin. Jack then closed the door to his office and left the men to their conversation. The two were in there for over three hours. Jack could occasionally hear muffled voices. Twice he heard McKeil raise his voice in response to something asked of him. At the end the door opened and McKeil walked briskly out of the station without saying a word to anyone.

Jack walked back to his office and saw Lieutenant Griffin packing his brief case. Jack asked: "How did it go?"

Griffin stopped what he was doing, looked up and paused for a moment. Then he said: "He is an interesting character alright. His sense of guilt over the loss is obvious but he blames everyone else for the sinking."

Jack asked: "Is he in trouble?"

Griffin shrugged: "It's not up to me alone to decide. I just gather all the facts. But there was a significant loss of life. He lost almost half the crew. He may have to go to a hearing to see if he gets to keep his license. He didn't load the Inland Mariner by the loading manual. Our merchant marine technical people in Headquarters will look at that and any construction issues with the lengthening the owners

35

recently did. If he had just ducked behind one of the Apostle Islands for the night we all never would have met."

Jack nodded his sad understanding.

Griffin added: "He is a heavy weather sailor. Every Great Lakes fleet has one or two. The owners love them as they keep to the schedule and timely move a lot of cargo. They ignore storm warnings and want nothing to do with anything that will delay them. He tells me he didn't tarp the hatch covers. While he blames the First Mate for that, it would have made them late leaving Superior. Captains like him take a lot of risks. A lot of risks."

Chief Mike Duggan arrived shortly after Thanksgiving to acquaint himself with station operations and meet the crew. His formal relief of Jack wouldn't happen for close to another month. The ice was heavy enough that Jack didn't launch one of the boats to show him some of their area of responsibility. But they took the station vehicle and saw what they could. Jack introduced him around the area to other first responders and law enforcement. Jack was pleased to see he was the same sailor he knew when they were much younger. Since he was coming from a life boat station on Cape Cod, Massachusetts the routine would not be that much different. The Coast Guard had standard operating requirements regardless where the station was located. The major change would be the longer winter.

Duggan's family had stayed behind to pack and let his two children who were in school finish up the fall semester. They all would be here before Christmas. Jack had him move into his side of the residence and take one of his open bedrooms. In the evenings the two would play checkers, smoke their pipes, listen to the radio or talk over their service experiences. Jack enjoyed the company.

One Friday evening Jack stood staring at the calendar hanging on his kitchen wall. It was December 5. Retirement was drawing closer. He was conflicted over it. He still didn't have a clear idea of what he would do. At times he felt like he was going into a tunnel and wasn't sure where he would come out at the other end. He had rented a room in Hancock and had started to move a few items over there. It would give him a place to stay for a few weeks while he figured out what his next career would be.

Duggan walked up behind him and said: "Chief, why don't you and I go visit that road house on the canal, the one on the way to town? It's not snowing so the road is good. Blackmore can keep an eye on things and we can give him the telephone number in case he needs to reach us. We can have a few beers and relive old times. The family will be here soon and my chance to go out will be limited."

Jack wasn't particularly excited by the idea but decided to be sociable saying: "Only if you let me buy you a drink. You've worked hard at getting settled in here so it's the least I can do."

Duggan laughed and said: "I never say no to free beer!"

About a half an hour later they were settled in the back booth of a country tavern sipping a couple of draft beers. Both of them took note the bar maid was particularly comely. Duggan knew Jack was troubled by his retirement and thought it might help if he could talk some of that through. Duggan started by saying: "Jack, the Guard is going to miss you. I know the crew here especially hates to see you go. I have big shoes to fill. There aren't many members of the old Life Saving Service still on active duty with the Coast Guard."

Jack gave a small smile. "I was only in the Life Saving Service for one season and then it was almost two years before I enlisted in the newly created Coast Guard. In some ways all that seems like ages ago. But at other moments it is as real as though it were yesterday."

Duggan knew Jack had been part of the crew at Vermilion Point that had their surf boat overturn with the loss of several members. He was smart enough not to pursue those memories. Instead he said: "The family and I want you with us for Christmas dinner. The kids will be all excited and the wife will cook the best turkey you ever had!"

Jack brightened at the thought. "Thanks Mike. That is very kind. I was going to throw some money in the mess fund and stop by the station for a Christmas meal."

Duggan said: "You can stop by the station anytime and you don't need to put money in the mess fund. They'll have their dinner at noon. Ours will be in the evening. So you'll be well fed on Christmas Day."

Jack looked up and saw the bar maid standing at their table and smiling at him. She had a cheer leader figure and a very pretty smile. Her long brown hair was stylishly done. She asked: "Another round fellas?"

Duggan answered for them both and said "Certainly. My friend here is about to retire from the Coast Guard and we are toasting his future."

The bar maid put her hand on Jack's shoulder and said: "Congratulations. But you don't look old enough to retire. I hope you stay in the area and stop here often."

As she walked to the bar to get the beers Duggan looked at Jack and said: "She likes you. You need someone to keep your back warm this winter and she looks like the perfect choice!"

Jack blushed a little and said: "I'm not sure a woman is what I need right now. Particularly if I ship out in the spring or go to the East Coast yet this winter. The war in Europe is causing the merchant fleet to grow and need lots of additional men. They say the Coast Guard may get bigger as well."

Then Jack's voice trailed off and he sat in thought for a moment. He watched the bar maid heading their way with the fresh beers. As he studied her he thought about the years that had passed since he last made love. The few times he had been with a woman after his wife died had not been anything he cared to remember. But he could not deny that he was lonely and after he retired that would become more difficult to bear. Jack shrugged, looked at Duggan, nodded in the direction of the bar maid and said: "I hope you're right about her liking me. I'm going to ask her out. I don't want to make a damn fool of myself."

The following Sunday evening Jack was sitting reading in his sitting room when Duggan came back from the main station building with a look of despair. He sat down heavily across from Jack. Then he spoke quietly: "Jack, something terrible has happened. Japanese planes have attacked the Navy base at Pearl Harbor and all the Army air fields. Hundreds, maybe thousands are dead. It was a surprise attack. Those bastards really got a twist on us. We didn't stand a chance."

Jack sat up straight. "How do you know this?"

Duggan said: "The crew had the radio on and the news came through an hour or so ago. Everyone is stunned. Do you know anybody out there? Shipmates? Friends or relatives?"

Jack stood up and paced across the room. He turned and faced Duggan. "No, I never was a West Coast sailor so I have no ties to Hawaii. How the hell did the Japs get planes to Hawaii?"

Duggan said: "I don't know for sure. Everyone thinks their aircraft carriers brought them within striking distance. There is a lot of confusion about the details. Some reports say the Japs are now heading for the West Coast. The crew's blood is up over this so I think you are the best one to have a talk with them. Calm them down and keep them focused."

Jack started to put on his hat and coat to go talk to the crew. He stopped and asked Duggan: "Has anyone contacted us about this — given us new orders?"

Duggan shook his head and said: "No." He paused, then added: "It's too soon. But we will be at war by tomorrow you can bet on it. Apparently, the Navy moved the Pacific Fleet to Pearl and they caught the battleships all at anchor. It was a slaughter. The only good news is our aircraft carriers were at sea."

Jack was stunned as the news sank in. He thought about what it meant to him personally. Then he said: "I wonder if I'm still going to retire in two weeks?" Duggan didn't respond and the two of them headed to the main station building to talk to their crew.

The next two weeks were a blur to Jack when he thought back on them. That Sunday evening he talked with the crew and told them to carry out their duties to the best of their abilities. He told the men who had Christmas leave coming to plan on going unless the station received orders otherwise. He told them the change of command would take place as scheduled and Chief Duggan would become the Officer-In-Charge. Finally, he assured them the Japanese were not going to attack the Keweenaw Peninsula in the dead of winter. That brought a chuckle.

As Duggan predicted President Roosevelt immediately asked Congress for a Declaration of War against Japan which was promptly approved. A few days later Germany declared war against the United States. This latter struck Jack harder than the news of Pearl Harbor. The Atlantic Ocean was now a war zone and German submarines would be waiting for American ships. Jack thought the Coast Guard would get part of the job protecting those ships.

When Jack was on duty during the time of America's involvement in World War I, his duty stations did not involve him in the war. He was glad. He had talked with other service men who had been in the fighting and knew they endured much hardship and sacrifice. This clarified Jack's feeling about retirement. A large part of him hoped his retirement would not be delayed. At this point in his life he did not want to go into combat.

In these final days Duggan essentially started running the station even though the leadership had not formally changed hands. Jack moved into his rented rooms and Duggan's family showed up to take Jack's residence. With Duggan well occupied Jack had time on his hands. He started going out with the bar maid Duggan and he had met. Her name was Dorothy and he asked her to have dinner with him on her nights off. He liked her and she him. He was much older than her but she didn't mind. Dorothy found Jack handsome and straight forward in his manner. He was polite to her and showed her respect. This was new to her in her dating experience. Dorothy took the lead in their first kiss. With all the patriotic fervor and uncertainty caused by the start of the war they both needed something stable to hang on to. Yet at the same time there was a feeling the old rules didn't apply anymore under the threat of uncertain futures.

One snowy night, after dinner, Dorothy and Jack went back to his room. Jack fixed them a brandy and soda and they sat together on an old love seat. Dorothy wanted him very badly. They shared several deep passionate kisses. She whispered: "Jack, I need you." Then she touched the front of his trousers and felt him respond.

Dorothy stood and slowly took off her sweater and her bra. She sat back down next to Jack and he kissed and stroked her breasts. Then he gently sucked on each of her nipples. He wanted her breasts endlessly, and she welcomed it.

That was the first of many nights they shared each other's sexuality. The first time Dorothy undressed Jack she was impressed with his slender legs, tight behind and muscular chest. Jack it seemed wanted her breasts as much as she wanted him deep inside her. She told him his erect penis fit her perfectly. They couldn't get enough of each other.

Having Dorothy in his life seemed to give Jack a greater sense of inner peace. He worried less about retirement and his future. What did cause Jack to pause and think was the difference in their age. He half expected her to walk out the door on him every time he saw her.

Jack thought for sure he would hear from the District or Headquarters canceling his retirement, but no new orders came. He tried to call his detailer in Headquarters but couldn't get through. He was sure the administrative demands on the Headquarters staff must be great with the war on. Plus, the Coast Guard was supposed to move from the Department of Treasury to the Department of Navy.

Pursuant to the orders Jack and Duggan had previously received, Duggan assumed command and Jack was discharged from the Coast Guard. The change of command ceremony and Jack's retirement party came off perfectly. There were smiles all around. Dorothy came and stayed at his side. There was a big buffet along with cake and ice cream. Jack was very touched and had trouble speaking when it was his turn to say farewell to the crew. His voice cracked with emotion. As he left everyone was inviting him to all types of Christmas dinners and celebrations to ease any loneliness he might feel at the Christmas season.

The Monday morning following the change of command Jack was sound asleep in his room. Dorothy was sleeping next to him with her arm around him. Through his sleep Jack heard a loud knocking at the door and someone saying: "Chief, Chief, are you in there?" Then more knocking. Whoever it was wasn't going away.

Jack tried to slip out of bed without waking Dorothy which wasn't successful. Dorothy said a little grumpily: "Who is that?"

Jack said: "I don't know but I will soon find out if I can find my briefs." Their clothes had been piled on a chair when they undressed last night and Jack couldn't find his underwear. Finally he just pulled on his pants.

Dorothy giggled: "You look good with your clothes off."

Jack ignored her, crossed the room and opened the door. Jimmy Spencer was standing there. Jimmy could look past Jack into the room and saw a very attractive nude woman getting out of bed. For a moment it left him speechless. Jack stepped out into the hall and pulled the door closed behind him.

Jimmy immediately spoke up: "Chief, am I glad I found you. Chief Duggan would have my hide if I hadn't." He handed Jack a well worn manilla envelop that was addressed to Jack and had been mailed several days ago from the District offices.

Jack took the envelope and asked: "What is this?"

Jimmy said: "I don't know. But Chief Duggan thinks it's important. He sent me right away to find you."

Jack said: "Thanks Jimmy. Tell Chief Duggan I'll be by to see him later today."

Jack turned to open the door. Jimmy leaned to his right hoping for another glimpse of Dorothy, until he saw Jack's stern look at him and he hurried out of the building. Jack went back into the room and sat on the edge of the bed. Dorothy had pulled her slip on but it still showed her breasts quite nicely. She kneeled on the bed behind Jack to read over his shoulder.

Jack took a number of pages of type written paper out of the envelope. Dorothy asked: "What is it?"

Jack read instead of answering. He immediately hit on the words 'Your discharge from active duty for purposes of retirement is hereby canceled. Your enlistment is extended for an indefinite duration based on needs of the service. Enclosed you will find orders assigning you to temporary duty at Coast Guard District Offices in Cleveland, Ohio.' It was all dated before his retirement date and had been tied up in the mails.

Jack stood up and looked at Dorothy and said: "I'm back in the Coast Guard and I haven't much time to get to Cleveland where I'm reassigned."

Dorothy came and stood in front of him. She took him in her arms and pressed her cheek against his. She asked quietly: "What will it mean?"

Jack put his arms around her and said: "I don't know dear. I don't know."

1944

CHAPTER FOUR
SEA SERPENTS

Admiral Ernest J. King walked briskly down the sidewalk from the side entrance of the White House towards his staff car and driver who was waiting for him on the street. Admiral King was the Chief of Naval Operations for the United States Navy which meant he was in command of all US naval forces around the world. It was a late winter day in Washington DC and as is often the case the morning sun shone brightly and the air was spring like. He was troubled by his meeting with President Roosevelt. He hadn't seen the President recently and he could see the demands placed upon him as a war time President were taking a toll on his health.

The United States was now in its third year of World War II. Great Britain had been at war for five years. But the tide was turning in their favor both in Europe and the Pacific. Still, Admiral King knew there would be thousands of men killed and maimed before Japan and Germany were fully defeated. It left him with a continually somber attitude.

The plans for the early summer of 1944 called for American, British and Canadian forces to invade the north coast of France with the ultimate goal of driving the German army out of France. The Allies would then invade Germany itself. It would be a massive effort with hundreds of thousands of soldiers and sailors involved and thousands of ships. The navy would be needed as all the men and material had to be transported from southern England across the English Channel to France. The tactical command of the operation was in England under General Eisenhower. However, an operation of this size involved the planners in Washington DC as well.

This was the reason President Roosevelt asked to see him this morning. The President expressed his concern about their ability to safely transport all the men and equipment to France. He could foresee attacks from German submarines, torpedo boats and aircraft taking a terrible toll on the invasion fleet before it even got to France. Then there were the underwater mine fields and obstacles the Germans had planted to snare landing craft as they approached the beaches. The President indicated Prime Minister Churchill, the head of Great Britain's government, had similar concerns.

Admiral King thought the two leaders might be losing faith in the success of the mission. Or maybe they were remembering the spring of 1940 when the British Expeditionary Force was driven across France by the German army to the beaches of Dunkirk. More than three hundred thousand men had to be rescued by the Royal Navy and hundreds of civilian craft. The German army and air force had put murderous fire on the waiting men and the ships trying to rescue them.

Admiral King kept his thoughts to himself. Instead he and the President agreed there needed to be an additional force of rescue craft to rescue men in the water, when inevitably, vessels would be damaged or sunk. The conversation only painted the nature of this rescue force in broadest terms and it was up to King to implement the concept. As he walked towards his car Admiral King was thinking about the U.S. Coast Guard. In times of war it becomes part of the U.S. Navy, but it's command structure remains intact. Yes, he thought, the Coast Guard is the solution to this problem. As soon as he got back to his office he would call Admiral Russell R. Waesche, the Commandant of the Coast Guard. He would ask him to present him with a plan to create a rescue flotilla.

It was Sunday afternoon. Diana Winter sat on the grass in the spring sunshine looking out over the English Channel. There was a series of low cliffs here and she was on top of one affording her a clear view of the beautiful blue water. She was watching a British naval vessel heading west, presumably for Poole's harbor. From her training she judged it to be a destroyer escort. Diana had been in Poole for about two and a half years and was well settled.

Diana was amazed at how much the war had changed. When she first came to Poole there was not much military presence. The planes of the German Luftwaffe had flown overhead regularly. At times Poole was the bombing target, but mostly the large flights were headed further inland for other targets. Still, Poole had a lot of damage. Her first flat had been badly damaged in a Saturday night bombing while she and other residents huddled in a nearby public bomb shelter. She identified with her neighbors around her, but was not feeling guilty about her countryman's planes dropping bombs on them. She knew British and American bombers were doing the same thing to Germany.

But those days were gone. There were still occasional air raids on Poole but the large flights of German planes were not seen. The Allied build up for the invasion of France had grown dramatically over the past year. The harbor had become a bustling place with troop transports, merchant ships, and naval vessels arriving. There were new military camps which Diana judged to hold two divisions of American troops. There were several additional British military camps. The rather sleepy reporting job of her early months in Poole were long over. Now she regularly reported troop movements and vessel arrivals on a large scale. Her job at the Lion and Cross gave her much information about specific army units and naval capabilities of the ships that came here. Soldiers and sailors couldn't help but talk after a pint or two. But no one knew when the invasion of France would start or where the troops would land on the French coast. Diana was worried someone might notice her frequent calls from public telephone boxes and her frequent mailings reporting in code her latest intelligence.

Diana met with her handler very infrequently. Her handler was a dowdy middle aged woman who dressed poorly. Diana presumed that her dress was designed to keep attention off her. The woman never revealed her name. She acted as though she did not like Diana and could be quite critical of Diana, without cause. The meetings were brief, in public places, and Diana was passed new codes and contact information. The addresses she sent her reports to, and telephone numbers she used to report, were frequently changing. Occasionally Diana was given some money. But Diana knew she was

45

expected to be self-supporting. The relationship met all essential needs, but made Diana feel isolated.

Diana was weary of war. She liked living in England and longed for peace to return. While the war continued she could not have any contact with her father. She missed him and was worried about him. Diana hoped he was not already dead from the bombs that fell on Germany. He too would be better off in England after the war. If she continued to keep her role secret, Diana wondered if she could find a way to stay after the war, even if Germany lost?

Diana could see that the tide had turned and Germany might not be victorious. The Allied buildup of men, material, and ships was stunning to her. And what she saw was only in the Poole and Bournemouth areas. The same buildup was going on all over southern England. It would overwhelm the German boys fighting to hold such a force back. She thought of her husband's wasted life and had little energy for any of it any more.

Diana strolled back to her bicycle as all of this turned over in her head. Tomorrow would be Monday and she had to go into Hawes' office in the morning and do some bookkeeping. Hawes was becoming a problem. He sometimes stood behind her when she was working so he could look over her shoulder and down the front of her blouse to study the top of her breasts. When she was standing he would walk up and brush against her behind or let his hand touch her thigh. But now he wanted time with her away from the office. So far she had brushed it off, but she thought every now and then he may be following her after she left the office.

The Lion and Cross would want her in the afternoon and evening and the soldiers or sailors would also be wanting her attentions. Diana was weary of this too. Many of the men were attractive, especially the American officers. But her sense of her own sexuality lay dormant.

Diana cycled back to her flat and tried to wipe all these thoughts and worries from her mind. It was hard to do so as she had nothing to look forward to. It would all just continue. She wondered if tomorrow would bring a change.

Monday morning came and brought wind and rain. Diana went to her bookkeeping job. She had a small cubicle down the hall from Frank Hawes' office. Hawes was not in when she arrived and she was glad. Diana had never particularly liked the man and now his pressure to be alone with her was concerning. Diana worked on the accounts and made the entries in the ledger. She realized she would have to bring some of the increased sales costs to his attention. The business was too successful. Maintaining the inventory of tobacco products was hurting cash flow. Diana started to write Hawes a note and then leave when he came down the hall towards his office. He was nicely dressed in suit with a white shirt and tie. They were the only ones in this part of the building and he stopped and smiled at her.

Diana smiled back and said: "Good morning Mr. Hawes. I was just writing you a note. There are some figures I want to bring to your attention."

Hawes, still smiling said: "Get the records and ledger and bring them to my office."

This was not what Diana wanted but she said: "Certainly. I will be right there."

Diana gathered the materials and went into Hawes office. As she entered he said: "Close the door, please. If someone comes by I don't want them hearing my financial information."

After closing the door, Diana stood in front of Hawes desk and laid the records out on the top of the desk. She spoke for a few moments when Hawes stopped her and said: "Come around to my side of the desk. It's hard for me to read upside down while you are looking at the pages from your side."

Diana was suspicious but didn't object. She came around to Hawes side of the desk and stood next to the chair he was seated in. She started again with her report and to her relief Hawes seemed to be paying attention. They had a brief discussion and then Hawes took a cigar from a humidor on his desk and without lighting it said: "Let me reflect on the cash flow problem."

The room was quiet and Diana remained standing beside Hawes. After a moment or two of quiet she leaned over the desk ever so slightly to begin picking up her materials. Then she froze. Hawes had his hand up the back of her skirt and was stroking the inside of her thigh just above the knee. Diana fought the sudden urge to turn and slap his face as hard as she could. The basic tenet of her training as an agent was to never bring attention to herself. That way she would not be caught. A row with Hawes could lead to the police being involved. Even worse, there might be some sly retribution from him that could expose her. Her subliminal fear of detection and perhaps execution rose to the front of her brain. She could not move.

Diana turned her head a little to look at Hawes. The cigar was no longer in his hand. His eyes were closed and his free hand was stroking his member through the front of his trousers. Diana closed her eyes and tried to believe this wasn't happening. Her head was swimming in conflicting thoughts when she heard herself say: "Mr. Hawes you are a married man. What would your wife think?"

Hawes still had his eyes closed and his breathing was a little quicker. He didn't respond to Diana's question but said: "Open up your legs."

Diana stared down at the desk and said nothing. To her amazement she moved one leg slightly to the side to allow Hawes to slide his hand upwards. Then he hiked up the back of her skirt. She could feel his fingers running over the lips of her vagina through her silk panties. Diana gasped. It was as though time stood still and this was all happening in slow motion. She glanced again at Hawes. His member was very large and very erect under the front of his trousers. Diana knew she had power over him through her sexuality. In some way, it pleased her.

Diana suddenly turned and stepped away from the desk. She gave Hawes a wild look and then said: "Mr.Hawes, this can never happen again."

Diana hurried out of the office to the lavatory down the hall. Diana knelt in front of the commode and vomited. She was in the lavatory a long time. Once she stopped shaking she washed her face, straightened her skirt, and stepped out into the hall. Hawes was there pacing back and forth. He was clearly agitated and looked worried.

Hawes immediately said: "Diana, I'm so sorry! Really, I am. It's just my wife no longer has any interest in love making. I know you are alone and I thought, well I thought we might be able to help each other in that way. Just some playfulness. I would never try to put myself in you, that is, unless you wanted it?"

While Hawes was saying these things he paced back and forth and looked at the floor and not at Diana. Diana watched him and thought he was somewhat pathetic. Diana wasn't sure how to handle this. The spy in her told her to smooth things over. Her sense of self respect urged her to quit as his bookkeeper. She decided to play for time.

Diana put a sharp tone in her voice and said: "I will never allow you to touch me in any way. I need to leave. Now. If I'm back Wednesday you will know I want to keep my position." With that Diana went into her cubicle and put on her coat.

Hawes followed her and said: "I trust you won't speak of this to anyone? That you can take what happened as a compliment?"

Diana didn't answer. She briskly walked down the hall and out of the building.

Diana lay in bed that night and thought about her day. After leaving Hawes she had a spot of lunch and then went to the Lion and Cross and did some office work. They were shorthanded so after she was done in the office she worked behind the bar and as a waitress until almost midnight. She was exhausted. Diana had decided she would go back to Hawes as the bookkeeper. The money from the job was good enough she didn't want to be without it. Diana often got information on military movements or unit identities from the route salesmen. Most importantly she did not want another potential employer checking into her work and education history as part of a job application.

As Diana drifted towards sleep she questioned why she had opened her legs at Frank Hawes request. Was it a feeling of sexual power she wanted to experience over this detestable man? Was it a longing for sexual attention after such a long time with no love? All she knew was that it was a mistake and if she did something like that again, it could lead to her being caught.

Senior Chief Jack Trevenen sat on the top of the forward cabin of his 83 foot long Coast Guard patrol boat. He was enjoying the spring sunshine. They were tied up to a wharf adjacent to the Coast Guard base on the York River in Yorktown, Virginia. Their home port was in the Elizabeth River but they made regular patrols out the Elizabeth River to the James River, then down the James to the mouth of Chesapeake Bay. Depending on their assignment, they might go out into the Atlantic for coastal patrol, or turn and go northwest up the York River. Jack liked the river runs. They had the Virginia scenery to enjoy and the rivers at this point were very wide and tidal. It was like having your own huge lake to patrol. They performed basic port safety and security functions observing vessel traffic and shoreline installations. Occasionally, they had a search and rescue case to assist with.

At the beginning of the war German submarines lay in wait just off the mouth of Chesapeake Bay. But those days were gone due to regular patrols by aircraft and increased numbers of coastal patrol vessels. Jack was glad they had never had to tangle with a surfaced German submarine. Its deck gun and secondary batteries could make short work of their wooden hull.

Jack had left the Keweenaw pursuant to his orders and taken a train to Cleveland and the District offices. There he was assigned to Operations and helped with various administrative tasks. To Jack it was boring and tedious. He had initially stayed with one of the other Chief Petty Officers due to a shortage of hotel or boarding house rooms. The war and wartime production had filled the city with workers and business travelers. He eventually found some overpriced dingy rooms down near the river. He rented one out of necessity. Jack was miserable. He was conflicted about being held on active duty for the duration and longed to get out of Cleveland to another ship or station. By calling his detailer in Headquarters enough times he finally was sent to this 83 foot patrol boat in Virginia. But only after a long six months in Cleveland.

Jack liked this duty. He was the Executive Officer on this boat. The Commanding Officer was Lt(jg) Robert Stonecliffe. He was a graduate of the Coast Guard Academy. Jack liked him. Like Jack, he would not put up with any nonsense when it came to performance of shipboard duties. But with this crew that was seldom an issue. Stonecliffe was easy going in his manner and not afraid to ask Jack for his opinion when confronted with new situations. Jack thought they made a good pair. The boat was so small and cramped that the crew of twelve all had to eat and berth together. Everyone had to get along.

The 83 foot patrol boat, as a class, had first been built in 1940 and production continued into the early part of the war. In all, 230 were built and assigned around the East, West and Gulf coasts of the United States. They were powered by two 600 horse power Viking gasoline engines. They were affectionately called the "Matchbox Fleet" due to their wood hulls. With the throttle wide open the boat could do 20 knots, but fuel economy was poor and the usual cruising speed was 12 knots. The boats were used for harbor and coastal patrol duties of all kinds. In the Gulf they occasionally did convoy escort duty. They were used for anti-submarine patrols everywhere. Individual boats had slightly different armament depending on duties and location but all could carry radar, sonar, depth charges and 50 caliber machine guns. Jack's boat had all of these.

As Jack sat deep in thought in the morning sun Robert Stonecliffe jumped from the wharf to the deck of their boat, snapped off a salute to the American flag on the stern flag staff, and walked over to Jack. "Chief, you look like you have the weight of the world on your shoulders. Are our new orders troubling you?"

Jack grinned a little. Lt (jg) Stonecliffe had told him earlier of their being ordered into combat. The rest of the crew didn't know yet. Jack said "I don't mind being sent overseas. I knew this duty was too good to last. But after two years of it I was hoping we would spend the rest of the war right here. What troubles me more is the vague nature of where we are going and what we are going to do. All we know is we are to be at the Brooklyn Navy Yard by the middle of the month for purposes of having the boat loaded on a transport. Then we get shipped across the Atlantic Ocean to support European operations of the Navy. Our operational command shifts to 'Coast Guard Rescue Flotilla One.' Whatever that is?"

Stonecliffe was a good looking young officer. He had brown hair, square facial feautures, and piercing blue eyes. He wore his uniform well. Putting on a brave face Stonecliffe started to speak: "Chief, I don't know much more than you. We are the only boat to be transferred from the Elizabeth River Squadron, but other boats up and down the coast are being sent too. By the name 'Rescue Flotilla' it sounds like search and rescue to me, but what our area of responsibility will be isn't being told to us. Apparently, there is a Coast Guard Commander who will be the Commodore of the flotilla. Myself and the other commanding officers of the boats will meet him on Governor's Island once we get to New York."

Jack just shook his head as if to clear his thoughts. He knew Stonecliffe was young and inexperienced and his attitude could affect Stonecliffe's. Jack didn't want to needlessly cause him concern. Jack took a more pragmatic approach and said: "Whatever it is we are asked to do, we are obliged to take it on, so we might as well make the best of it."

Stonecliffe smiled and said: "I know we will Chief. We have a good boat and a good crew. Keep this change of duty to yourself until we brief the crew tomorrow. If nothing else, this will give us something to tell our grandchildren."

Jack laughed and said: "I don't think grandchildren are in the cards for me."

Stonecliffe asked: "Whatever happened to that girl from the Keweenaw you used to write when you first got down here? I think Dorothy was her name?"

Jack just shrugged and said: "There was too much geography and too much age difference between us, so we both let it go."

Stonecliffe nodded his understanding and then decided to change the subject. He had just returned from the Coast Guard Base up the bluff from where they were tied up. "Chief, I met with the Base CO about the cook who will be transferring to us. The CO is going to work with us to get him on board without any delays. The cook is young but excited about sea duty."

Jack said: "I hope he can cook! Nothing helps morale like good chow. I have a feeling we are going to need all the good morale we can get."

Stonecliffe then said: "Well, let's get underway and go down to the Naval Weapons Station and make sure all is well there. Then head for home." Looking around at the tranquil river and beautiful shoreline Stonecliffe added: "You are right Chief, we are going to miss this duty."

The next day Lieutenant Stonecliffe had all the crew gather topside so he and Jack could address the coming changes in assignment. Stonecliffe read them the orders sending them to New York for further transport to the European Theater of war. Then he turned the discussion over to Jack.

Jack looked out at the ten faces he knew so well. There was Mike McCauley who was a First Class Gunner's Mate. Mike handled all the armament and was their weapons expert. Mike had been in the Coast Guard since the 1930's and had lots of sea time. He was a good man to have around if trouble started. He was of average height and had light brown thinning hair. His face was weathered from years of time at sea. Unless the smoking lamp was out, McCauley always had a cigarette dangling from his thin lips. Jack knew McCauley was married and would be concerned about these sudden changes in duty.

Sitting next to McCauley was Harry Turner. He was a Third Class Gunner's Mate having just made the rate. He was a round faced pudgy youngster that followed McCauley around like a puppy. Jack wasn't sure how Turner might react if they were in combat. But there was no doubt he was a crack shot with a rifle or pistol.

The First Class Engineman was Sam Ritt. Tall and thin there was nothing he couldn't fix when it came to their Viking gasoline engines. He had blond hair and liked to drink. He liked to think of himself as a ladies man. Jack kept an eye on him for alcohol use while on board. So far there hadn't been a problem. But Jack was told by others in the crew he had a mean streak when he drank too much and could be a vicious fighter.

Sam's assistant with the engines was Sean Flaherty. He was only a Fireman, but Jack thought the young Irishman had promise and tried to mentor him all he could. His red hair and fair complexion made him popular with the girls. Jack didn't want any of Sam's bad personal habits to rub off on him. Jack noted they always went on liberty together.

Their Radar and Sonar operator was Jeffery Carpenter. He had just made third class and didn't have a lot of experience. Carpenter was intense and worked hard to get better at his job. He had jet black hair and had a rather handsome face. He was quiet and kept to himself. Jack hoped they were not going to be sent chasing German submarines until Carpenter got more experience.

The topsides were maintained by Boatswain Mate Jimmy Spencer, Jack's old crew member from Station Portage. It was more happenstance than planning that got him on the boat with Jack, but Jack was glad to have him.

Spencer had a Seaman to help him by the name of John Bollinger. He had joined the Coast Guard about a year earlier when he turned 18. He knew he was going to be drafted and decided the Coast Guard was better than the Army. He was a big sailor, both tall and strong. He had been a wrestler in high school. Jack kept an eye on him as he wasn't motivated and sometimes outright lazy.

To help with the charts and navigation they had a First Class Quartermaster. His name was William Russell. He was part Cherokee and his facial features and complexion reflected his heritage. Jack liked him and thought they lucky to have him.

The Radioman was Paul Vincent who was very good at his job. He wanted to make the Coast Guard his career and he looked forward to the change created by their new orders. The only problem was he was newly married and his young wife wouldn't want him going overseas.

Finally there was the new cook, Carl Williams. He had literally just stepped on board and was meeting everyone for the first time. He had his hair cut very short, was plump, and had fat fingers and hands. Jack thought he must have spent too much time eating his own cooking!

These were the men that Jack's future was sown with. In the moments before he spoke he thought they weren't a bad crew, given wartime needs of the service. And in a strange sort of way that was saying a lot.

Jack started out giving more detail: "As you know from the orders we are going to be sent overseas with the boat and all its equipment. That's all we know formally. Mr.Stonecliffe understands from discussions with other officers we are not the only boat involved. We will run up to New York and then be shipped overseas from there. I caution you not to discuss our move with anyone. You can tell your immediate family the boat is being reassigned. That's it. You'll get in touch with them after the move. We've read a lot in the newspapers that there is going to be an invasion of France this spring or summer to drive the Germans out. This may have something to do with that, but it is only speculation on my part."

The crew had paid rapt attention and now stood before Jack with very serious faces. Jack continued: "Russell, I want you to check and make sure we have all the charts and coastal pilots we need to get to New York."

Russell answered: "Aye, aye Chief."

McCauley asked: "Are they going to make us off load the depth charges and other ammo?"

Jack said: "We haven't been told to do so. For now, let's just plan on getting underway as we are."

Jack pointed at the new cook Carl Williams and said: "This is our new cook, Carl Williams. Make him welcome. And Williams, I want you to look over the galley and draw stores if we need them. At least enough to get us up the coast and a few days in New York. If we need more after that we can draw them up there."

Williams said: "Aye, aye!"

Finally, Jack added: "We leave tomorrow night at dusk. Bring a full issue seabag. Wrap up all your affairs ashore. This assignment could test us all, individually and as a crew. Everyone needs to do their duty. We all depend on each other."

Jack looked at the ten somber faces and then looked at Stonecliffe to see if he wanted to add anything. Stonecliffe just shook his head 'no'. Jack looked out over the Elizabeth River and wished he was back on the Keweenaw. Then he quietly said: "Dismissed."

CHAPTER FIVE
SEA CHANTY

Senior Chief Jack Trevenen stood on the dock at the Brooklyn Navy Yard. He looked up, studied the deck load of 83 foot patrol boats that were being loaded on the dark grey Navy transport ship. His boat had already gone on board and been tied down in its cradle. Another was now being 'nested' in its cradle along side Jack's boat. Jack wanted to make sure the cargo boom operator didn't have any accidents. Jack's boat had the depth charge rackets stripped off and all ammunition, provisions and personal items removed. The side arms and a 50 caliber machine gun were left on board, properly stowed. All fuel had been removed. But the boat would be easy to make operational again once put in the water in southern England.

Their trip up to New York from Virginia had been uneventful. Lt(jg) Stonecliffe had left Jack to oversee the loading of their boat while he attended another meeting with the other patrol boat captains and the Coast Guard Commander in charge of the flotilla. Jack understood sixty boats and crews were going to be shipped. They had been transferred from locations up and down the East Coast and Gulf Coast. Some were being loaded over on the Jersey side on civilian ships. They would then all proceed north to join a convoy off Newfoundland and then head for England. Jack and the rest of the crew would berth on the Navy transport and ride it to England. Stonecliffe had learned they would be off loaded at Poole on the English Channel.

The loading being completed, Jack decided to go on board and take a good look at the way the boats and cradles were secured. They were crossing the North Atlantic after the winter weather, but they could still run into some pretty good seas. Jack was about to go up the gangway to the cargo deck when he saw a Coast Guard officer coming down the dock in his direction. Jack prepared to snap off a salute when he looked hard at the sandy hair and smiling face and recognized Lieutenant Griffin. He had last seen him at Station Portage when he was conducting part of the investigation into the loss of the *SS Inland Mariner.*

Jack saluted and smiled saying: "I'm glad to see you again Lieutenant. You are the last person I expected to see in the Brooklyn Navy Yard. This is still a small service despite the wartime expansion."

Griffin, also smiling, returned the salute and said: "Senior Chief Trevenen, it's good to see you again. You are just the person I'm looking for. Can I interrupt your duties for a few minutes? I have an issue I want to talk over with you."

This response interested Jack, and he said: "I was just going aboard to check the Navy's work stowing our patrol boat! But don't tell them I said that! I have lots of time as we are not sailing until tomorrow night."

Griffin nodded in the direction of the end of the pier and said: "Let's take a little walk and let me tell you why I sought you out."

Jack was good at taking direction from officers so he simply nodded his agreement and they started walking.

Griffin explained: "I'm presently the Executive Officer on the Coast Guard Cutter Campbell. She's a Secretary Class cutter built in the 1930's. Because of the war we are assigned to the US Navy and have been doing convoy duty, including the Iceland shuttle, for several months now. We have had a lot of sea time and have engaged with German submarines several times. Frankly, the crew is tired and not at their best. I lost the Chief Boatswain's Mate who was running the Deck Department to a broken arm. The First Lieutenant is a young reserve officer with little experience. Despite the wartime growth of the Coast Guard, Chief Petty officers such as yourself are hard to come by. Instead of riding the transport to England I'd like to give you some temporary orders to serve on the Campbell for this trip. The Campbell is one of several escort vessels guarding your convoy. You would rejoin your unit when we get to England. By then maybe the Navy can find us a new Chief Petty officer. From what I saw on a previous trip there sure are enough Navy ships in English ports to share a crew member with us."

Jack didn't know what to say. He didn't relish the idea of going to the Campbell. It would be tough, demanding duty for the two weeks or so the entire commitment would last. He was looking forward to taking it easy on the transport for the trip over. Once they were off loaded in the war zone Jack thought the duty could be hard. Still, the German submarine threat existed. If he was going to be part of this convoy he would rather be one of the hunters rather than the hunted. The transport would sink like a rock if torpedoed in the right place.

After pausing to reflect on this Jack said: "How did you find me? We just arrived from Virginia?"

Griffin said: "I got access to the patrol boat crew rosters since we will be one of your escorts. I was hoping to find a replacement for the trip back to England from the Chiefs who would be accompanying their boats. When I saw your name I knew you would be right for the job."

Jack said: "You flatter me Lieutenant. There is nothing special about what I can do. If you have a good First Class Boatswain's Mate on board he should be able to step up?"

Griffin didn't respond to the question but simply said: "We would be better off with you aboard, especially if we have to go to General Quarters because of a submarine attack."

Jack nodded his understanding. Then he said: "You would have to get permission from Mr. Stonecliffe who is my commanding officer, and I assume the Commander in charge of our flotilla."

Griffin looked down at the dock and then a little sheepishly said: "Already done. Your orders should come by messenger this afternoon. We are tied up at Governor's Island. If you have trouble getting a ride over there just call the duty shack on the Island. I'll send one of our small boats."

Jack appreciated the fact Griffin took the time to talk it over with him and let him decide before he was simply given orders. It all gave him pause though. He was not as young as he used to be and he didn't know how much hard sea duty his body would take.

Jack looked at Griffin and said: "I'll be there timely. Just tell your OOD I'll be coming. But there is something I want to know. The last time I saw you, you were looking into the actions of Captain McKeil of the *SS Inland Mariner*. Whatever happened to all that?"

Griffin said: "Eventually he was charged with hazarding the vessel in light of the weather and his safe harbor options. He fought it and it went to a hearing. He was acquitted due to the issues surrounding the seaworthiness of the vessel and the lengthening of her the prior winter. Our Headquarters people thought there were questions in that regard. He kept his license and is sailing oceans today. We recently escorted a convoy where he was in command of a troop transport. I don't know what you are going to be doing in England but you might see him again."

Jack answered: "I don't know what we are going to be doing either. Top secret I guess! But I hate to think of a ship full of troops in his hands."

Griffin turned and started to walk away. Then he stopped, turned back, and asked one further question: "Chief, when I saw you on the Keweenaw you were about to retire. What did you do? Ask to ship over when the war started?"

Jack shook his head: "Not hardly! They pulled me out of a warm bed with a good woman to tell me my retirement orders were cancelled and I'm here for the duration."

Griffin got a big grin on his face and said: "Welcome aboard Chief! Glad to have you with us."

Diana looked around the pub from behind the bar. It was early afternoon and they were beginning to get a few customers. They were all sailors off duty and off the ships in the harbor. They were mostly military but there were a few civilians. She had been tidying up and washing a few glasses in readiness for the evening business. As the inevitable invasion drew nearer, southern England, including the Lion and Cross, seemed to be bursting with soldiers and sailors keyed up and tired of waiting for the big day when they would invade France.

Diana was under constant pressure from her handler to find out the answer to two over riding questions — when and where would the Allies land? Each time she worked at the pub she eavesdropped on as many conversations as possible hoping to hear something she could report. Diana carefully observed the patrons looking for persons of authority she might engage in conversation. So far her attempts to penetrate the secrecy surrounding the invasion had not been successful.

A tall man in a ship captain's uniform came in and Diana took note. He had grey hair and a grey beard. His face was weathered and looked like it had seen hard days. He had been in before but Diana had not had a chance to speak to him. She did recollect that he drank a great deal. He now sat down heavily at a table by himself and took off his hat and put it on the chair next to him. He motioned for Diana and she went over to him.

Diana asked: "What can we get for you this afternoon?"

The man answered: "I'll have a porter to start with, then maybe go to an ale."

Diana recognized the accent as American. She decided to confirm her judgment that he was in command of his own merchant ship. She said: "We don't get many ship captains in here. We are glad to have you. Your services keeping Britain supplied in the face of wartime dangers is appreciated."

The man shook his head and said: "I'm master of a troop transport. I haul men, although I have commanded cargo ships. This is my third trip. Now I'm just waiting for sailing orders."

Diana couldn't believe her luck. This man could very well be the source she needed. Diana said: "Those are important duties as well. What is the name of your ship?"

"The *John J. Southland* is my command. My name is McKeil. This war leaves me weary. Not that I'm not enjoying your conversation miss, but that porter would go down well if I could have it?"

Diana said: "Of course. Forgive me. Our barkeep Roger will be taking over for me as I have office duties. He will keep you in good order. Please visit us often."

McKeil nodded and said rather gruffly: "I'll be back as my duties allow."

Diana had to make some bookkeeping entries and pay some bills in the pub's cramped office. She had no further contact with McKeil that day but noted he was still drinking when she left.

That night in bed Diana couldn't stop thinking about how her role would change if she really did find opportunities to talk with McKeil and he began to trust her with information. Up to now she was simply reporting her observations to her handler. McKeil could result in her becoming a more traditional agent working sources. Her risks of detection certainly would go up, but so did the potential rewards. Diana was not going to report any of this until it developed further, if at all. Finding subtle ways to talk with McKeil alone would not be easy. Diana rolled over on her side and decided to stop thinking about it and try and sleep. It was a warm spring night and she was sleeping nude. She slid her hand over the soft curls between her legs and then touched the lips of her vagina. For a moment she thought of using seduction but the distastefulness was too much to bear.

Jack went up the gangway to the deck of the Coast Guard Cutter Campbell and snapped off a salute to the American flag on the stern and then to the Warrant Officer who was the OOD. The Warrant returned the salute and said: "Welcome aboard Senior Chief. Mr. Griffin said you would be reporting in. Let me get the messenger to take you up to see the Exec and then the Captain."

Jack said: "Thank you." Within a few minutes he was shaking hands with Lieutenant Griffin who once again assured him he was glad to see him. Shortly thereafter he stood at attention in front of Captain Dawson who was the Commanding Officer of the ship.

Dawson looked at Jack's orders and then flipped through the pages of Jack's service record which Jack had also carried and presented. Dawson held the rank of Commander but due to his position he was referred to as 'Captain'. He was tall and looked much older than what Jack knew he must be. He looked tired. His hair was almost entirely grey. As he sat at a steel desk studying the information in Jack's service record he ran his hand through his hair as if to help him understand the man he had in front of him. Jack watched as he lit a cigarette and took a deep drag. Jack noted the ash tray was full of butts.

Dawson closed the service record and turned to Jack saying: "At ease Senior Chief. You have an impressive service record. I see you have had sea duty and command experience. Griffin says he tried to get you for more than this voyage but your CO and the Flotilla Commander said no. In the short time you are here I need to get the ship as ready as possible for anti-submarine combat. I'll send Mr. Jenkins our young First Lieutenant to find you. I want you and he to tour the ship. You need to make a mental note of all you want to do before we get underway and afterwards, if it can be done safely with available crew. You'll be worked to death but there is nothing else for it."

Jack replied: "Aye, aye sir. I'll do anything I can Captain. These Secretary class cutters were pretty ships when they were painted white but the wartime grey and black camouflage on the hull makes it look mean and ugly."

Dawson gave Jack a knowing grin: "You'll like mean and ugly when we are half way across the Atlantic and in a U-boat's sights. This trip we'll have a big convoy and lots of other escorts. All in preparation for the invasion of France. The Germans know that and the U-boats are particularly aggressive. We have air cover on each side of the Atlantic which really helps. But for two days or so in the middle it is just us versus them."

Jack didn't know what to say so he just stood quietly for a moment.

Dawson looked at him and said: "The crew is tired. We have had more patrols than we should have for the sake of the crew and the vessel. But the war makes demands on all of us. Give us your best Senior Chief. Our Deck Department needs your talents."

Jack replied: "Aye, aye sir." He then began a progression of activities which made an indelible impression on him.

Jack berthed in the Chief's Quarters and the other Chiefs welcomed him warmly. They were glad of all the help they could get—especially new additions to the crew. They teased him endlessly about his "booking passage to Europe on their ship"! They were close lipped about what happened at General Quarters in a U-boat attack. But Jack was able to get a picture of the needs of the ship by talking with them. He and the Chief Quartermaster would work well together. Unfortunately, the Chief Quartermaster had injured his back and had trouble standing for a four hour watch. He was their best helmsman. When Jack heard this he knew he would get bridge watches, and possibly time on the helm.

63

After touring the ship with Mr. Jenkins, the First Lieutenant, he knew where he would start. The davits for the four lifeboats and the standing rigging on the after mast needed attention. He wanted that work done in the short time before they sailed. Jack met the enlisted men from the deck department and introduced himself. He asked all their names and experience. They appeared tired and some were sullen. They had been pushed hard and liberty had been short and was now over. Despite that Jack put them to work and lent a hand himself which made a positive impression. Jack went into the engineering spaces and found an engineman to help check the engines in the lifeboats.

The Chief Gunners Mate turned out some of his men and made sure all the secondary batteries and depth charge equipment was in working order and then secured it for sea. The Campbell was 327 feet long and had a 5 inch gun enclosed in a turret forward. Behind that was a twin 40 millimeter mount. Back aft there were two 20 millimeter mounts and two rows of depth charge racks. There were also five depth charge launchers down each side of the main deck, aft of the life boats.

The Chief Quartermaster oversaw the final repair and readying of the navigation equipment. The surface radar and sonar all were in good condition. By the time the Campbell slipped her lines and headed out of the inner harbor all was as ship shape as possible. Jack had other chores of less importance his men could work on while underway, weather and watch standing permitting, but the worrisome issues had been addressed.

The Coast Guard Cutter Campbell waited outside the entrance to New York harbor for the transports with the Coast Guard patrol boats on board to come out and take stations to form a small convoy. After that they all sailed for Newfoundland to join the other vessels in the larger convoy for the trip across the Atlantic.

As Jack lay in his bunk the first night at sea he realized he needed to get use to the movement of the ship. This class of cutter rode well but Jack felt slightly nauseated. He was also anxious. Despite all his years in the service this would be his first time in a war zone and potentially engaged in combat. Jack thought back on his life in the service. In some ways it allowed him to escape personal responsibilities and challenges. The Coast Guard kept you busy regardless what ship or station you served at. It provided all your needs. Jack didn't have time to think about his wife Catherine who died so tragically and so young. He didn't have to make an effort to find a new wife or start a family. He always had the duties that were immediately in front of him and the assurance he would be transferred to a new assignment and location every two or three years. Now as he lay there he felt very lonely and actually had a sense of regret that he had no family and no warmth of home to return to when this was all over.

Jack laid awake for a long time and had just drifted off to sleep when the claxon went off and a general quarters drill was called. Jack immediately rolled out of his bunk and pulled on his pants. Everyone scrambled to their assigned station for this type of emergency. Depending on the type of emergency, duty stations could change and were posted on the watch quarters and station board in the main passageway. Jack had three emergency stations. For some he was assigned to the bridge, but was also part of the forward damage control party for collision or torpedo damage to the forward part of the ship. In an air attack he was to report to the 20 millimeter batteries back aft.

Jack was fully dressed when he got to the bridge. The Captain was on the bridge as was the Mr. Jenkins who was the OOD. The quartermaster of the watch had the helm. There was a lieutenant Jack hadn't met who apparently served as navigator. He was standing in the hatch leading to the operations center which held the radar, sonar and radios, all of which were also manned. Jack took a position off to one side to get out of the way.

When all the parts of the ship reported they were manned and ready the Captain turned to Jenkins and the lieutenant and with a stern look said: "That was too slow. The crew has lost its edge while we were in New York. We need to come to general quarters much faster. If we had had a contact with a German sub it could have put a torpedo into us. Pass the word I want improvement. I'll talk to all the other department heads in the wardroom tomorrow morning."

The officers answered smartly with an "Aye, aye sir".

Then the Captain turned to Jack: "Senior Chief, you are out of uniform. Mr. Jenkins will see to it you have a steel helmet and life vest to turn out in for general quarters. I also want you to take a turn or two at the helm while we are in the open ocean. I want to see your skills in that regard. Since you aren't a regular member of the crew I may assign you a lot of different activities if we are at general quarters. You will see things can happen fast."

Jack said: "Yes sir."

The Captain nodded and said to Mr. Jenkin: "You have the con. I made entries in the night order book. Unless trouble arises our course won't change until daybreak. Keep an eye on our flock of merchant and transport ships. I'll be in my cabin if anyone needs me." Mr. Jenkin saluted and the Captain left the bridge. Jenkins then had 'secure from general quarters' announced over the ships loud speakers.

Jack turned to Jenkins and asked: "Sir, how often do we do this?"

Jenkins took off his helmet, wiped his brow with the back of his hand and took his work cap from a binocular rack and put it on. He responded: "We do this all the time. Every drill you can imagine until we are about a day out with the main convoy. Then our real worry is the convoy and U-boats and if we go to general quarters it is for real. Captain Dawson wants us well trained so when the real thing happens we know where to go and what to do."

Jack nodded his understanding and after asking permission to leave the bridge and return to his bunk he went below. He didn't sleep anymore that night. He just lay there thinking. Jack didn't know it yet, but for the entire time he was on the CGC Campbell he never got more than four hours sleep due to watches, drills and calls to general quarters. And drill they did. All the way to Newfound Land and in the initial stages of the Atlantic crossing with the main convoy-- fire drills, collision drills, air or surface attack drills, and of course anti-submarine drills. At one point Jack didn't think he would ever be able to sleep for eight uninterrupted hours again.

Diana stood in front of the small mirror over the sink in her flat. She had just gotten out of bed and was nude. The mirror only allowed her to view herself from the waist up. She ignored her breasts and studied her face. She looked pale and tired. Diana noticed some small wrinkles around her eyes. She was aging. All the hours spent working in the cigarette smoke filled pub didn't help. She was tired of the stress of having to hide her true identity and role as a German agent. She was tired of the war and wanted it all to end. Diana regretted staying with Hawes as his part time bookkeeper. After she had reacted so indignantly to his touching her Hawes had been afraid to come near her. But the fear was wearing off and she was very tense when she was working and he was around. She knew he stole glances at her when he thought she wouldn't notice.

Diana lowered her view from the mirror and thought about her day. She wanted a bath. Her legs needed shaving. Razor blades were expensive and hard to come by, but she couldn't go any longer. The lavatory was down the hall and she would have to check and make sure none of the other tenants were using it. Diana splashed some water on her face, put her hair up and put on her robe. She went to the door to go down the hall and check the lavatory when she heard a small knocking on the other side. Diana paused. She never had visitors. She looked at the clock. She had gotten up late after working until closing time at the Lion and Cross. It was mid-morning. Diana made sure her robe was fully closed and slowly opened the door.

There stood the woman who was her handler. Diana was surprised to see her. They had always met in public before. Still, as her handler she had authority over her and could control their meeting places. Diana hoped nothing was wrong. Their relationship had not gotten any better with time. The woman was in her fifties, overweight, and not attractive. Diana thought maybe she resented her good looks. Today she was wearing a wool hat and a long dark green coat. She carried a small leather suitcase. Her coarse facial features displayed no emotion.

The two of them stood staring at each other for a moment. Then the woman spoke up in perfect English: "Have you no greeting for your cousin Anna?"

Diana hadn't used the code words for a face-to-face meeting in ages. She had to think a moment, then she said: "Cousin Anna, I'm glad to see you are well and able to go out."

The woman responded: "Your good wishes have brought me health." With that the woman stepped through the doorway and Diana quietly closed the door.

The woman looked around the room, then turned to Diana and in a scolding manner said: "You need to be more correct in your use of our code words. What if it hadn't been me but someone testing you. The enemy perhaps?"

Diana said: "You took me by surprise. It took me a moment to recognize you. Won't you sit down. I can make you some tea."

The woman looked at her severely: "I will not be here that long. I do not hear much from you that is of merit. You know how important it is we know when and where our enemies will land in France."

Diana sat down and leveled her look at the woman saying firmly: "You have all the information on the buildup in this area—the number of troops, units, ships in the harbor—everything. If I get any hard information on the invasion I will contact you."

The woman sat the small suitcase she had been holding on the table in the center of the room. She opened it and Diana saw it contained a shortwave radio. The woman said: "This is yours. You have been trained in such things. If you get information about the timing or location of the invasion you are to send it over this. The frequency is set. The codes for the transmission are on top in the folder. Read everything, memorize the codes and then burn the folder. Do not use this for other purposes. You must wait for a confirmation if you transmit."

Diana nodded her understanding. Then she said: "Doesn't the use of that increase my chances of being caught, I mean, aren't the British monitoring such transmissions and then locating their source?"

The woman scoffed at Diana and said: "Fool. Do you not think there is risk in what we do. You have grown soft. The few transmissions you will make will be of no consequence to your being discovered."

Diana bristled at the insult. Diana stood, looked the woman squarely in the eye, and firmly said: "I will do my duty. You may be assured of that."

The woman gave Diana a very small knowing smile and said: "Good."

Diana moved to the door, opened it, and said: "If that is all I will bid you good day."

Without another word the woman walked briskly out of the flat and down the hall. As Diana closed the door she hoped it would be a long while before this woman paid another visit.

Later that morning Diana sat soaking in a bath tub of hot water. She thought about the radio and it frightened her. She would have to have learned specifics about the invasion before she would use it. Nothing less. With all this military presence in the area she was sure the British would pick up a transmission. She was even afraid to keep it in her flat.

Diana's flat was on the top floor of her building and there was a small door leading to the attic. The landlord said the attic was not to be used. Despite that, Diana had opened the door and put the radio in the shadows in the attic where it would not be seen from the doorway. She had read the materials in the folder but not memorized the codes. She had put the folder on the bottom of the dresser drawer where she kept her lingerie. Diana thought that was the best she could do with it for the moment. She had to go to Hawes after lunch and then work at the pub after that. It would be another long day.

The Coast Guard Cutter Campbell with her flock of transport ships carrying their deck cargo of 83 foot patrol boats headed east past Long Island and Cape Cod and then turned northeast for St. Johns Newfound Land. Sant Johns Newfound Land is the most easterly location on the North Atlantic coast of Canada to depart by ship for Great Britain. That made it a popular location for the formation and departure of North Atlantic convoys supplying Great Britain and the American, Canadian and British armies located there. It has a good harbor and many safe anchorages. Vessels could fuel, take on potable water and other supplies. The ships forming the various convoys came from New York, Boston, The Saint Lawrence River or even Hampton Roads.

Jack Trevenen was impressed with the number of different nationalities represented by the ships gathered there. It was a sampling of the countries of the world. He was also impressed at the organization and effort that went into the creation and management of each convoy. Their convoy would have about forty merchant ships in it including the ones with the Coast Guard patrol boats. There would be ten escort vessels from the US Navy, Coast Guard and Canadian Navy. These would be destroyer and destroyer escort class ships. They were fast and armed for anti-submarine warfare. There would be a Convoy Commander in charge of the merchant ships. There was another senior naval officer named as the Escort Commander.

The ships would sail in five lines of approximately eight ships apiece. The ships on the inside of the formation carried cargos such as gasoline, oil or munitions. This gave them some added protection against being torpedoed as they were screened by the outer ships. The merchant vessels sailed within a few ship lengths of each other with the escort vessels taking positions on the outside of the convoy to provide protective screening and engage any German submarines that attacked. Their convoy would be a fast one as the goal was to maintain 12 knots, although that could change with weather or submarine attack.

The ships were blacked out at night so no light would lead a German submarine to them. It was essential that all ships maintained the correct course and speed to avoid collision. If attacked, course changes or zig zag sailing patterns could be employed and danger of collision increased. It was a nerve wracking trip for ocean sailors who thought they should always be miles from the nearest vessel. Even on a quiet night watching for the darkened ship ahead or behind yours was tension filled. The officers and men of these merchant ships could only take comfort in the fact 60% of vessels sunk by U Boats were not in a convoy.

During the trip to Newfound Land the weather had been good and the seas calm. Jack was able to get the deck department work done between drills. At one point he even asked Mr. Griffin to ask the Captain to hold off on afternoon drills as his work party needed to tear down and repair a forward deck winch that handled the raising and lowering of the port anchor. Jack advised he needed the whole afternoon. He didn't know if his request made any difference, but drills were held off until after the evening meal.

Naval ship patrols and air cover along the coast had just about eliminated the threat of U Boats on the Atlantic Coast. So they had no call to go to General Quarters other than for drills. Griffin told him that early in the war coastal defenses weren't in place and they would have been dealing with German submarines.

Jack was also falling into the shipboard routine. He stood a lot of watches on the bridge in various roles. The Captain wanted him wheeling so he stood several helm watches and was a natural at handling the cutter. The Captain assured him in an emergency evolution he wanted his best man on the helm and he wanted to know who that was.

When they got to St Johns the Captain went to several meetings with the Convoy and Escort Commanders and they got some brief liberty. Jack grabbed a young Boatswain's Mate and took a small boat over to the transport with his patrol boat on it. He went aboard and checked on everyone in his crew. They were not required to stand any watches so they were happy. The patrol boats rode well and hadn't moved at all in their cradles.

Mr. Stonecliffe asked: "How are you being treated on the Campbell?"

Jack smiled and light heartedly said: "They work me endlessly! The cooks put down some good meals. Lots of watch standing. But I'm not in the lap of luxury like you men!"

Stonecliffe said: "Seriously, is it going okay?"

Jack was touched by his concern. He looked at Stonecliffe and said: "Yes sir it is. I'm getting use to the routine of a larger cutter. I'm learning a lot about the war against U Boats in the North Atlantic. When Lieutenant Griffin pulled me into this temporary duty I told myself I'd be better off as the hunter rather than the hunted. This transport will flood and sink rapidly if torpedoed. We will do all we can to protect you, but make sure the men keep their life jackets handy if we are attacked. I'm told the escorts can't stop to pick up survivors in many circumstances—it's too dangerous. The escort vessel can then become the target."

Stonecliffe looked quite somber. Jack put his hand on his shoulder. "Don't worry Lieutenant. We are going to get through this trip".

Stonecliffe didn't say anything but firmly shook Jack's hand.

As Jack turned to go he smiled and said: "It's not this trip I'm worried about. It is what they have in store for us once we get to England that bothers me!"

Late the next afternoon, the convoy sailed. One by one the merchant ships and transports with the patrol boats on board left St Johns harbor and found their predetermined locations in the convoy's organization. The escorts, including CGC Campbell, took their stations outboard of the cargo carrying ships. As the Canadian coast disappeared behind them in the growing darkness, a Canadian Air Force multiengine aircraft droned slowly overhead keeping a safe watch over the ships below.

Diana stood behind the bar at the Lion and Cross and looked up at the clock. It was almost 11 pm and she could leave for home soon. It had been a long day and her legs were tired. She went into the office to get her coat and coming out she met the bar keep who encouraged her to go on home. The crowd was thinning out and most of the regular patrons were gone. Diana could walk the few blocks home and wasn't bothered by the darkness or the fact she was alone. Despite all the soldiers and sailors about, she had been treated with courtesy. Tonight, the street looked vacant and there was a light drizzle falling. Diana turned up her collar and puled her coat tightly around her. She quickened her step to get in out of the damp.

As Diana turned the corner and headed away from the quay she noticed a man in the shadows of a doorway. He was bent over and had vomited on the sidewalk. Diana stopped to observe him. The man straightened up and started walking down the street. His gait was unsteady and at times he would stop and lean against the front of a building to keep from falling. Since there was a black out Diana could not make out the man's features, but he was obviously drunk. Diana decided to stand still and let him get well down the street from her before she started walking again. She didn't want trouble with him.

Just then a nearby door opened and a man came out and went down the street in the opposite direction. The light that shown into the street from the brief opening of the door allowed Diana to recognize the features of the drunken man. It was Captain McKeil. This caused Diana to pause and think. This might be the opening she had been looking for to gain his confidence and learn what he knew about the invasion.

Diana walked quickly to catch up with McKeil and came up behind him. In a gentle voice she asked: "Captain, are you alright? Can I help in some way?"

McKeil turned and with glassy eyes looked at her without recognizing her. Quite gruffly he said: "Who are you? What do you want with me?"

Diana answered: "Captain, it's me, Diana from the Lion and Cross. I've waited on you. You've become one of our regular guests."

The explanation sank in and McKeil seemed to recognize her: "Oh, yes. I know you now. Sorry I didn't remember you." Somewhat embarrassed over his condition McKeil tried to stand up straight but needed to brace himself against the wall of the building to do so.

Diana asked: "Where are you going? Do you have a way to get back to your ship?"

McKeil took a moment to answer and then said: "Liberty boat went back to the ship without me. I need to find rooms for the night."

Diana gave him a concerned look and said: "Captain, you are not going to find any place to stay here in Poole at this time of night. Why don't you come home with me? I have a nice warm flat and I can make you a nice hot cup of tea?"

McKeil hesitated but then decided to accept direction: "Yes, that would be good. I could get my sea legs under me again and then figure out what to do."

Diana said: "Come Captain. You can lean on me and we'll walk to my flat. It's is only a short distance." With that the pair headed down the street with McKeil leaning heavily on Diana, his arm over her shoulder.

By the time they got to Diana's McKeil seemed to have sobered up some. He no longer needed to lean on her. Diana brought him into her small one room flat and sat him at her small wood dining table while she made some tea. Neither spoke and McKeil's head fell forward with his chin resting on his chest. He seemed to be dozing. At last the tea was ready and McKeil drank it without a word.

Diana finally decided she couldn't learn anything from him in this state so she decided she would keep him and engage him in conversation in the morning. Diana went and stood next to McKeil's chair and said: "Captain, why don't you sit in my arm chair. You'll be more comfortable and you can get some sleep. If you need the lavatory it is down the hall. Please don't be sick in here."

McKeil rose and crossed the room sinking heavily into the upholstered arm chair. All he said was: "Thank you." He closed his eyes and fell asleep. Diana put a blanket over him and he was set for the night.

Diana slept in her bed on the opposite side of the room. She kept her bra and panties on and put her robe tightly around herself before getting under her blanket. She did not want to give McKeil the idea this was a seduction if he woke up in the night.

The next morning McKeil woke and saw Diana fully dressed and making eggs. The tea was made and a place set for him at the small table. He groaned and suddenly felt very ashamed of himself and his behavior. He tossed the blanket aside and said: "Thank you very much for taking me in. I apologize for my behavior."

Diana said: "No need to apologize. The lavatory is down the hall. Why don't you go down there and get cleaned up. By then some breakfast will be ready. By the way, here are two aspirins. You will need these."McKeil nodded, took the aspirins and went down the hall. After he came back they had a light breakfast. McKeil was hung over and had very little appetite.

Diana started the conversation by saying: "Captain you need to be more careful with your drink. If I hadn't come along the military police would have picked you up and held you. Are you in trouble anyway for not making it back to your ship.?"

McKeil shook his head 'no' and said: "I'm the Captain. We are at anchor awaiting the invasion. I'll get one of the small boats in the harbor to take me over to her this morning. Your bar tender introduced me to half and half's—a stout and ale combination that was more powerful than I realized." McKeil then looked down and rubbed his face with his hands as if to clear the cobwebs. He continued: "Just before the United States got into the war I was Captain of a merchant ship on the Great Lakes. I lost her in a storm. There was a serious loss of life. At times I can't stop thinking about it and I drink too much." He was silent and then looked up at Diana imploringly.

Diana looked at him and said: "We all have moments we want to forget but just can't. The war creates many. I lost my husband in the air war during the summer of 1940. My bitterness over his death can surface in me at times when I least expect it."

McKeil paid little attention to her attempt to show him understanding. He continued, taking an angry tone: "The bastards in the Coast Guard blamed me for the ship sinking. Tried to take my license. But I beat 'em. I'm still sailing and I hope they've all gone to hell."

Diana didn't say anything for a moment, then decided to see what she could learn. "What will you do in the invasion?"

McKeil said: I'll load part of the American 29th Division and take them across the English Channel. We'll then load them into landing craft that will take them ashore."

Diana asked: "When will you take the troops on board?"

McKeil shrugged: "Who knows. They don't tell us a damn thing until the last moment."

Diana said: I'll wager they haven't told you where you are going either?"

McKeil said: "You have that right. They think we are all spies or will talk in front of the enemy."   McKeil shook his head in frustration: "More shameful treatment by my superiors."

Diana decided she would make a point of keeping in touch with McKeil. While he didn't know anything now, he would in the future. Diana stood and told McKeil he needed to go as she had to go to work. He rose and again thanked her. They parted and Diana promised him she would keep an eye on him at the Lion and Cross.

CHAPTER SIX
GROUND SWELLS

Senior Chief Jack Trevenen stood on the bridge of the Coast Guard Cutter Campbell and looked out at a quiet moonlit sea. Lieutenant Griffin was there as well. He was taking the watch as OOD due to one of the other officers being sick. Normally, as Executive Officer, he didn't stand watches. Jack wasn't sure he had a title, but at the moment he was keeping track of the radio transmissions and radar and sonar contacts in the Combat Information Center located just behind the bridge. He kept Griffin informed of any contacts as well as incoming messages. All was quiet so Jack could stand at the after bulkhead of the bridge and talk quietly with Griffin about less urgent matters. Tonight's topic was Jack's experiences on Lake Superior while he was in the US Life Saving Service.

Griffin shook his head in wonder and said: "I can't imagine you and six others rowing a 26 foot wood surfboat into a raging Lake Superior to try and save someone."

Jack was a little embarrassed as he didn't like telling sea stories about his career. He gave Griffin a small smile and said: "We didn't look forward to it but we went out when we had to. Most of the time we were successful in getting survivors and ourselves back safely. The old surfboats were made for rough weather and they could take a beating and still get you home."

Jack paused and then continued: "Sir, to change the subject for a moment, could I inquire about how I'm to be reunited with my command and the crew of my patrol boat?"

Griffin grinned at him: "Don't worry. We get to take you to jolly old England and drop you on the dock at Poole. We need some liberty in an English port for the crew. We have been on convoy duty endlessly. For a while we were stationed in Iceland and came south to pick up convoys mid-Atlantic and get them through the 'gap' where there is no air cover. The winter trips were awful regardless where we started from. Seas could get so big the convoy had to slow and we would be lucky if we got 4 or 5 knots of speed over ground. The Campbell would climb 30 foot waves—breaking out of the crest and slamming her bow down into the trough—it shook the whole ship. We took solid water back to the bridge. Everything was secured. No hot food. It seemed never ending."

Jack looked out at the calm moonlit evening and thought he was glad he missed those trips. Then he said: "I know now why some of the men in the deck division didn't look too enthusiastic over my work assignments."

Griffin nodded: "Yes, they have had a hard time. Punctuated with U Boat attacks."

Both men were quiet for a moment. Then Griffin added: "Normally we hand a convoy off to British escorts when we get closer to England. Then we head back to Iceland or the East Coast with ships returning to the United States. But because your patrol boats are part of the cargo in this convoy, someone in Headquarters thought this should be a Coast Guard operation and escort you all the way. Whether we stick around for the invasion or go home has not yet been told to us."

Jack said: "What earthly use can there be for a flotilla of wooden patrol boats in the middle of history's biggest amphibious landing?"

Griffin answered: "I don't know. But I'll bet you will be in the lead of whatever is planned. Seems to me they would want your search and rescue skills. The English Channel could be your new Lake Superior."

Just then Captain Dawson came up the ladder and on to the bridge. Jack and Mr. Griffin stopped chatting and Jack went back into the CIC. Mr. Griffin announced: "Captain on the bridge."

Captain Dawson asked for course and speed which Griffin promptly told him. Griffin further advised the Convoy Commander had the convoy zig zagging and the ships had just executed a turn to port. The escort ships like the CGC Campbell were in a protective circle around the outside of the convoy and they too modified their course and speed to stay on station. The Captain nodded his approval in response to Griffin's information. He had concerns about the safety of the convoy tonight The seas were relatively calm and the moon, almost full, caused the merchant ships to appear in silhouette against the horizon. It was perfect for a submarine attack.

The convoy had lost its air cover from the west and was not far enough east to fall under the protection of British air patrols. Two of the Canadian escorts had turned back for home and been replaced by a single Coast Guard cutter assigned the 'Iceland Shuttle'. They had come down from Reykjavik, Iceland where they were temporarily stationed to assist in escort duties. This was the dangerous part of the trip. Mid-ocean with no protection other than what they provided themselves. Jack was glad the transports with the Coast Guard patrol boats on board were sailing in the center columns of the convoy. The outboard merchant ships were more at risk.

The convoy was making good time. They weren't averaging the twelve knots the Escort Commander wanted but they were doing close to eleven. They had good weather so far and had only zig zagged once when they had air cover. Zig zagging involved predetermined course changes to the left or right and then back again. On a quiet moonlit night the turns by convoy ships sailing in close proximity, and in columns, were relatively safe. On a dark night, in bad weather, or in the confusion of torpedo attack, ships could easily collide. But zig zagging was important. It helped throw off a torpedo set up by any U Boat that might be lurking in their path. However, there had been no radar or sonar contacts with U Boats and no U Boat sightings. The circle of escort ships and their radar and sonar created a protective ring. The CGC Campbell's station was on the starboard side of the convoy near the rear of the outboard column of ships.

The Captain went back into the CIC. He nodded to Jack who promptly said: "Good evening Captain." The Captain looked at the radar screen. The positions of each ship in the convoy were visible and appeared to be maintaining their stations well.

The Captain pulled a clip board off the bulkhead that had all recent radio messages typed and attached. He flipped through them and finding nothing he hadn't already seen he turned to Jack and said: "I'll be in the wardroom. If you haven't looked at my night orders do so. I want to be called for any contact you pick up. We need to be on our toes tonight. The conditions are perfect for an attack."

Jack said: "Yes sir, I understand. We'll keep you informed."

With that the Captain went below.

About an hour later Jack was looking forward to the end of his watch. He looked up at the ship's clock mounted on the bulkhead and figured he only had 20 more minutes and he should be relieved. His rack would feel good. One thing he learned from his time on the Campbell was he could sleep anywhere at anytime. He was glad all was quiet. Griffin was also still on watch and he was standing next to the young quartermaster who had the helm. Both men were looking out the bridge windows at a starlit night. In fact, it was so clear the stars seemed three dimensional—as if you could reach up among them and touch them. It reminded Jack of Lake Superior.

Jack decided he should ask Griffin what assignments he had for the deck department the next day when a bright white flash lit up the sky on their port side. Then the sound of a deep loud 'crump' came across the water. The sky on their port side turned orange from the flames of a burning ship. They were all startled by the sudden nature of the U Boat attack. Griffin put his binoculars to his eyes and said: "Those bastards have hit one of the inboard ships. Sound general quarters – battle stations. Jack, call the Captain."

They sounded the alarm but didn't need to call the Captain as Dawson was on the bridge the moment he heard the explosion from the torpedo striking the ill fated ship. Jack noted he was very calm. He asked for course and speed and checked to make sure they were on station. Then he looked at Jack and asked: "Do we have any contacts?"

Jack said: "Nothing, sir."

Jack went back into the CIC. The radioman said: "The Convoy Commander is sending out a message ordering a new zig zag pattern." Jack wasn't sure what to do. To his relief a young Lieutenant (jg) appeared who was their Operations Officer and Navigator. He relieved Jack.

The Captain called out: "Chief Trevenen, I want you on the helm. The quartermaster will take the sound powered phones."

Jack said "Aye, aye Captain." Taking the helm, Jack checked the heading and waited for the course changes that were sure to come. He could see they were rapidly leaving the stricken ship behind. The convoy was moving away from them on a new zig zag pattern. The captain asked for a new course and speed to maintain station and the Operations Officer promptly gave it. Jack heard the Captain say to him: "Left ten degrees rudder, steady on 085." Jack turned the helm in response.

Suddenly, another explosion lit up the night as another ship on the far side of the convoy was hit by a torpedo. The sickening sound of the explosion came through the night. For Jack it was hard to realize men were dying. It seemed surreal.

Griffin turned to the Captain and said: "Wolfpack." Jack knew this meant multiple submarines were attacking.

Dawson nodded his agreement.

Then the Operations Officer advised they had a sonar contact south of their position and off their starboard quarter. The rest happened very quickly. The Captain said "Get a message off to the Escort Commander and let him know we are leaving station to intercept and attack a U Boat south of our position. Give its relative bearing, course and speed."

A moment later Jack was being ordered to put the helm hard over and then steady up on a heading to intercept the U Boat. Dawson rang down to the engine room for full speed ahead. The Campbell heeled over in response to the sharp turn and her big propellors bit into the sea. Her bow wave flared. The battle ensign stood straight out as the Campbell turned to attack her enemy.

Carl Gromek stood in the doorway of a chemist shop that had yet to open for the day. It was just now getting light and he was sheltering from the rain. Carl's real name was Ernst Wehling and he had been a member of the Kriegsmarine in the late 1930s. He had spent part of his youth with relatives in America and as a result spoke English perfectly. German intelligence recruited him. In early 1939 his superiors had him change his legal residence from Germany to Great Britain. He was to be a sleeper agent that could be called upon if war broke out. Now he was part of a clandestine group of German agents working southern England for German intelligence. Gromek was short and stocky, but very strong. His black hair was neatly cut and combed straight back. His round face seldom smiled. He chain smoked cigarettes.

Unlike Diana, Gromek had no permanent assignment. He moved between locations as directed performing the more unpleasant tasks, such as eliminating someone who had become a problem. When needing a cover story he claimed to be a sales representative, or wholesaler looking for customers. He had multiple identity papers to explain his location to anyone in authority who might ask.

This particular morning Gromek was watching the windows of Diana's upstairs flat. Her handler had become suspicious of her after their last meeting and delivery of a shortwave radio. Diana's loyalty was in question and she needed some watching. Gromek had started early as he did not yet know her routine and he did not want to miss her if she left early for any daily activities. Eventually he would make contact with her, but for now he would just see who she met and where she went.

Gromek had a long wait as Diana did not come out of her building and start walking briskly down the street until mid-morning. He followed her to the wholesale tobacconist where she worked part time. He had been told of this employment and it was nothing out of the ordinary. He now knew he had some time so he returned to her building, went upstairs, and opened the door to her flat. He entered and closed the door quietly behind him. It was essentially one room with a kitchen area and table off to one side. There was a bed on the opposite side and an arm chair and small lamp in front of the window. Simple but very clean, neat and organized, betraying her German background.

Gromek looked in the closet, drawers and under the bed. He noted there was no radio but that was smart. He made a point of not disturbing anything so his presence would not be known. There was nothing he observed that would be of concern. He went to the door and listened to make sure the hall was empty. Then he left the flat and quickly went down the stairs and out onto the street.

Diana was busy all morning at Frank Hawes'. She made her bookkeeping entries, had questions for the route salesmen, and had a long discussion with Hawes about the business. Hawes was impressed with her understanding of his business—how to cut costs, maximize sales, and forecast trends and ordering needs. If truth was told, he thought she was better at it than he was.

They had their discussion in her cubicle. Diana had worn a suit, but the day had warmed and she had taken off her jacket. She had on a sleeveless blouse and she knew the top button was undone. She also knew Hawes would stand by her shoulder periodically so he could look down her blouse at the top of her breast that amply filled the bra cup. Their period of estrangement after he had touched her was passing. Diana didn't mind him studying her if it brought stability to the relationship. But she was not going to allow Hawes to touch her.

When Diana was done with everything she wished to tell Hawes about, she pushed the office chair back from the desk and stretched her arms over her head. Hawes saw her bare arms and thought them very sensual. Her skirt had hiked up from sitting all morning at her desk and Hawes could also see her knees and part of her thighs. Diana crossed her legs and said: "I am at the Lion and Cross every day now. All the soldiers and sailors have time on their hands as they prepare for the invasion and they get regular passes to come into town. It certainly improves business. So I must go."

Hawes was still looking at what he considered a lovely pair of legs. Then he said: "I'm glad we are getting on better since that unhappy moment. I appreciate your thoughts about the business. You seem more relaxed lately and more open to conversation."

Diana simply gave him a level gaze and said nothing.

Hawes continued: "I have a chance to buy some nylon stockings and silk under things for my wife—would you like me to see if I could get you some as well?"

Diana knew these items were both scarce and expensive when available. She looked at him sternly and said: "Black market?"

Hawes looked a little embarrassed and answered: "Where they come from is my secret. If you want me to get them for you write down your sizes on a slip of paper."

Diana thought for a moment. It would be very nice to have new silk under wear. All hers were prewar. And all her nylon stockings had runs in them. It would be a small delight, but it would make her feel good about herself. Diana knew this would encourage Hawes and his sexual overtures. But her desire for a little joy in her life overcame her better judgement. Diana took a note pad and wrote the sizes down. She tore the paper from the pad and handed it to Hawes.

Then she said: "I want to pay for these, even if it requires a little taken from my salary each week."

Hawes smiled at her and said: "We'll worry about that later! Your insight into my business matters is worth a little reward."

Diana thanked him and rose to put on her jacket and go to the Lion and Cross. Hawes wished her a good day and studied her beautiful hips and legs as she walked out. One day he hoped to see her in nothing but the silk panties he was about to get for her. He couldn't stop thinking about it.

The Coast Guard Cutter Campbell completed her turn towards the German submarine and steadied up on a course to intercept it. Shortly thereafter the sonar operator advised the U Boat was going deeper and changing course to parallel the convoy. Dawson immediately knew what was up. The U Boat would briefly parallel the convoy and then turn and go under it. It would surface on the other side to either launch torpedoes from its stern tubes or simply wait for a new opportunity to attack.

Dawson ordered a new course to move between the convoy and the U Boat. He turned to Jack and said: "Chief, we are going to go thru a series of quick maneuvers, do you have enough feel for her if I just gave you the heading without the rudder commands?"

Jack promptly answered: "Yes, sir."

Dawson gave a small smile and said: "Good, now you know another reason why you are here."

Then Dawson said to Griffin: "Mr. Griffin launch six depth charges set at 200 feet from our starboard launchers. Let's see if we can drive the bastard away from the convoy."

Griffin said: "Aye, aye captain." Shortly thereafter Jack heard the concussion of the launchers firing the depth charges into the air off the starboard side. As they splashed into the sea and sank there was a brief pause and then there was a dull roar, a heavy concussion and geysers of water shot upward off the starboard quarter. Jack had never heard anything like it. He was glad he was not underneath those depth charges. The concussion briefly disrupted the sonar return but soon the sonar operator advised the Operations Officer the submarine was still paralleling the convoy.

The Operations Officer came out of the CIC and said to Dawson: "The sub hasn't changed course. The Escort Command wants to know if he should detach another escort to help us?"

Dawson asked the Operations Officer: "Do you have a recommendation?"

Jack had the helm and couldn't really study the faces of the other men on the darkened bridge, but he got the feeling the Operations Officer and maybe others were feeling the danger of the moment.

The Operations Officer nervously said: "Attacking with two escorts would be normal protocol. After all, the U Boat has the advantage in these chases."

Dawson turned toward the convoy which was now beginning to fall astern and put his binoculars to his eyes. The convoy was partially lit up by the orange glow of at least two burning ships. Dawson thought he had heard a third ship torpedoed but couldn't see for sure from his present distance.

Dawson said: "Tell the Escort Commander we don't need assistance at this time." Dawson then added a note of explanation for those on the bridge: "The convoy is being attacked by multiple submarines and the men in those merchant ships need the remaining escorts for protection."

Then began a long night of cat and mouse between the crew of the CGC Campbell and the submarine. Every half an hour to forty-five minutes the Campbell would run up on the subs position and drop depth charges, usually from its stern racks. Then the Campbell would drop back. The submarine never turned toward the convoy and eventually went deep and headed out to sea. The CGC Campbell lost sonar contact with the U Boat. Dawson reported the situation to the Escort Commander who ordered them back to the Campbell's station with the convoy. CGC Campbell secured from general quarters.

Jack was relieved by another quartermaster shortly before daylight. Griffin left the bridge at the same time. They went below together. Jack asked: "Why would the submarine have an advantage over us in an attack like last night?"

Griffin said: "One on one, the sub still has stealth in its favor. The sonar is not exact. The sub has bow tubes and stern tubes that can launch torpedoes. The sub can change depths. That was probably a Type VII. It can go to six hundred feet, although they prefer not to go to those depths. It carries fourteen torpedoes. On the surface it has an 88mm deck gun which can do a lot of damage in a hurry, even to a ship like ours. Still, I'm assured that being in a sub that is being depth charged is one hell of a terrifying experience."

Jack nodded his understanding and headed for the Chief's quarters. The crew stood down from General Quarters and got breakfast and some rest. Jack was too wound up to sleep. As he lay in his rack a sense of anxiety crept over him. He had been too busy during his watch to be anxious. But now the U Boat chase was over it hit him how dangerous this duty was. He also noticed he had a slight tremor in his hands. Jack put it down to lack of sleep.

Captain Dawson had been reluctant to give up the chase because he thought the U Boat wasn't finished with the convoy. But the Escort Commander's orders had given him no choice. The U Boat attack sank three merchant ships. None of them carried the Coast Guard patrol boats. There was loss of life.

During the initial stages of the attack many of the merchant ships in the convoy got out of position. In the confusion and darkness there had been a serious collision between two of them. One ship was not very badly damaged and could keep up with the convoy. But the other was a cripple and had fallen behind the convoy. It was flooding and it was about to lose all propulsion. It would sink, or be spotted by a U Boat and torpedoed. The Campbell was soon ordered to leave its station and go back to take the crew off the crippled merchant ship.

In peace time this would be routine for the crew of the Campbell. In wartime, it was much more dangerous. Escort vessels that stopped to pick up crewmen of a torpedoed ship could find themselves torpedoed as well. Therefore, Captain Dawson sent a message to the crippled merchantman to tell the crew to get in the life boats, launch and stand off their vessel so CGC Campbell could do a quick recovery.

Jack had only three hours rest and had gotten a quick breakfast when he was summoned back up to the bridge. Jack looked around as he came above deck. It was a cold but clear spring day. The sun shone brightly and there was only a scattering of small waves on a beautiful blue sea. The Campbell was riding well and going some place in a hurry. Jack could see the convoy disappearing astern as they headed in the opposite direction.

Jack entered the bridge and relieved the quartermaster. Captain Dawson was on the bridge with his binoculars to his eyes scanning the horizon to the south west. He looked at Jack and said: "Good morning Senior Chief. We are supposed to take a crew off a sinking member of our convoy. She is quite a way off so we are on our own. I want to do this in as short a time as possible. We'll put a cargo net over the lee side and we'll take enough way off to get the crew out of their life boats. Then we are going to get the hell out of there. There may be a lot of helm commands."

Jack said: "I understand."

Dawson smiled and said: "Glad you could make the trip Senior Chief."

It took close to two hours to get back to the cripple. The sonar was pinging away regularly listening for any contacts. As the CGC Campbell closed on the vessel they could see a cargo ship about five hundred feet in length. It looked like it had three cargo holds forward and two aft with superstructure and tall smokestack amidships. It was down at the head, severely, and listing heavily to starboard. One life boat was in the water but not filled. The other was still in the davits. The Campbell closed to within a hundred yards and with a bull horn Captain Dawson told the men standing by the davits to abandon ship.

Captain Dawson cursed under his breath: "Damn them for not being in their boats already." Then he turned to Jack: "Senior Chief, keep bringing me around in a big circle but keep me upwind of them."

Jack answered: "Aye, aye sir."

Dawson ordered slow ahead. Then the crew of the Campbell waited while the crew of the cargo ship climbed down a rope ladder and entered the life boat that was in the water. It seemed like it took forever to Jack, who, like everyone else on the Campbell, felt like they had a target on their backs. Finally, there was no one left on the cargo ship's deck. The oars came out and the life boat began to pull away from the sinking freighter.

Then the Operations Officer stepped out of the CIC onto the bridge: "Captain, we have a contact. It's a sub. Coming up from the south east. It could be our contact from last night. At the moment it is running on the surface."

Captain Dawson asked: "Are they close enough to see us."

The Operations Officer said: "Not sure, but I expect so."

Captain Dawson said: "Send a message to the life boat by flashing light. Tell them we are engaging a U Boat and will come back for them. Then give me a course to intercept that submarine. Sound general quarters. Full speed ahead." The Campbell turned to once again face her enemy.

Jack had a clear view forward, and half expected to see a submarine coming straight at them. But he didn't. The submarine dived shortly after they turned and headed toward it. It fired two torpedoes from its bow tubes as the two ships headed toward each other. Sonar gave them a warning there were torpedoes in bound. Jack looked at Dawson for a helm command but his eyes were glued to his binoculars that were trained on the sea ahead. At the last moment Dawson calmly said: "Right full rudder." He then gave Jack a course to steady up on.

Jack handled the helm as ordered. The jog in their course was enough to save them. The bridge crew watched the two torpedoes speed by off their stern. The Campbell then turned back and ran over the sub's position with the stern racks dropping depth charges. As soon as the sonar recovered from the effects of the depth charge concussions it was apparent they had damaged the submarine. It slowed and veered sharply to port. Dawson was tempted to take another run at it but hesitated for fear he might collide with a surfacing sub.

Then everyone on the bridge saw the submarine begin to surface less than a mile off their starboard bow. Then it stopped moving forward and was dead in the water. Dawson asked: "Are all guns manned and ready?"

The OOD answered: "All manned and ready. Sir."

Dawson said: "I want our 40mm trained on their deck gun. Chief Trevenen, start maneuvering us to starboard, bow on. I want to be a slender target. OOD, slow ahead."

Before anyone could acknowledge an order the deck gun on the sub fired and a shell rocketed over the bridge of the Campbell. Dawson yelled: "All guns, open fire." The Campbell's five inch gun barked and the 40mm opened up as well. The Germans got off another round with their deck gun. This round was lower and hit the sea and exploded just short of the starboard side of the Campbell. The concussion of the exploding shell could be felt throughout the ship and a large geyser of water shot high in the air. Jack thought, they have us bracketed and the next round will hit us.

At that moment the Campbell's 40 mm mount got the range. The sub's deck around its deck gun splintered into small pieces as the rounds from the 40 mm hit the sub. The German sailors manning the deck gun were caught in the gunfire. The Campbell's five inch gun came into action. The first shot from the Campbell's five inch gun was high. The Campbell's second shot with its five inch gun hit the sub amidships with a bright orange flash and loud explosion. There was no further fire from the submarine.

A cheer went up from the CGC Campbell's crew. Captain Dawson wasn't smiling. He knew the sub was still afloat and could potentially still fire torpedoes. He repeated his order: "Keep firing. That damn thing could still put a torpedo in us." The Campbell's guns continued to fire and the five inch gun had another hit on the stern of the sub. It was only when the stern of the sub sank and the bow stood straight up out of the water that the Campbell's guns fell silent.

The crew of the Campbell waited to see if any German sailors got out of the submarine. Two came out of a forward hatch and dropped into the sea. The bow of the submarine then slid downwards and the U Boat was gone forever.

Diana lay on her bed in her robe. The front of her robe was open and her legs were free. She was waiting for another tenant to finish in the bathroom and then she was going down the hall and take a bath herself. Hawes had given her the silk underwear and nylons the day before. When he gave them to her she purposely gave him a troubled look. She also had repeated her desire to take money from her pay each week to pay for them. Hawes was gracious and wouldn't tell her the cost. He told her not to worry and simply enjoy the items. Then he left her alone with her work.

Diana was going to wait to try on the bra and panties, but couldn't resist pulling on one of the nylons. She extended her leg straight up in the air and admired the black nylon which fit her perfectly. She thought her legs still looked good even though she was aging. Diana knew she no longer had the figure of her youth. She lowered her leg and pulled the nylon off.

Diana wasn't sure why but the emptiness of her situation hit her at that moment. Hawes only wanted to get between her legs—the same was true of many of the soldiers and sailors who flirted with her at the Lion and Cross. Given the fact she was a German agent, it was impossible to attract or keep a good man who truly cared for her. Such a relationship would have to be based on lies and would not last. It could even get her turned in to the authorities. It exhausted her to think about it. Diana pushed herself up off the bed, closed her robe, and went down the hall for her bath. She had to reconcile herself to her isolation.

Hawes was anxious about his situation with Diana. He wanted her in his bed very badly. He had hoped his recent gift of intimate apparel would cause her to be more receptive towards him. Unfortunately, she only looked troubled when he gave her the present. He knew if he angered her she might go to his wife and that would be disaster. But still, he couldn't stop thinking about being with her in various sexual situations. These thoughts were becoming an obsession with him. About a week or so after he gave her the lingerie he found himself following her. He made sure he stayed back from her so she wouldn't notice. He pretty much had her routine down when he decided he wanted to visit her flat when she was at work.

This particular afternoon the opportunity presented itself. He quietly went to the second floor and into Diana's flat through the unlocked door. He closed the door behind him and looked around. It was neat and clean but very plain. He thought she needed new furniture. He sat on her bed and thought of her lying there. He put his face to her pillow and could smell her scented soap.

Hawes then crossed the room to her dresser and opened the drawers until he found her lingerie. He felt it. He lifted it too his face and it aroused him. He wanted to rub his member on her panties but was afraid he would lose control and leave a stain. He dug deeper in the drawer to see all she wore when he felt a paper folder. He pulled it out and opened it up. There were instructions for a radio and what looked like codes. All the printing was in German. He took one of the pages, folded it, and put it in his inside jacket pocket.

Frank Hawes knew he would have Diana. As often as he wanted.

CHAPTER SEVEN

SQUALLS

After the German submarine sank Captain Dawson briefly stopped the CGC Campbell in the fuel oil and small debris field floating near where the sub sank. He picked up the two crew members and had them taken below under guard. One was badly injured. Dawson secured the crew from General Quarters.

The Campbell then headed back to the sinking merchant ship to pick up the crew in the life boat. Upon their return Jack could see the ship was much closer to going under. The bow was completely under water and the list had grown sharply. The lookouts quickly spotted the life boat. Dawson stuck his head into the CIC and asked: "Any contacts?"

The Operations Officer said: "Not near us, but there is some radio traffic. The convoy is getting hit with another submarine attack."

Captain Dawson said: "Send a message to the Escort Commander. Advise we have engaged and sunk an enemy submarine. Also advise we will pick up the crew of the cripple and expect to be back with them by 20:00 hours."

With that being accomplished Dawson said: "Alright Chief Trevenen, let's just bring her upwind of that lifeboat and do this quite handily."

Jack answered: "Aye, aye sir."

Captain Dawson ordered the engines to slow ahead and a cargo net was draped over the Campbell's side for the men in the life boat to climb up. With only a brief stop the life boat was emptied and all were brought aboard. Captain Dawson asked to have the ship's captain brought to the bridge. Then, Captain Dawson made another decision. He told the OOD: "Tell the five inch gun crew I need their talents again. We are going to sink that ship. Have them man the turret and aim low on the starboard side."

91

The merchant captain appeared on the bridge and saluted Dawson. Dawson remembered him from the organizational meetings in Newfound Land. He was quite old and a good Scotsman with a heavy brough. Captain Dawson returned the salute. Then he said: "Captain, your ship is too far gone to save. I don't want to leave her still afloat. It could endanger another vessel. We are going to sink her." The merchant captain listened in stony silence, understanding what was being said but shaken by the loss of his command.

The merchant captain raised his hand and once again saluted saying to Dawson: "Captain, if you don't mind I would prefer not to watch, and would like to go below with my men." As he finished speaking the five inch gun fired and a shell rocketed through the air hitting the freighter. There was a flash as the shell hit the hull and exploded, followed by a column of water shooting upwards.

Captain Dawson returned the salute and simply said: "Of course. It may interest you to know we sank the German sub we had to leave you for earlier. Two of her crew survived and they are on board under guard."

The merchant captain turned to leave the bridge, and with a wry smile said: "You are too much a gentleman. It the tables were turned the crew of that submarine would have machine gunned any survivors of your lost ship."

The excitement that traveled through the CGC Campbell after they sank the sub was cut short for the bridge crew. They saw the sadness in the old merchant captain's eyes and watched another ship sink as the five inch gun crew made short work of it. Jack later confirmed through Griffin that German subs regularly machine gunned crew members of the merchant ships they sank, if they were lucky enough to get off the sinking ship in a life boat or on a raft.

The crew of the CGC Campbell headed back to the convoy at full speed. By the time they came up on the convoy the attack was over, but the formations were scattered and it took until nightfall to begin to get the formation back in order. Jack was told no ships carrying Coast Guard patrol boats had been hit, but another ship had been lost. The Campbell spent a long and active night on the starboard side of the convoy ranging back and forth with her sonar looking for enemy contacts.

Late the next day they were far enough east to pick up air cover from the Royal Air Force. At dusk Jack was standing on the after deck by the depth charge racks talking with the First Class Boatswain's Mate from the Deck Department. An aircraft was approaching from the northeast. Jack looked towards the front of the ship half expecting to see men running to General Quarters. But no one was running and no claxon sounded. The plane made a low pass overhead and wagged its wings up and down to say hello. It was am RAF flying boat. Jack was glad to see the British insignias on its wings. He thought they might be safe at last.

There were no more U Boat attacks. Some of the American escorts were relieved by Royal Navy destroyers and destroyer escorts. Later, as they passed south of Ireland the convoy broke up into smaller groups of ships. Some headed north to English ports on the western side of the country. The CGC Campbell, the ships with the Coast Guard patrol boats, and a few other merchant ships headed for the entrance to the English Channel that lay between France and England.

Jack was glad the trip was almost over. The constant drills and then time at General Quarters had taken a physical toll on him. He couldn't do as much in his fifties as he had in prior decades. He had a slight tremor in his hands and had no appetite. He had some discomfort in his gut. His sleep was disturbed and even when he could get four hours sleep, he was restless. He put it down to stress. He thought if he could get to England and get on dry land he would be fine—assuming he could get eight continuous hours of sleep. Still, he thought he made a contribution to the ship and was actually going to miss some aspects of the routine. He knew he would miss some of his shipmates and prayed they survived the war.

The CGC Campbell and the other ships in its now much smaller convoy neared the westerly entrance to the English Channel at dusk. They intended to stay close to the English side of the Channel and run it at night. The German Luftwaffe was not much of a threat since Allied aircraft largely controlled the skies. But no chances would be taken. They would enter Poole Harbor on the south coast of England about daybreak.

Jack took the time to look at the navigation charts for the English Channel. He studied the coast of Cornwall which they would move along first as they headed east up the Channel. Jack was the descendant of a long line of Cornishmen, many of whom were miners. They got their training in the tin mines of Cornwall and then migrated to other countries with similar mining needs. That was how Jack's father had gotten to America, and the copper mines of Michigan's Upper Peninsula. Jack wondered if he would have time to visit Cornwall and look up members of his father's family. Poole was east of Cornwall and looked like it would be somewhat of a trip to get down to Cornwall.

Looking at the navigation charts for the English Channel, Jack noted it was quite wide at its western end. It would take several hours to cross from England to France by ship depending on the nature of the vessel. He also noted the Channel narrowed at its eastern end and the crossing between England and France at Dover and Calais was much shorter. Jack figured that was where the Allied army would probably cross in its invasion attempt. The ships leaving Poole would have to go east to this narrow point and then turn south for France. Jack wondered what his part in all this would be? One thing was certain. They would be facing a determined enemy and invading France would be difficult.

It was late in the afternoon and Diana was washing glasses behind the bar at the Lion and Cross. They had several customers but the evening rush had yet to arrive. A short stocky man with black hair was drinking a brandy alone at the end of the bar. He was smoking a cigarette. He was well dressed and had on a light tan raincoat open at the front. Diana approached him to ask if he wanted another drink. As she approached he smiled at her and said: "Good Afternoon. I send greetings from your cousin Anna. She misses you and would like to see you."

Diana was taken by surprise and didn't know what to say. She never expected to be approached at work by someone in the network. She was wary. Was this person really British Intelligence? Since she had not given a code word in return the man said nothing further

Finally, Diana said: "Tell cousin Anna I miss her as well and will be talking with her soon."

The man slid a small piece of paper towards her and said: "Tomorrow morning at nine would be convenient. At her country house outside Bournemouth."

With that the man raised his glass and drained it. He put the price of the brandy on the bar, smiled, and walked out. Diana looked at the piece of paper. It was a residential street number. Diana presumed this was her destination tomorrow morning. She memorized the information, crumpled the paper and threw it in the trash. She would have to rearrange her schedule tomorrow morning which aggravated her. She had no choice, particularly since her relations with her handler remained troublesome. She would take the early morning train to Bournemouth.

The next morning Diana was walking up the front walk to a nice home tucked away in the country just east of Bournemouth. She had trouble finding the location and was a little late. Diana rang the front bell and waited. She half expected the door to open with British military police standing in the doorway. But when the door opened, it was her handler who stood there. Diana noted she hadn't grown any more attractive and was poorly dressed in a cheap frock.

The woman scolded her: "You are late. You again display a lack of commitment to your duties."

Diana decided to let it pass and simply said: "I'm sorry." She was directed into a formal front parlor. There she saw the black haired man who came to the pub yesterday afternoon. There was another man with white hair and a white moustache smoking a pipe. He looked quite distinguished. He reminded Diana of her father. He stood by the fireplace. The black haired man sat in an overstuffed chair. Her handler stood.

What Diana didn't know was that Gromek's report to these two on Diana had been positive. He saw nothing that would indicate she had been 'turned' by British Intelligence and become a double agent. He thought she should be well positioned to gather news of the invasion. This had not sat well with her handler who frankly hoped Gromek would find reasons to get rid of her. The handler thought Diana was not hard enough for the work and had said so before Diana arrived. The older man who had authority over all of them wanted to observe for himself.

Initially there was an awkward silence. Diana didn't like the fact the others seemed to know her name and duties, but she didn't know the same about them. Then her handler started the conversation by saying: "We are concerned about a lack of information on the timing of the invasion and the location of the landings. That is your job to supply such information. Yet we get nothing. You have not used your radio once. There is no excuse for this failure."

Again, there was a silence. Then Diana spoke up: "I cannot report what I do not know. There is a ship's captain who comes to the pub. His vessel will carry part of the American Army's 29th Division to France. We have become friendly, and he drinks too much. He will be my best source. When he starts to take troops on board the invasion will be launched within a few hours. He will also be given his destination. But at the moment he knows nothing about either."

Dianna paused and then continued: "The route salesmen for the tobacco wholesaler mention news of changes in troop dispositions. I will know when they prepare to board the ships. I listen to every conversation I can at the pub hoping to learn something. At the moment all the soldiers and sailors are anxious to invade but the details are only known at the highest levels of command. No one locally knows. Yesterday I heard there will be a new arrival--patrol boats from America. They will be moored on the quay near the Lion and Cross. This is something I will learn more about-- to see if it gives us new clues."

The woman handler responded: "We need to know before ships sail where they are going. Our defense forces need time to react and position themselves to throw these invaders back into the sea."

Diana gave her a steely look in return and said: "The ships will take hours to get to France. Even a warning when they are loading could make the difference. I cannot make up information I do not have. I will only use the radio when I have something reliable to report. I'm surrounded by military forces. When I use the radio the chances of being detected are good. If I'm caught you lose my observations and sources. That risk cannot be taken lightly."

The woman handler was angry at this response and her face grew red. She was about to accuse Diana of being a coward, but the older gentleman raised his hand and she remained silent. He walked towards Diana holding the pipe he had been smoking in one hand. He stopped a few feet from her and said: "Fraulein, please, sit."

Diana did as directed and took a seat on the edge of a nearby upholstered chair.

The older gentleman toyed with his pipe and thought about his words. Then he said: "Fraulein, your services are valuable and I have looked over all your reports from the years you have been in England. You are observant and your reports are clear. You have maintained your cover remarkably well. I do not want to lose you. From now on you will report to Gromek. He will be in your area to assist you in any way he can. You and he can work out the ways to contact each other."

The older man turned to Gromel who smiled and nodded his understanding. Then the older man turned again to Diana. He added: "You are correct that your information must be accurate or it is useless, or even worse, damaging. But do not think you must have the complete picture before you report. Bits and pieces can be helpful in creating a complete picture. Do you understand?"

Diana said: "Yes, I understand. I will do better. Thank you for your trust in me."

With that the older man said: "We are done. Nodding toward Diana he continued: "You will leave first."

Diana rose, politely shook the older man's hand and said to Gomek: "Come by the Lion and Cross and let me know how cousin Anna is doing."

Gromek smiled at her, admiring her beauty. Then he added: "I will be in touch."

As she went down the front walk Diana was sure the three of them were continuing to discuss her. Diana thought she would give anything to know what they were saying.

Frank Hawes had given considerable reflection to his find in Diana's flat. His first reaction that she had to be a German agent, was fading. There could be other reasons she might have the codes and instructions for a German short wave radio. There was nothing identifying where they came from. He certainly wasn't going to report her to the authorities. At least not until he had confronted her himself and watched her reaction. The thought she might not be able to say no to his sexual advances aroused him deeply. It preoccupied a good part of his day as he fantasized about how he would force her to satisfy him. If she didn't, he would threaten to turn her in.

But the more he thought about it the more he realized blackmailing her for sex could get him in trouble for not promptly turning her in. Even worse, if she was an agent and still continued to send messages to Germany serious harm could result. Harm he could have prevented. He certainly could be in trouble. Disgraced and maybe imprisoned. All this went around and around in his head broken only by thoughts of her nude. Finally, Hawes decided he would confront her and study her reaction. He would decide what to do thereafter. He might just turn her in. If he forced a brief sexual encounter on her before he reported her, it could be denied. Who would believe a spy over a long standing businessman such as himself? Now all he had to do was wait for the right moment.

Diana had also been doing some hard thinking about her own situation. When she first left the meeting in Bournemouth with the other members of the network she thought the whole thing was a waste of time. She also thought she had handled herself quite well. But the more she reflected on it the more she thought she may have been in greater danger than she initially thought. Perhaps she was no longer necessary, and could be eliminated. What was Gromek's role in this? Diana had worked alone for years and now she had a partner? Clearly, they wanted information from every available source on the timing and location of the invasion of France. Maybe they would get rid of her after the invasion took place?

Diana had other issues to keep her occupied. The business at the Lion and Cross had picked up. A new group of American sailors had arrived and business was too good for her liking. Diana was there from mid-afternoon to late at night most days. She had little time to speak with Captain McKeil which frustrated her. She dropped into bed dead tired each night and did not wake up refreshed.

The mornings she went to work at Hawes' didn't help cheer her. Hawes was acting strangely. He continually had a serious look on his face as though he was lost in deep thought. At times she thought he was going to scold her. He said very little to her, but studied her body when he thought she wouldn't notice. All in all, it was getting

to be too much for her and she decided she would give her notice to Hawes. It was just a question of finding the right moment. Their relationship had to end.

Jack arrived at Poole, England just as Lieutenant Griffin had promised. The USCGC Campbell escorted the transports into Poole and then anchored as well. Jack was given a set of orders transferring him back to Rescue Flotilla One. Before he left the ship he stuck his head in Griffins tiny cabin and said: "Thanks for the ride. I'll miss the Campbell."

Griffin looked up from what he was doing and gave Jack a smile and a firm handshake. Then he added: "We are sorry to see you go. The Captain liked the way you handled the helm for close maneuvering. You looked like you were driving a motor lifeboat!"

Jack smiled in return and said: "Old habits die hard. I hope our paths cross again and you and the crew stay safe. Chasing submarines is dangerous work."

Griffin was quiet for a moment and then said: "We are going back out for escort duty. I'm not sure what convoy we'll pick up or where it's going. I hope it's not to Russia. The Murmansk run makes our last assignment look tame. The Germans can attack by air from bases in Norway. Air attacks worry me more than U Boats."

Jack replied: "I thought they might leave you here as part of the invasion fleet?"

Griffin shrugged. "Who knows. I doubt we'll invade before summer. We could be back for that. Speaking of which--is your patrol boat been unloaded from its transport?"

Jacked said "Yes, after unloading they are towing them over to what must be a fuel dock to get fuel and potable water. They are rafting them out three abreast from the stone quay on the east side of the harbor. It looks like my boat is in the front row. I need to get going. One of your small boats is waiting to take me ashore."

Griffin walked Jack back up on deck. Jack stood for a moment at the top of the accommodation ladder before he descended to the motorized lifeboat waiting for him. He looked up and down at the deck of the Campbell and was glad she brought him safely to Poole. Jack saluted Griffin, then the flag and went slowly down the ladder to the boat. As he got in the boat Jack recognized the young boatswain's mate who was serving as coxswain.

The young coxswain said: "Sorry to see you go Chief."

Jack said: "I'll miss you men as well. Take good care of the Campbell. Stay safe and fair weather."

With that the coxswain started the engine and headed the boat towards the stone quay across the harbor. Jack noted it was a beautiful spring day with blue skies and warm sun. The harbor was a fine large natural harbor that could hold a large number of ships. At the moment it had a mixture of warships, merchant vessels and military transport ships riding at anchor. The harbor was surrounded by the town on the north and east, and then beyond were high rolling hills. It was a peaceful and beautiful location.

After the short trip across the harbor Jack headed for the patrol boats that were already moored after being unloaded and fueled. The boats were all painted wartime grey and any distinctive Coast Guard marking or paint were gone. There was a large numeral painted on their bows. There were sixty patrol boats brought over and each had its own number between one and sixty. Jack's boat had a large number "6" painted on its bow in white paint. Just behind the numeral and in much smaller letters "USCG" was painted. The crew of each boat could be seen getting their boats ready for sea.

Jack quickly spotted Lieutenant Stonecliffe who also saw him at that same moment. Jack quickened his pace in his direction, glad to see a familiar face. Jack saluted. Stonecliffe returned the salute. He thought Jack looked like he had lost weight and his face was more drawn. He said: "Damn, am I glad to see you. I was worried we might not get you back." Then with an earnest look on his face he quietly asked Jack: "How bad was it? We saw the Campbell briefly but you were on station on the opposite side of the convoy. We heard you got a U Boat?"

Jack replied: "Well Lieutenant, it wasn't port security duty in Hampton Roads! The men on the Campbell are really being put to the test with endless watches and having the constant tension of U Boat attack. The North Atlantic can be rough anytime and the Campbell is only 327 feet long. You really feel the effect of the seas. Still, I was glad to be on her when the wolf pack hit us."

Stonecliffe nodded his understanding. "Those two or three days in Mid-Atlantic when we were under submarine attack were hard on the men. We slept in our life jackets. We were helpless and just hoped our ship wasn't in the periscope of some German sub."

Jack asked: "Did the boat and all the men make it alright?"

Stonecliffe smiled: "We are all fine. The boat seems no worse for wear. We are going over her from top to bottom to make sure everything is ship shape. We haven't started the engines yet. We were towed here. Chief, are you well? You look a little worse for wear. I need you to get the men organized and oversee all aspects of our readiness."

Jack nodded and said: I'll be fine if I can get a couple of nights sleep and a few good meals. Before I do anything I need to report in and get my orders endorsed. Where has the Command set up shop?"

Stonecliffe pointed: "They are on the second floor of the building next to that little hotel. Just up the street from us."

Jack said: "I see it. I'll be back shortly. By the way, do you know any more about what they plan for us?"

Stonecliffe answered: "Nothing official. Since they call us Rescue Flotilla One I assume we will do search and rescue missions once the invasion begins. The Germans will be expecting the invasion and I expect the invasion fleet could have a lot of casualties or sinkings. No doubt there will be men in the water."

Jack looked up at the bright blue sky, then over at the patrol boats rafted out from the quay. He smiled at Stonecliffe and said: "Well, we are good at that, but we may need a helluva lot more boats. From just the little I've seen there will be hundreds, maybe thousands of ships heading to France."

Stonecliffe shrugged and said: "We do what we can."

Jack turned and walked across the street towards the buildings on the other side. He passed a pub with the sign Lion and Cross over the door. He thought this might be a good spot to have a beer or get a meal.

CHAPTER EIGHT
HEAVY SWELLS

Jack's crew had worked hard for two days to get everything on board the 'Six Boat' as it was now called, operational. Jack had them make a couple of runs in and out of the harbor so he could get the exact bearings and distances to get out to sea in darkness or fog. He also didn't want to be caught in the harbor at night when an air raid suddenly appeared. The pier head lights wouldn't be showing in a blackout.

They were only carrying a single 50 caliber machine gun mounted mid-ship on the after deck. This became the subject of some humor. Jimmy Spenser said: "At least we can throw a few shots back at an enemy chasing us as we run for home!" Despite that, Gunners Mate McCauley stressed how helpful it could be against an attacking aircraft.

Jack stressed the need to have the engines in perfect operating order. He told his senior Engineman Sam Ritt to tear anything out and replace it if it even looked like it would break. Jack got a couple of small life rafts from the Navy and tied them down on the forward deck. He figured if they were picking survivors out of the water it would be helpful to have them.

Lieutenant Stonecliffe had been in a series of meetings with other patrol boat captains, the Flotilla Commander and the Navy. He had been silent about what was discussed.

Jack had been sleeping better. The first night at Poole he went to bed early in his bunk in the patrol boat. It was cramped and there was no way to keep him from hearing the men talking. He had trouble sleeping. But after that first night sleep seemed to come more easily and he stayed asleep. He felt more relaxed and at times his appetite came back. His hand tremor still remained.

Aside from Stonecliffe and Jack, there were ten men in the crew. Jack divided them into two watch sections of five men each. At night only one of the watch sections would be on duty. The other section could go on liberty. The work day normally ended at 4 pm unless they were running familiarization patrols along the English coast. Stonecliffe allowed the men not on watch liberty until 11 pm. Without knowing when the invasion would happen Stonecliffe wanted to be able to recall his men quickly. He would not allow excessive drinking and ordered the men on liberty to stay in Poole so they could hear the recall signal blown on the patrol boat's horn.

This worked into a pattern where they all usually ate together on the boat and then the men on liberty drifted over to the Lion and Cross. There, they took a table and spent the evening. They became popular with the staff and Carl Williams would occasionally help the English cook who wanted to learn how to cook hamburgers and hot dogs! They all commented on a raven-haired woman who looked in her 30's and had an hour glass figure. Sam Ritt was particularly taken by her and asked her out repeatedly without success.

One particularly busy night Diana was at the Lion and Cross to help with the serving. Some of the crew from Jack's boat had a table. Jack came in and stood next to the table and ordered a porter from Diana. Diana had seen him in the pub before. He wore a peaked cap and a khaki uniform. He appeared to be a person of some authority. He never drank much and always left after talking with his men for a short while. His men seemed relaxed around him, but they clearly paid him some deference. Diana thought him handsome. He had broad shoulders and a narrow waist. He had a pleasant smile and a small dimple in his chin. His light brown hair was flecked with some grey. His face had the lines one might see in a sailor, but he didn't look old by any means. Diana wondered if he could be a new source of information about the invasion.

When Diana arrived with Jack's drink she smiled and said to Jack: "Here you are, one porter for the US Navy."

That brought loud laughter from the other men at the table. Jimmy Spencer was one of them. He immediately piped up and smiling said: "Miss, you are talking to the United States Coast Guard! We are the hard core around which the Navy forms in time of war! Senior Chief Trevenen here is the senior enlisted in our flotilla."

Diana was confused. She said: "I think our Coast Guard is a volunteer force that man local life boats?"

Jack spoke up: "What you just heard from Boatswain's Mate Spencer is a little burst of service pride." Jack cast a slightly scolding glance at Spencer. He looked back at Diana and continued: "In the time of war our Coast Guard becomes part of the Navy, but we retain our separate organization. Our Coast Guard has a variety of jobs, search and rescue is just one of them. If you haven't figured it out already, the patrol boats tied up along the quay are all manned by Coast Guardsmen." Jack smiled at her and raised his glass slightly. "If nothing else we seem good for business."

Jack was taken with her attractiveness, and her refined English diction. The men were right when they praised her good looks. Diana reminded him of the English women who had come to the Keweenaw to live. A place he was thinking more and more about as his home. Jack wanted to talk to her more, but was interrupted.

Captain McKeil came striding into the Lion and Cross having visited two other pubs before arriving. He was enjoying his alcoholic glow. He glanced around the room and noted the tables were all taken, but there was room for him to get a drink at the bar. Then it hit him that he knew the man in the Chief Petty Officer's uniform standing by one of the tables. The loss of the SS *Inland Mariner* came back to him in an instant. Inwardly, a horrible sense of anxiety, then rage swept over him. He went straight toward Jack and in a loud voice said: "Well God Almighty, if it isn't the damn matchbox navy. Who the hell let you sons of bitches into this country!"

In a moment all of Jack's crew was up out of their seats and heading for McKeil ready to shut him up any way necessary. Jack dived between them and McKeil. He raised his voice at his men saying: "Belay that!" Jack grabbed the lapels of McKeil's merchant marine officer's jacket and started pushing him towards the door. McKeil took a swing at Jack, but was too drunk to land his punch. Diana grabbed McKeil's arm and shouted into Mckeil's face: "Stop Captain, stop. You must not behave like this."

Jack and Diana pushed McKeil through the outside door and Jack pinned him up against the outside wall. Diana was impressed with how much upper body strength Jack had. Under his breath McKeil had been repeatedly muttering : "God damn Coasties."

Jack tightened his grip on McKeil's lapels and shook him saying: "Listen McKeil, you have no enemy in me. You need to let go of the past. If you can't there are a few dozen Coast Guardsmen in this harbor who will be happy to take you apart. Now you are going to behave or this young lady next to me is going to call the shore patrol. What's your pleasure?"

Diana added in a quiet voice: "Please Captain, you must behave yourself."

The comment from Diana seemed to have effect and McKeil pulled away from Jack's grip and tried to straighten his uniform. He started to turn to walk away, but said quite bitterly to both of them: "I'll remember this and I'll take my business elsewhere. But Trevenen, I wouldn't spend a whole lot of time in dark alleys. I have a crew too, and they are loyal." With a slightly staggered gait he walked off into a light rain that had just begun to fall.

Diana and Jack went back inside. The room was smoke filled and noisy. Jack preferred the cool air of early evening and the smell of the new rain. Jack said to Diana: "Sorry about that. There is some history between us that I will share with you one day."

Diana responded: "There is no need to apologize. I appreciated your quick response. We normally have an orderly crowd. Captain McKeil has a problem controlling his drink and has come to my attention before." Diana extended her hand and said: "I should introduce myself. My name is Diana Winter."

Jack smiled at her and took her hand. He hadn't felt the touch of a woman in ages. He felt self- conscious. Then he said: "I'm a Chief Petty Officer, Senior Chief Petty Officer. My name is Jack Trevenen."

Diana said: "That is a good Cornish name. How did you get here?"

Jack replied: "Despite my Cornish last name, I was sent here as part of the invasion force. Both my parents immigrated to the Upper Peninsula of Michigan from Cornwall. I was born there. I'm the Executive Officer on the Six Boat tied up across the way."

Diana wanted to know more about Jack but didn't have time for an extended conversation as the bar keep was motioning her to come to the bar to pick up orders. As she stepped away she said to Jack: "Meet me here for lunch tomorrow? I have to do the books and make a deposit in the morning. Then we could go to a nice little tea room around the corner and have sandwiches."

Jack nodded his approval and said: "If we aren't out on patrol, I'll be here. Thanks"

Diana went back to her serving duties, but stole a glance or two at Jack as he finished his porter and left to return to his patrol boat.

The next day Jack wished he hadn't agreed to meet Diana for lunch. Stonecliffe and he kept a close eye on the men and due to the pending invasion kept everyone close to the boat. They didn't allow the crew to go into Poole for lunch. Jack felt awkward about doing so himself. He didn't like the idea of creating standards for the crew he didn't adhere to as well. However, he felt he couldn't stand Diana up and not meet her.

In the end Stonecliffe told him he was worrying too much and told him to just go. Jack had reported the incident with McKeil to Stonecliffe and Stonecliffe wanted Jack to find out from Diana what McKeil's history in the port was. Stonecliffe also remained a little worried about Jack's health and thought a break away from his duties might help.

When Diana got up that morning she felt happier than she had in months. She knew why. She was going to meet a handsome sailor that she was attracted to. Diana told herself it was ridiculous for her to feel this way. After all, she had asked him to lunch. He hadn't shown any special interest in her. Her job was to get information and relay it as soon as possible. Her role as an agent prevented any real relationship.

They met outside the pub and walked up the street together. Jack wasn't sure what to say so he let Diana lead the conversation. After a few brief comments about the weather Diana asked: "I take it you and Captain McKeil have met before?"

Jack said: "That is a bit of a long story. McKeil used to be a captain on Great Lakes freighters hauling bulk cargos from Lake Superior to ports on the southern lakes. The Great Lakes are great inland seas. In the fall they can get quite stormy. He lost his ship in a fall storm and there was significant loss of life. At the time I was in charge of the nearby life boat station. My crew and I responded to the sinking with our life boat. In fact, we pulled him out of the water."

Diana looks puzzled. "Why would any of that cause him to not like you or your service?"

Jack said: "McKeil is a heavy weather sailor. Storms don't bother him. When most captains would stay in port or seek shelter and anchor, he pushes through. This causes contentious relations with crews. However, the ship owners like him. He can make more trips with less disruption to shipping schedules. That is profitable for the shipowners."

Jack paused, and then continued: "Because there was a sinking the Coast Guard investigated and held a hearing to potentially take away his sailing license. His decision to chance the storm was the basis of the hearing. In the end he was acquitted due to concerns there may have been problems with the seaworthiness of the ship itself, over which he had no control."

Diana said: "I think I understand. He is angry at you because he believes he was unfairly treated?"

Jack said: "In part. But he carries a lot of guilt over the drowned crew members. After the sinking He began drinking heavily, and from what I saw last night, he still does. Personally, I think he showed poor judgment in not seeking shelter and going to anchor the night he lost his ship. If he had, everyone would be alive and he never would have been investigated." Jack paused then asked: "What do you know about him?"

Diana said: "He certainly does drink too much. I had to help him one night when he was in his cups. He is the captain of one of the troop transports. The one that will carry part of the American 29th Infantry Division to France. I hadn't seen him recently—until last night. I'd hoped he would have changed his ways. But don't you think much of it is all this waiting for the invasion to start? I mean, there are thousands of soldiers and sailors just waiting with nothing but time on their hands. Time to miss their loved ones and contemplate all the dreadful things that might happen to them in the coming fighting."

Jack said: "Yes, I suppose so. I keep a close eye on my crew and have projects for them every day. We all eat and berth together on our little boat so we are pretty close knit. In fact, I would never let them go into Poole for lunch on a weekday. I'm breaking my own rules. But do me a favor and let me know if you learn more about McKeil. I want to keep an eye on him. If the invasion had started last night he was in no shape to command a ship."

Diana nodded her understanding and added: "It isn't for me to decide, but the owner may want him banned from the Lion and Cross if anything like last night happens again."

They reached the tea room and went in. Once settled at a table Jack felt more relaxed than he thought he would. He asked Diana about her background. Diana gave her well rehearsed cover story. Jack noticed she wore no rings of any kind. He wasn't sure why he was so bold, but asked: "Are you married?"

Diana paused and an honest sadness swept over her and was evident in her face. Jack immediately regretted asking the question, but it was too late to take it back. Looking away, Diana said: "My husband died in 1940 during the air war that summer. He was a pilot. He was shot down." Diana looked back at Jack and there was a silence between them. Then she said: "Tell me about your upbringing and your time in the Coast Guard. Trevenen is a good Cornish name."

Jack told about his early years with lots of information about Michigan and the Cornish miners who immigrated to the Keweenaw Peninsula. He explained his parents were among these. He gave a short version of his Coast Guard career. Finally, he explained he had been stopped from retiring due to America's entry into the war. Jack ended by saying: "I don't mind telling you I don't have the energy I once did. I hope the war ends soon." With a wry smile he added: "Allied leaders are predicting the invasion will result in Germany surrendering by Christmas."

Diana looked at him very seriously and said: "I don't believe this war will end by Christmas. The German Army is prepared for hard fighting. But like you I wish this were all over and we could just meet as any peacetime couple might. You look fit and healthy to me, far from being past your prime. You handled McKeil quite nicely and he is not a small man. What will your role be in the invasion?"

Jack said: "We don't know for sure. Our boats are very lightly armed and we aren't big enough to carry troops. My guess is we will perform our traditional role of search and rescue-picking people out of the water or helping survivors of sinking or stranded vessels. But like everyone else we don't know when or where the invasion will take place."

Diana asked: "Why did McKeil refer to you as the matchbox fleet?"

Jack laughed: "That is a term applied to our patrol boats because they are made of wood. The term can either be a good-natured jest or an insult depending on who is using it!"

They chatted some more while they finished their lunch. Jack was watching the time. As enjoyable as this was, he didn't want to be away too long. Finally, Jack said: "I'm sorry but I must get back to the boat. They'll give me the dickens for meeting you for lunch. Let me pay for the tea and sandwiches."

Dianna smiled at him and said: "Do your rules apply on Sunday afternoons? If the weather is nice a picnic along the shore can be enjoyable. There is a spot that is just east of the harbor. You could easily return if you had a recall."

Jack said: "I'm not sure. Let's wait to see what demands the Coast Guard places on me. I'll know where to find you. Thanks for today. I enjoyed it. You were good for me."

With that they shook hands and went separate ways. Jack headed back to the quay and his waiting crew. Diana headed to Hawes office to make the weekly bookkeeping entries. Today might be the day she gave Frank Hawes her two weeks notice.

Jack took some good-natured teasing about meeting Diana. Ritt, who continued to think of himself as a ladies man was jealous and his remarks had a harder edge to them. Jack glossed it all over by saying he was getting whatever history he could from Diana about McKeil. Jack hadn't ruled out bringing his drinking to the attention of higher military authority. Stonecliffe was against it. He didn't want to stir up trouble right before the invasion. He reasoned McKeil's First Mate and other crew members had to be aware of his drinking and they could take steps if McKeil was drinking on the ship.

When Jack thought back over his conversation with Diana he wondered why he hadn't mentioned his marriage to Catherine, or her sudden death shortly after they were married. All that had happened many decades ago and he was past the feelings of intense grief. Still, he often thought about Catherine and their short time together. Maybe talking about her to another woman gave him a sense of betrayal? Or maybe he liked Diana more than other women he had met over the years? Certainly, he felt no need to explain his history with Catherine to Dorothy. But in hindsight, he thought both he and Dorothy knew their relationship would be short lived.

Diana seemed to touch him in a way that would require him to explain his intense love for Catherine. It was the kind of love he did not think he would ever know again. And now, was it possible? Or maybe he was just swayed by her good looks and lovely accent. All in all, Jack thought it best if he stayed away from Diana and the Lion and Cross for a few days while he thought it all over.

Diana had spent the afternoon at Hawes' with her usual accounting and bookkeeping work. She found her train of thought kept drifting away from her work to wonder about Jack. Diana knew her interest should be strictly related to gathering information to pass on. But she found him a very interesting man. His role as part of a rescue flotilla intrigued her. Plus, he was handsome and was a perfect gentleman. She couldn't help but think about the joy she might know in making love to a man like him.

When she finished she looked at the clock and saw it was a little after 5 pm. The other workers would be gone. If Hawes was in his office she would give her notice. Diana was nervous as she walked down the hall to Hawes' office. She told herself there was no reason to be as she could replace the income by working longer hours at the pub. While she had learned about the local military displacements from talking to the salesmen, there was very little new to be learned from them that would be of interest to German intelligence. No, it was time to leave. She wanted to put an end to Hawes leering at her.

Diana walked through the open door to Hawes' office and closed it behind her. Frank Hawes was sitting at his desk and looked up at her. He noted she had a serious look and he also noted she had closed the door. He thought maybe he wouldn't have to show her the German codes he had taken from the folder in the lingerie drawer in her flat. Maybe she needed him in her as much as he wanted to penetrate her.

Diana started the conversation saying; "Mr. Hawes, I have to talk to you. I hate to say it but I'm giving my notice. My work at the Lion and Cross is too demanding and I have to leave here to give that business my attention on a full time basis. I can stay for a couple of weeks until you get a replacement."

Hawes stood up behind his desk and motioned with his hand for Diana to sit in the chair in front of his desk. Diana sat down waiting for a response. Hawes said: "Don't be hasty about leaving. There is something I want to share with you." Hawes pulled an envelope from his desk drawer and opening it took out a sheet of paper with printing on it. He held it up so Diana could see the printing was in German. She studied it for a few more moments and recognized it as codes for encrypting messages.

Diana was confused and asked: "Where did you get this?"

Hawes gave her a small smile and said: "From the lingerie drawer in your flat."

Diana had a flash of honest anger and said: "What were you doing in my flat!"

Hawes said: "I came to see you one day but you weren't in. The door wasn't locked so I let myself in. I wanted to get some sizes from you to buy you some more lingerie—so I looked in your dresser. I discovered this in a folder. There were other documents in German. I believe they were to explain the operation of a short wave radio."

Diana felt the panic rising in her chest. For a moment she thought she might pass out. She tried to think. Diana had forgotten about the folder in her drawer. Since she had no information of an immediate nature she hadn't used the radio. She was passing whatever she had through Gromek. Diana knew she had to come up with an explanation.

Diana tried to keep the edge in her voice and said: "I don't know what those documents are. I found the folder in the hallway of my building. I thought someone might come looking for it so I put it away for safe keeping. That was weeks ago and I hadn't thought of it since. More important is you entering my flat when I wasn't there. Never do that again. Is that clear?"

Hawes could see Diana was flustered. He decided to play this out. He ignored her question saying: "I think I should turn these over to the police anyway--so they can get to the bottom of all this. I'm sure they will clear you if all is as you say."

Diana felt even more desperate: "Mr. Hawes, Frank, please don't involve me in a police investigation. It would be too upsetting. I would lose my position at the Lion and Cross. No one would hire me if that were pending."

Hawes came out from behind his desk and stood in front of Diana. Diana knew if she tried to rise from the chair her legs might give out from under her. Hawes said: "Well, it seems you want something from me and I want something from you. You should stay right here working as you have, but giving me some special attention as well." Hawes put his hand on his groin. "I'm quite large you know. Much bigger than most men. You will enjoy it. I know, in our past moment, I took you by surprise when I touched your vagina. But you opened your legs so I could—so I know you wanted me."

Diana turned her face away from him and said: "Frank, we have been over this. You are married. What would your wife say?"

Hawes chuckled a little. "We all have our secrets my dear. My wife will never know. She has no interest in intimate matters." Hawes paused still touching the growing erection in the front of his trousers.

Still smiling Hawes said: "We need to discuss raising your salary. Before we do let's get you more comfortable. Let's get your blouse and your brassiere off."

Diana felt trapped. She couldn't think of anything to do but let him undress her. She tried a small protest. "Frank, someone could walk in on us. Please don't."

Hawes said: "Everyone has left but us. Don't be shy my dear."

Hawes started to undo the buttons down the front of her blouse but his anticipation was rising and he was having a hard time undoing them. Diana pushed his hands away and with a brief moment of strength stared him in the eye as she finished unbuttoning her blouse and pulling it off. She then reached behind her back and undid her brassiere. She slowly slid one strap, then the other over her shoulders. The brassiere fell to the floor.

Hawes stared in awe at her beautiful breasts. They were high and full with perfect nipples. Her skin was flawless and her nakedness aroused him even more. His hands went instinctively to her breasts and he began to touch them and squeeze them. Then he stopped. He took a half step back and undid his belt and the front of his trousers. They fell to the floor. He pulled down his under shorts and then stepped out of them and his trousers. Diana looked at his penis. It was stiffening, although he wasn't at full erection. Hawes took his penis in his hand and stroked it.

Hawes smiled at Diana and said: "See my dear, I really am quite large." Hawes put his hand behind her head and pulled her face towards his penis and said: "Put it in your mouth and suck on it."

Diana couldn't do it. She pulled away and said: "No Frank, not here, not now. Maybe one day but not now."

Hawes said: "Touch me."

Diana took his huge member in her hands and stroked it. He got very hard. She continued stroking it giving him the benefit of what she had learned from her short married life. She rubbed it faster and then she felt a wetness on her palm and his shaft spasmed. The semen ran out between her fingers. Hawes gasped with pleasure and pushed his groin against her bare breasts. They stayed like that for a few moments with Hawes breathing hard. Finally, he started losing his erection. Diana let go of his shaft and pushed him away.

Hawes looked down at her breasts and saw his semen glistening on one of them. With a wry smile he said: "It's been years since I came like that."

Diana stood. She held tight to the arm of the chair to keep from falling. Hawes approached her to kiss her on the mouth, but she turned her face only allowing him her cheek. He might be able to take her body but she would not give him the intimacy of a kiss.

Diana turned and started for the door saying: "I need to visit the lavatory." She didn't cover herself but picked up her blouse to take with her. Hawes said nothing but watched her walk through the door admiring the contours of her bare back.

Diana was stunned. She walked down the hall to the lavatory dragging her blouse on the floor behind her. As she got to the lavatory door she noticed her shoes were off. She didn't know when she took them off. Diana entered the lavatory and closed the door behind her. She looked at her breasts in the mirror. There were red marks where Hawes had squeezed them. Diana thought she would have bruises.

Diana washed Hawes's emissions from her breast and hands. Twice. She was nauseous. She sat down on the toilet and held her face in her hands. An hour or so ago she was in control of her life. Now she was facing a British prison, maybe even a death sentence. Either that or she must continue performing vile sexual acts for this despicable man. She was filled with regret for her actions that would have encouraged him. Worst of all, she knew he would turn her in when he was done with her, or when she refused him some particular act. A tear coursed down her cheek and through her fingers.

After a few minutes she stood up and washed her face. Her hair was all askew. She unpinned it, shook it out and rolled it up and pinned it to the back of her head. Diana put on her blouse and headed back to the office. She was glad to see Hawes had put on his trousers. He said nothing as she entered. Diana took a cigarette from a box on the desk and lit it. She stood there smoking, then finally said: "Can we discuss my raise in salary now?"

Hawes looked at her nipples that were showing through her blouse. Her brasserie still lay on the floor. Her breasts were still young and high and he thought she didn't need a bra. While he didn't believe her story about finding the folder, he also wasn't convinced she was a spy. One thing he knew was she aroused him deeply and he wanted her again. But he didn't want to push too hard. Not this first time. She might just up and leave Poole and he would never see her again.

Hawes finally spoke: "Diana, we need to continue the discussion about your raise-and other things, away from here. Some place where we won't be interrupted and we can have privacy. My wife is going to Cornwall to visit her sister next week, midweek. She'll be gone over night. You can come to my house for the evening and stay the night. That way we are free to take care of our intimate needs." After a pause he added in a harsher tone: "Make sure you get the time off from the pub."

Diana said nothing. She put out her cigarette. She reached down and put her bra in her purse. Her shoes were under the chair. She put them on. Then she said: "I'll be there. But I won't be back here in the late afternoon or evening due to the demands at the pub. We won't be able to have what happened here today again."

Hawes shrugged then said: "Inventive people will always find ways."

Diana turned and walked out. As she went through the door Hawes said: "Oh Diana, don't bother to bring any pajamas next week. You won't need them."

Diana hurried straight home. She and Gromek had arranged a signal. If the shades on both her windows were half drawn, he was to contact her. Diana drew each shade half way and hoped he would see the signal. Diana had to talk to someone.

Lieutenant Stonecliffe had just come back from a planning meeting with the other Coast Guard officers and the Navy. He and Jack were standing by themselves on the quay by their boat. No one was around and they could talk in private.

Jack asked: "Can you tell me anything about what was discussed at the meeting?"

Stonecliffe said: "This is not to be repeated, but I think they are looking at early June to invade. The higher ups in London are still not telling us where we are going. But they will create shipping lanes in the Channel to get all the vessels across in one piece. The ships will be assigned a shipping lane and a place in line. The warships go first so they can be off the coast for a bombardment ahead of everything else. Then come the transports with the men and landing craft. We go with them. There will be screening ships—destroyers and the like, but we'll have our radar and sonar on too. We will be doing any necessary rescue work if some of the ships get in trouble. Jack, there are thousands of ships involved from ports all along the southern coast of England. We are not the only Coast Guard involved. Many of our larger cutters will be screening. Hundreds of Coast Guardsmen will serve as crews for various landing crafts and Higgins Boats."

Jack was impressed but still questioned their role. He said: "What do we do if we get an enemy contact? We have no armament."

Stonecliffe grinned at him and said: "We call in the Navy!"

Jack looked disgusted. Stonecliffe continued: "Look, we are here for search and rescue. I honestly do not see the German Navy or Luftwaffe attacking us on the way over. You saw how the convoy system worked. Ships will be close together and can collide, just as in peacetime. We need to be around for that—or if there is an enemy attack. We need to get men out of the water and get them to another seaworthy vessel. And we can do that better than any other outfit in the world."

Jack nodded his understanding. It would just be a short time before he would be back in combat. His thoughts went to Diana. He wondered whether she still wanted to go on that picnic.

CHAPTER NINE
BREAKING SURF

Gromek had seen Diana's half drawn shades. They were now sitting on a park bench in an out of the way part of town. Diana had rather haltingly told Gromek about her relationship with Hawes. She left out any part of the story that reflected any encouragement she may have given. The rest was an honest portrayal of what happened. Gromek smoked his cigarettes and listened saying nothing before she finished. Then Diana sat there waiting, expectantly.

After he thought about what he had heard for some time, Gromek asked: "Why didn't you memorize the codes rather than keeping the papers?" Then somewhat irritated he added: "Now we will have to change our codes."

Diana wrung her hands a little. Then she said: "I didn't think I would need the radio for some time and I didn't want to learn codes I might later remember incorrectly—due to the passage of time. My judgment about the radio was correct. I've had no information come to me that would require it."

Gromek kept smoking, thinking. Then he asked: "Does this paper with the codes, that this Hawes has, does it have any information on it tying it to you, or anyone else in our network?"

Diana answered: "No, nothing."

Gromek knew Diana was lying about some aspect of the relationship—something she felt she needed to conceal. This British businessman would not have let himself into her flat when she was not there and gone through her under garments if they did not have some form of personal relationship.

Gromek looked straight at Diana and asked: "Do you know what my orders are about you.?"

Diana answered: "Yes, you are to help me, but also keep an eye on me since my former handler doubts my effectiveness and my loyalty."

Gromek lit another cigarette and gave a small nod of agreement. Then he said: "You must know the simple solution to this problem?"

Diana body tensed up like a piece of sprung steel. She wrung her hands. Then she looked Gromek in the eye and with as clear a voice as she could manage said: "Yes, you could eliminate me."

There was silence between them. Then Diana continued: "But if you did that you would lose my sources and you will not be able to get anyone in place before the invasion. I have two contacts that may give us key information. One is the Captain of a troop transport ship that I have told you about before. The new one is a senior crew member with the patrol boats that undoubtedly will go to France with the other ships."

Diana knew in a strange way she was begging for her life.

Gromek asked: "Have you gotten rid of all the other papers that refer to the radio?

Diana said: "Yes, and the radio is hidden in the attic away from my flat. If I need to transmit you will have to get me new codes."

Gromek nodded his agreement. Then he said: "We end this discussion for today. I will look into this and then contact you. Just go about your normal routine. If this Hawes was going to turn you over to the police he would have done so."

Diana looked at him somewhat imploringly: "I need to know what to do before next week when I am to meet him and spend the night with him. He will turn me in after that."

Gromek shrugged and simply said: "I will be in contact with you. But I remind you sharing your body to get information—or to stay alive, is part of your duties." Then he stood up and walked away.

Diana sat there for a long while, her heart pounding. She didn't know what she had expected from this meeting, but it left her feeling just as helpless and vulnerable as before. If Gromek was going to kill her she prayed it would be both quick and painless.

Gromek took the next couple of days to watch Hawes and learn his routine. He talked with his superiors. It was decided that if he could quietly eliminate Hawes he was authorized to do so. They would then keep Diana around through the invasion to see what value she was. After that they would decide what to do with her.

Gromek saw no easy way to kill Hawes. He thought about trying to stage a robbery at his home. He contemplated a kidnapping—but when and where? And what to do with the body? No, Hawes was too prominent and had too many people around. Gromek took some amusement from the fact Hawes had no idea who he was dealing with when he attempted to blackmail a German agent. The fool, he doesn't deserve to have a beautiful woman like Diana.

About five o'clock on Friday afternoon Gromek was loosely tailing Hawes who had left work and was heading to the bus stop to get a bus home. Since it was the end of the work week there were several people in a long queue waiting to get their bus. It was a nice spring day and Hawes, along with some of the others, was chatting while they waited. The queue was not only long but two and three people wide. Hawes was closest to the curb.

Gromek saw an opportunity. Gromek waited for a bus to approach the stop. He walked along the sidewalk until he was nearly opposite Hawes. He then stumbled forward as though he had tripped. He knocked the person between him and Hawes out of the way and as he was falling forward he hit Hawes hard in the center of the back. Hawes pitched forward into the street. The radiator and bumper on the front of the slowing bus hit Hawes with enough force that it slammed him to the pavement. Hawes looked up in time to see the bus, and felt a searing pain when his head hit the pavement. Then all went black.

Gromek was on all fours and stayed down looking at the sidewalk to hide his face. The accident caused an immediate commotion. No one was paying attention to him. The crowd focused on Hawes. Gromek waited for the right moment to stand and amble away, the brim on his hat pulled low.

Diana was working at the Lion and Cross making bookkeeping entries and paying some invoices. It was a late Friday afternoon and the evening crowd was beginning to arrive. The barkeep stuck his head in the door of the small office where she worked. He said: "Listen dearie, I got news for you! Your other boss, Frank Hawes, just got run over by a bus. He is dead as can be. Drove right over him it did!"

Diana was stunned. Her first thought came in the form of a question. Was this Gromek's work, or simple fate? She realized she needed to show not only surprise, but grief as well. Looking up with a sense of sadness in her face Diana said: "Oh, my God, no! He was such a good employer for so many years! Tell me what you know about it."

The bar keep answered: "I don't know much more. It's all the talk on the street. Some bloke tripped on the sidewalk and when he fell it knocked old Frank out in front of the bus! Tied up traffic and knocked the buses off their schedule. I got customers to get back to— just thought you should know." With that he was gone out to the bar to serve the thirsty patrons.

Diana knew she had been saved by Gromek when she heard the circumstances. Her relief overwhelmed her. She wished Gromek were here. She would thank him endlessly. She would do anything for him. It wasn't until later she realized she had a part in the taking of another life. Strangely, it didn't bother her. In fact, she was pleased. Now the task was to get some meaningful information. The kind that had importance, that would cause the network to see her value. The kind of information needed to keep her from being eliminated.

Jack made a point of seeking out Diana. After he learned from Stonecliffe they may be sailing with the invasion fleet in two or three weeks, he found her serving at the pub. She was glad to see him and smiled broadly at his arrival. Jack didn't take a table but stopped her on her way back to the kitchen and said: "Does that offer of a picnic still stand?"

Diana honestly brightened at the thought. She answered: "Of course! This Sunday would be good. My boss at my other job just died, but I don't think that should cause a problem."

Jack said: "I'm sorry to hear of your loss. Had you worked for him long?"

Diana said: "Yes, but it was a business relationship. I will be sure to be free."

Jack smiled and said: "Great. I'll make sure I don't have the duty. I'll see you about noon. Where should I meet you?"

Diana wrote the address of her flat on a paper napkin and gave it to Jack. She was busy and had to go, but reached out her hand and touched Jack's hand, holding it for a moment. She looked into Jack's eyes and said: "Stay safe. I want you with me. We could have our own world-at least for an afternoon."

On Sunday Jack had Stonecliffe's blessing for an afternoon of liberty. The boat was as ready as it could be. All that was to be done now was wait patiently for orders that would take them to France. Jack borrowed a jeep from the Navy and drove the short distance to Diana's flat. He had his khaki uniform on. The sun was warm and he needed no coat even though the jeep had no top or sides. He parked in front of the building and quickly climbed the stairs to the second floor and her flat. He felt a little nervous. Like he was on his first date. But he figured what the hell. Even if this didn't turn out as well as he expected, it passed a long afternoon.

Jack knocked on her door and he heard her say: "Come in!"

Jack opened the door and saw her finishing putting their lunch in a basket. She had on a white blouse and a fashionably short navy blue cotton skirt. Her clothes showed off her figure nicely. Jack was impressed. He asked: "I hope I'm not too early? I didn't have anything else to do. I borrowed a jeep so we can go wherever you like."

Diana looked up and gave him a smile. "You are right on time. I have us a lunch—the best I can do with rationing." She held up a bottle of wine. "You owe the Lion and Cross for this next time you are in."

Jack said: "My pleasure! Let's go enjoy the sunshine."

With that they were off. Diana directed Jack to drive to a quiet bit of coast east of Poole. There was a grassy knoll with a sweeping view of the English Channel. The sun was high in the clear sky and the Channel waters were a dark blue. A beautiful setting Jack knew he would remember. The best part was they had it all to themselves.

They ate lunch and drank a little wine and lay next to each other in the sun. Mostly they made small talk, but finally Jack thought he should say something about Catherine, his deceased wife. He wasn't sure where to start so he just began talking: "Diana, I remember you told me your husband died early in the war. I had a wife who also died. I met her at my first posting with the Coast Guard--in those days it was known as the US Life Saving Service. I was at an isolated station on the south shore of Lake Superior in Michigan's Upper Peninsula."

Jack paused finding it hard to keep speaking. Diana lay on her side in the grass close to Jack and reached over and touched his cheek. She whispered: "Go on, dear"

Jack continued: "It was 1913 and I was very young—never even kissed a woman let alone made love. Anyway, we met and fell in love. The ice forms on Lake Superior in late fall and the station closed. We went back to my home on the Keweenaw Peninsula about two hundred miles to the west. Unfortunately, there was a miner's strike going on which tore the community built on copper mining apart. My wife was at a Christmas party for the miner's children on the second floor of a two-story building. Someone falsely yelled fire and there was a stampede down the stairs. There were two or three hundred people trying to get out and dozens were trampled and killed in the stairwell."

Jack paused again. Then said: " My wife, Catherine, was one of those that died. She was pregnant with our child at the time."

There was silence between them for some time then Diana said: "Did they ever catch the person who did this horrible thing?"

Jack shook his head no and added: "Many thought it was someone working for the mine owners but no one knows for sure. Not a day goes by that I don't think of Catherine. Don't you think that is odd? We weren't even married six months."

Diana said: "No I don't think it is odd for you to think of her often. You still love her. People don't really die as long as they are in the thoughts of those who knew them and loved them. I'm sad your child also died. He or she would have had a wonderful father. My question though, is why you have never married again?"

Jack thought about his answer. It was a question he had asked himself many times over the years. Finally, he said: "I'm not sure. Some of it may be not wanting to repeat the pain I felt on losing Catherine. I didn't want to love a woman that deeply again from fear of losing her. Plus, the Coast Guard moved me around a lot. I was stationed in the southeastern United States, the Great Lakes, Virginia. I was at sea some of the time. None of that makes for stable relationships."

Diana smile at him. She asked: "What will you do when the war is all over?"

Jack laughed: "Well, I hope they let me retire from the service, again! They pulled me out of retirement for this little party. What about you. What will you do?"

Diana lay back and looked up at the sky. "I guess that depends on who wins. Like everyone else I'm biding my time and waiting for the damn war to end."

Jack said: "Don't worry. We'll win. The question is when and with how many casualties."

Diana kept looking at the blue sky. Then she asked: "Do you really think the Allies will win? The Germans are a powerful enemy. They have had years to build their defenses against invasion."

Jack said: "The reason the Allies will win is the size of the force we will throw against them. Just look at the buildup in our area alone. Ultimately, they have to surrender."

Diana turned back on her side so she was facing Jack. A worried look crossed her face. She asked: "Jack, how safe are you in that wooden patrol boat? It would seem to me you could pretty easily be sunk?"

Jack looked at her very seriously and said: "The same thought has crossed our minds too. I can only hope we play a support role and aren't in the thick of the fighting. I worry more about my crew than I do me. They are young. Some are married and starting families. They are good kids and I want to bring them home safely."

Diana asked: "And you still don't know when the invasion will start or where you will go in France?"

Jack answered: "I'm sure some Admiral knows but I don't. We are just waiting for orders."

There was silence between them for some time. Then Diana leaned forward and kissed Jack, deeply. He responded and kissed her back, taking her in his arms. Diana gently broke the embrace and stood up, pulling Jack to his feet with one arm saying: "Come on Senior Chief Trevenen, there is a pretty walk along the top of the cliff we can take. It's safe to hold my hand and even steal a kiss or two."

Their walk was filled with the joy of being together and sharing intimate kisses. After they came back to the little knoll where they left the picnic basket, it was getting to be late in the afternoon. Jack had to get the jeep back. Jack said: "It's time to go back to reality."

Diana said: "This is reality. The rest of life is what we have to live through so we can have these moments."

They packed up the picnic basket and headed back to Poole. To get to Diana's flat they had to pass part of the harbor. Jack noticed a new ship sitting at anchor. It was the US Coast Guard Cutter Spencer. It was of the same design as the USCGC Campbell that he rode to England.

Jack slowed and pointed to the Spencer and said to Diana: "That is the Coast Guard Cutter Spencer. It is like the one I came over on. Those men have tough duty escorting North Atlantic convoys. I don't know if it is going to be part of the escort for the invasion fleet, or simply making a port call after bringing in another convoy. My one patrol on convoy duty was enough for me."

To Diana the Spencer looked like a variation on other destroyer escort class ships that visited the harbor. She asked: "Is this a sign the invasion is nearing?"

Jack said: "I don't know. But it has to be soon. Full summer is almost here."

They rode in silence until they got to Diana's building. Then Jack escorted her upstairs to her door. Diana smiled and said: "Come in and I will make us some tea."

Jack studied her smile for a moment. He wanted to go in and not leave until morning. But he couldn't bring himself to say yes. Instead, he said: "I have to get the jeep back. Thank you for a great day. I will long remember our time together."

Diana said "I understand. It was wonderful for me too. Please come and see me again."

Jack said: "I will." And they held each other and kissed deeply. Then Jack turned and went down the stairs.

Diana went into her flat and sat down. She truly did have a good day. Jack made her forget the war and her role in it. Briefly, they had known their own world. She was very attracted to him. But reality came flooding back. Guilt over her attraction to Jack. Guilt over her growing certainty Germany could not win. Anxiety over her status in the network of agents.

Diana told herself she needn't report about the lack of armament and wood construction of the patrol boats in the harbor. The information was of no consequence. She would point out the arrival of the Coast Guard Cutter Spencer when she next spoke to Gromek. It didn't merit a radio message.

With heavy heart she undressed and lay down. She closed her eyes and touched herself. She tried to imagine Jack naked, opening her legs, and entering her.

The following Monday Frank Hawes' widow, Francis Hawes, came in to the business and introduced herself to the staff. Diana had made a point of going in early on Monday to see what she could learn. Francis Hawes let everyone know they should all go about their business quite normally. She intended to keep the business open and functioning.

Francis was in her fifties and somewhat heavy set. She had a round face that had a little too much makeup. She had blond hair that was greying, but styled nicely. She was very well dressed in a suit and low heels. Francis was quite interested to meet Diana and took her up to Frank's office. Diana hadn't been in the office where Frank had made her undress and fondle him since that had happened. Being there again raised her anxiety level. She wondered if Francis was about to accuse her of having an affair with her husband? Diana forced herself to remain composed and let Francis take the lead in the conversation.

Francis started by saying: "Diana, I'm so pleased to meet you. Frank told me what a good head you have for business and how good you are at keeping the accounting straight. I need to keep this business going if I can. I need the income. I'll depend on you to help me understand the finances. The route salesmen know what they are doing so all should be fine."

Based on what little she had heard of her, Francis didn't strike Diana as being much of a business woman. However, she hadn't mentioned anything about a sexual relationship with Frank. Diana was willing to support her.

Diana spoke up saying: "I'm happy to help anyway I can. Ordering is the tricky part, but I can show you the history and you'll see what sells and what doesn't. But I must say you should be home taking care of any final arrangements. You have good people here. The business can run itself for a few days."

Francis said: "Yes, you are right but I worry so about it all. His passing was so sudden."

Diana softened a little and said: "We are all very sorry about Mr. Hawes' passing. Do you know any more about what happened?"

Francis shook her head and her voice choked a little with emotion: "No, the police can't find the man who fell and knocked poor Frank into the street. It makes them suspicious, but with the war and all that is going on right now, who knows. There are so many people coming and going. I meet with my solicitor this afternoon. I told the authorities to talk to him."

Diana said: "I'll be in my office for a little while if you need me. I usually come in three half days a week. I also work at the Lion and Cross and due to the needs there I'd like to be here in the mornings."

Francis said: "Of course dear. Anything is fine. Thank you for all you've done."

Diana was quite pleased. She had kept her job and there had been no mention of Frank Hawes' sexual misbehavior. She was in a position to keep tabs on Francis Hawes and her knowledge of the investigation into her husband's death. Gromek was grateful. He had given her new codes to use in sending radio messages. She promptly memorized them and then destroyed the paper copy. Gromek decided to get out of sight for a few days, and left for Bournemouth. Diana would use the radio to report anything of consequence that might come up before he returned.

The rest of her week went well. Jack came by the pub some evenings and walked her home. If there was time before he was due back at the boat he would come in for tea. He smoked his pipe and they talked about life in Michigan's Upper Peninsula. Diana was fascinated with the vast size of the largely undeveloped peninsula and the harsh winters. She wondered if one day she might live there? Jack claimed he would go back to Virginia when the war was over. He liked the more temperate climate.

Diana wanted him in her bed. The more she saw of him the more she wanted him. One evening while Jack was visiting she went to the bathroom and returned from it without her bra and with the top buttons of her blouse open. The outline of her breasts was clearly visible under her blouse. But Jack made no comment. When it was time for Jack to go their embrace and kisses grew longer. Diana longed for him to touch her, but Jack simply took his leave. There was no new information about the invasion in any of their conversations.

One afternoon Diana was working at the Lion and Cross and Captain McKeil came in. Diana hadn't seen him since the altercation with Jack. McKeil took a good look around to make sure no Coasties were in the bar. Once he satisfied himself there were none he sat down and waved Diana over to his table.

Diana went right over and said: "Good afternoon Captain. It is good to see you again. What can I bring you?"

McKeil looked up at her with a sour expression and answered: "I didn't think you wanted me in here again?"

Diana said: "You are always welcome, but you must be well behaved—just as you have been most times in the past. You know I like to talk with you and hear of your experiences. I hope we can get back to that kind of friendship."

McKeil felt a little foolish for staying away and said: "I'll be in to see you more often. This damn waiting to invade is getting to be tiresome. There is nothing for me or my crew to do. I know I drink too much at times, but there are reasons."

It was early in the afternoon and the pub was largely empty so Diana took a chair and sat next to McKeil saying: "What do they tell you about the invasion? There must be something they say to help with your understanding of the situation?"

McKeil said: "Nothing. Not a damn word. If I were running this show we'd be in France by now."

Diana put her hand on McKeil's forearm and said: "Don't worry Captain. You can always come and talk to me. Now let me get you a scotch. That will ease some of your irritation."

It was the second of June. There were no orders about the invasion. Time weighed heavy on the crew of the Six Boat. Jack had begun to wonder if the invasion was being reconsidered by higher command. Jack thought the coming weekend might be a good time for he and Diana to head out to the country and have another afternoon together. It had been two weeks since they had done that. Last weekend Jack had the duty as Stonecliffe went up to London.

Jack was sitting on a bench on the dock by their boat splicing a piece of line. The rest of the crew were doing chores associated with the weekly cleaning of the boat. Today it was cool, but there was broken sun and clouds so they were airing bedding topside on the open deck. Gunners Mate McCauley had disassembled their machine gun and was cleaning the various parts. Stonecliffe was off at another meeting of officers, but Jack expected him back soon. After he got back and the cleaning done Stonecliffe would inspect the boat. Then they would get underway for a short patrol—just to make sure all was in good operating order.

Stonecliffe came down the quay with a smile on his face. He had what looked like maritime charts rolled up and tucked under his arm. He came up to Jack and said: "The Six Boat looks like its manned by a bunch of pirates with all the bedding out for airing."

Jack said: "They will have it stowed shortly so you can hold your inspection. Williams has some fresh fish he is baking for lunch so it should be good. We'll be ready to get underway by 14:00."

Stonecliffe said: "Come below with me." They went to the interior pilot house and operations center. Quartermaster Russell was standing at the chart table checking any recent changes to their charts. Stonecliffe held on to whatever he was carrying and said to Russell: "Russell, let's see all our large and small scale charts for the English Channel."

Right then Jack knew something was up. He felt a tightness in the pit of his stomach.

After looking over the charts Stonecliffe said to Russell: "Thanks. I think we have everything we need. If that changes I'll send you to draw additional charts from the Navy. Now let Chief Trevenen and I talk alone."

Russell left and Stonecliffe turned to Jack: "Well, we don't know when we go, but we do know where we are going---it's Normandy."

Jack said: "Normandy—are you sure? That has to be the widest part of the English Channel. It will take five or six hours to get these troop ships to Normandy."

Stonecliffe unrolled the chart he had been carrying. It showed the shipping lanes that would be used to direct the various vessels from the different English ports to Normandy. There were five invasion beaches. The three easterly ones known as Gold, Sword and Juno would be assaulted by British and Canadian forces. The Americans would land at the two westerly beaches known as Utah and Omaha. In all, the assault would cover many miles of coast.

Jack let out a low whistle. It was a massive undertaking.

Stonecliffe said: "There are thousands of ships and hundreds of thousands of men involved in this. You are right. It will take a while to get there. But Normandy is almost directly across the Channel from Poole. They want to sail after dark to avoid tipping off the Germans we are coming. Even with summer daylight that should give enough time to be on station by 5:30 am. The briefing didn't say anything about when we sail, but my read is it is very close. Maybe this weekend. So no liberty after tonight—and tonight, everyone stays close and must be back aboard by 22:00."

Jack nodded his understanding. Then asked: "What's our part in all this?"

Stonecliffe said: "We will help the destroyers screen the troop ships during the crossing. Then we stand by the troop ships for search and rescue after we are off the invasion beach. Thirty patrol boats go over to help the Brits and Canadians. Thirty go with the American forces to Utah and Omaha beaches. We are in this group and assigned to Omaha."

Stonecliffe added: "For obvious reasons what I have just told you is top secret. I will lock up the chart showing the shipping lanes for the invasion fleet. You are not to repeat any of this for any reason. When we know what day we are going I will brief the crew."

Jack said: "I understand. But if you cancel any weekend liberty they will know something is up."

Stonecliffe said: "Let them speculate. I'll brief them at the proper time. I won't tell them weekend liberty is cancelled until they are back aboard tonight. Then there won't be grousing about losing liberty in the pubs. That could tip off the wrong people that something is up. When we get underway this afternoon I want to check all systems. Everything needs to be in perfect order. When we come in we'll go to the fuel dock and then back here."

Jack said: "Aye, aye sir."

Stonecliffe smiled at him and said: "I'm glad you are here. We all depend on you. I have a good feeling about this. It truly is an historic moment." Then he turned and went topside.

Jack stood there alone for a moment. Then under his breath he said: "God help us now." Then, he too headed topside. It was time to stow the damn bedding.

The same morning Jack learned of their destination, Diana stopped by Hawes' to make sure Francis Hawes was holding up. One of the route salesmen told Diana: "Something is up. Some of those army camps look like they are packing up."

Diana didn't pay it much attention having heard such rumors before—especially as the spring had wore on. That evening she was working at the Lion and Cross. Some of the crew from Jack's boat came in, but no Jack. Diana was disappointed. The crowd seemed lighter than usual and she was tired. She left early and went out the back door and up the side street in the direction of her flat. She jumped when she heard someone say her name. Then she recognized Jack coming up behind her and she stopped walking.

Jack said: "I'm glad I caught you. I can't stop by tonight. We call it the needs of the service! I'd hoped we could get away this weekend but I have the duty again so no luck."

Diana couldn't see Jack's face clearly due to the blackout, but she knew him well enough that she could sense something was troubling him. She stepped close to him and put her arms around him. She pressed her cheek to his. "That's alright dear. The weather is supposed to be bad anyway. I work tomorrow afternoon but I'm free the rest of the time if you can stop by the flat."

Jack put his arms around her sharing their embrace. He held her tight and said quietly in her ear: "I'm sorry Diana, but that won't be possible." Then he kissed her deeply.

Diana gently pushed herself back from Jack and whispered: "You are going to France aren't you?"

Jack answered: "I can't talk about such things. The Coast Guard is just going to occupy all my time for a while. I wanted to let you know that and tell you I will miss you until I see you again."

Diana was scared now. She cared for this man and didn't want him killed. But she had to know, was the invasion starting? Almost begging she said: "Darling you must tell me, are you off to France?"

Jack wanted to pour his heart out to her but knew he had to end the conversation. Jack kissed her deeply again and said: "I will be thinking about you." Then he turned and hurried away.

Diana was left standing there, upset, worried and at a loss as to what to do. Finally, she turned back toward her flat and started walking. When she remembered the comment from Hawes' salesman, and Jack's behavior, she was sure the invasion had to be near. But where would the Allies land? What day would they embark? She didn't have enough information to let her superiors know of her suspicions. As frustrating as that was since her future and her safety might depend on her ability to learn such information, it was Jack she couldn't stop thinking about.

Diana accepted the fact she cared deeply for this man. No man, including her husband, had ever been as kind or gentle with her. Diana liked the fact Jack was older. He was not enamored with the glory of wartime victories as the younger men were. He was calmer and more stable. She was sure that if they made love she would find a smoldering sexuality that would come alive and give her the pleasure she needed.

As Diana walked and thought about Jack she realized more than ever that information she might pass on to her superiors could result in Jack being hurt or killed. She told herself that she was so far removed from the conflict there could be no direct harm to Jack from anything she gave German Intelligence. There were many others like her watching the embarkation ports for movement of men and ships. She wouldn't be the only one reporting.

It troubled her deeply.

Saturday June 3 was a blustery day with more clouds than sun. A front was moving in from the west spoiling the spring weather. Jack could tell they would be heading for France soon. Men were beginning to appear on the docks and board ships. Equipment was also beginning to be loaded. The town which was usually full of soldiers and sailors on liberty was quiet.

Jack's crew had grumbled loudly at being restricted to the boat and immediate area on the quay. There was a nearby hotel that had been taken over by Navy and Coast Guard officers that wasn't off limits. Everyone from the patrol boats could go up there and shower and shave. The boat was very cramped and potable water very limited for these purposes. Underway there was no shaving or bathing at all. Jack told everyone to take advantage of the facilities as he had no idea what would happen once the invasion began. The men sensed change was in the air and the grumbling was short lived.

After lunch Lieutenant(jg) Stonecliffe came back from another meeting and gathered the crew in the galley. He gave them all the information he had given Jack earlier. He gave the chart with the shipping lanes on it to Quartermaster Russell and told he and Jack to start laying out some courses and distances to get them to screening positions on the west side of the convoy heading to the American beaches.

Stonecliffe gave individual crew members assignments for when they arrived off Omaha Beach. Gunners Mates McCauley and Turner along with Boatswains Mate Spencer and Seaman Bollinger would be responsible for getting survivors on board. The Six Boat's single machine gun would be locked and loaded but Stonecliffe saw little use for it. Jack would serve as OOD. Radioman Vincent and Quartermaster Russell would do his usual job. Radarman Carpenter was to have the radar on. Engineman Ritt and Fireman Flaherty would man their usual stations in the engine room. Carl Williams could keep the coffee hot and make light meals.

After everyone acknowledged their role, Stonecliffe asked for questions. Jack spoke up: "Mr. Stonecliffe, I'm sure everyone would like to know when do we get underway?"

Stonecliffe looks at the eleven serious faces all studying him. He smiled. "I thought you might want to know that. We go just after dusk tomorrow night. We need to be on station off Omaha Beach by

5:30 am Monday. And gentlemen, that is secret information. You don't repeat it."

Jack turned and said to the crew: "Let's run our normal watches and try and get some sleep tonight. I think it will be a hard few days after tomorrow."

Stonecliffe paused before dismissing the men. He added: "This is a massive operation. Every piece of it has to work smoothly. You are a good crew and I depend on you to do your duty. This is truly an historic moment. God go with us. Dismissed."

Saturday saw Diana go into the Lion and Cross in late afternoon. Earlier, she had ridden her bike around part of the harbor and could tell the ships were beginning to load men and supplies. Diana came in the back door, hung up her coat, and went out into the pub. The barkeep immediately stopped her. He pointed down the bar to a man hunched over the remains of a dark beer. He was swirling the liquid around the bottom of the glass and muttering to himself. The barkeep said: "Your friend is back. In his cups already he is. And him a captain of a ship. Get him out of here before I cut him off."

Diana recognized the man. It was Captain McKeil. She walked down the bar and stood next to him. Quietly, she said: "Captain, you need to get you drinking under control. You may have to put to sea soon and you can't risk your ship because of drink."

McKeil looked at her and brightened: "Listen Diana, they have done it again. Given me orders to take those young soldiers, boys really, and drop them in Normandy. It will take hours to cross that width of English Channel. Do they think the Germans will just welcome us? I can see the Luftwaffe and torpedo boats waiting for us. Bah! Then they think they will resupply them from England… with ships like mine running the gauntlet each time we go back and forth because they need something. Madness." Looking up at the barkeep McKeil added, with a little slurring of words, "Give me another dark beer."

The barkeep looked at Diana before he poured the beer. She nodded her approval and then just above a whisper said: "Captain, do I understand you to say the invasion will take place tomorrow and you are heading to the Normandy beaches?"

McKeil nodded his head up and down. Then he mumbled: "No harbors, no Cherbourg, no Le Havre, just beaches."

Two men dressed in American merchant marine uniforms came in to the pub. They made straight for McKeil. One turned to Diana and said: "Excuse us miss, but this is our Captain and the Mate has sent us to bring him back aboard. We have had a hard time finding him. Don't pay any attention to his mutterings. Does he owe you any money?"

Diana said: "No, the drinks are on the establishment. Take good care of him. He is pretty far gone."

The two sailors got McKeil between them and half carried him out of the pub.

The business was slow again that night as all liberty and passes for town had been cancelled by the various military commands. Diana left early. She went back to her flat. She went down the hall and got the radio from the attic. Diana took it back to her flat and closed and locked the door. She pulled the antenna out and in what she hoped was the correct encryption, sent a message to German Intelligence advising the invasion was to take place in Normandy on June 4. She waited a few minutes and then the transmission was acknowledged.

After that she poured herself a brandy and sat on the edge of her bed staring at the floor. Diana prayed she hadn't just killed Jack.

CHAPTER TEN
RAGING SEAS

On Saturday night, June 3, Jack was on edge. Tomorrow night they would go to France with the invasion fleet. He didn't let himself think about what could be waiting for his boat and its crew. If he did all he saw was his dead body floating face down in in the English Channel. This was the second time he was going into combat within a few weeks. Once again he was beginning to have trouble with anxiety. His hand tremor was back. His sleep was restless at best.

Since they were restricted to the boat, the crew was below deck playing cards, smoking and drinking coffee. The endless conversation around what the next day would bring irritated Jack. Finally, he decided to get out of the cramped spaces below and go up on deck and smoke his pipe. When he got outside he looked around. It was dark and there was a blackout but he could still make out the outline of some of the many troop transports and other merchant ships filling the harbor to overflowing.

It seemed to Jack most of the troops were done loading. The U S Army 29th Infantry Division was among these. They were headed to Omaha Beach and would be the Six Boat's responsibility. Jack thought about the German Luftwaffe. Wouldn't they have a prize if they bombed this harbor tonight. Jack was inclined to believe the assurances command had given that the German Luftwaffe would not be a factor in this fight. While staging at Poole there had been no air raids. Diana told him of some very scary ones earlier in the war, but those days seemed to be largely over.

The weather was still not settled and there was a good breeze coming in from the English Channel. There had been a light rain shower earlier in the evening. The Sixteen Boat had gone out to look at sea conditions in the English Channel just before dark. When it came back in the crew said there was a good chop running, but not enough to limit the use of the landing craft that would be taking the men and supplies from the ships to the French beaches. The moon was almost full but partially obscured by broken clouds.

The breeze was stiff enough that Jack got behind the highest part of the superstructure and lit his pipe. He pulled his foul weather jacket a little tighter around him. He wondered what Diana was doing. He thought how nice it would be to be holding her and feeling her warmth against him. He bet there wasn't much of a crowd in the Lion and Cross. That would be a dead giveaway to the locals that something was up—as if the troop loading wasn't! Jack was surprised by the chilly, blustery weather in June. It reminded him of the Keweenaw, where summers were short and could be cool. Jack wondered if he would ever see Michigan again after tomorrow's events.

Soon, some of the younger members of his crew came up to join him. Harry Turner, Jimmy Flaherty and John Bollinger gathered around. Flaherty started the conversation: "Chief, what do you think we are going to have to do at Omaha Beach?"

Jack was quiet for a moment then said: "I think we'll do what we are trained to do. We'll live up to our title, Rescue Flotilla. No one knows what we'll run into. There will be thousands of ships in the armada heading to France. There will be a great many warships as well as the transports. The warships will take on the heavy stuff. We'll just grab any men in the water when things don't go so well."

Jack's calm demeanor and simple explanation of their role was reassuring to these young men. Bollinger asked: "What happens on the way over?"

Jack said: "For the most part, your normal duties. Bollinger, you might get a turn at the helm. Turner, you and Gunners Mate McCauley may have things quiet until we get to France. The Six Boat will be part of the screening vessels for the part of the convoy heading to the American beaches. There will be destroyers with us and they'll have their radar and sonar going and will chase any contacts since we are essentially unarmed. We stay with the other ships in case one of them gets hit and needs help abandoning ship."

Flaherty thought about this for a moment, then said: "Chief, how many men can we take out of the water before we are full?"

Jack looked grim. Then he said: "About thirty or so. We'd have to take them to another ship, off load and go back for more."

Turner said: "But Chief, there are hundreds and hundreds of men on each troop transport. What if one of them is hit?"

In a solemn voice Jack answered: "We do the best we can and save the ones that have the best chance for survival."

Everyone grew quiet. Finally, Bollinger asked: "Chief, what are our chances of coming back from this?"

Jack knocked the ash out of his pipe and responded by saying: "I won't pretend there isn't going to be a helluva fight when we get to France. There will be. We all have to do our jobs and look after one another. That gives us all our best chances. If you haven't done so write your letters home. Fill out your form wills. Get as much sleep tonight as you can."

Jack turned to go below and then stopped and turned back to the men. He added: "There will be a chaplain giving a short service tomorrow morning right here on the quay for all Coast Guard crews. You might want to attend."

Captain McKeil woke up early on Sunday morning with a bad hangover. His head hurt. He was nauseous. He had drunk quite a bit while ashore on Saturday, before his crew members brought him back to the ship and put him in his cabin. He had a couple of bottles of scotch hidden there and he had drunk half of one of those before he went to sleep.

McKeil also had a nightmare. In it, he was standing outside on the bridge wing of his ship and watching an artillery shell arcing towards him. It kept descending, and getting larger, until it exploded in his face. It was so real he awoke from it in a cold sweat. The fear he felt was palpable.

McKeil sat on the edge of his bunk and thought he needed another drink. He reached for the half empty bottle of scotch and took a big swig. The alcohol soothed his anxiety. He stumbled across his cabin and sat down heavily in a chair. He wanted to get out of taking his ship to Normandy. But he couldn't see any other choice. All he could do was say he was sick, but everyone would know he was just drunk, scared, or both. The pain of that kind of humiliation was worse than facing enemy fire. He had to pull himself together. He took another pull on the scotch bottle and then rang for the cook to bring him some coffee.

Jack was up early on Sunday morning as well. He left the berthing area and went forward to the pilot house. It was just getting light. Jack thought tomorrow this time it won't be this quiet. He tapped the barometer. It was falling. Jack went topside. He looked around at the crowded harbor, then at the sky. There were a lot of clouds visible. There was a light breeze from the east.

Spencer had the watch. Jack greeted him: "Good morning Jimmy. Everything quiet?'

Jimmy smiled and said: "Sure is Chief. Have you ever seen so many ships in one place?"

Jack shook his head and said: "Not in my lifetime. Not much like the old Portage Canal Station is it?"

Spencer said: "Not at all. Did I tell you I got a letter a while back from one of the guys stationed there. We went to boot camp together. He says they built temporary barracks and a big galley and are using it to train new recruits in the warm weather months. As much as I liked patrolling Hampton Roads, I miss Lake Superior and I would like to be looking at it right now."

Jack nodded his agreement and added: "If we were on Lake Superior I would say we are in for some weather. The barometer is dropping and I think the wind will back north throughout the day. But since this is my first trip to England I don't know the weather patterns."

Spencer asked: "Do we go, even in bad weather?"

Jack answered: "I guess it depends how bad it gets. The landing craft taking the troops in to the beaches can't take much wave action. What I've been told is we need clear skies and a full moon tonight for the precision bombing inland and the paratroops that will be dropped behind the beaches. Tomorrow morning we need low tide so the landing craft won't run into any obstructions the Germans placed on the beach to prevent a landing. If we don't go now the moon and tides aren't right again for a few weeks."

Spencer said: "Chief, the Germans have weather forecasters. They can read an almanac. Don't they know all that. Won't they be waiting for us?"

Jack paused. Then he said: "You'll be off watch before the chaplain gives his service on the quay. Why don't you come over to it with me?"

Spencer looked worried, but said: "Sure Chief. I'd be pleased to."

Diana had a restless night and she too got up early on Sunday morning. She dressed and went out to study the harbor. To her surprise there had been no ship movements. Everything looked as it did on Saturday. It worried her. Had she sent the wrong information in her radio message? McKeil was drunk. Maybe he didn't know what he was talking about? Her first reaction was to worry she would be in trouble with German Intelligence. Then she remembered her meeting with her fellow network members. The older man, who was senior to the others, had encouraged her to send on information, even if it didn't represent a complete picture of what was happening. That thought seemed to calm her. Then she remembered the British military monitored radio transmissions. Did they hear hers?

More than ever she wanted to see Jack. But she knew that was impossible. He would be on duty and there would be other crew members around. Diana went to where she could see the Coast Guard flotilla tied up on the quay. They were all still there. She tried to see Jack but he didn't come into view. She wanted to beg him not to go. To tell him the German forces would be ready for them. But that wasn't possible, for many reasons. Finally, she was swept with sadness and resignation and went back to her flat to await events.

Most members of the Coast Guard crews attended the chaplain's service. It was short and interdenominational. His sermon explained the need for them to be there and gave them hope for their well being during the next few days. Jack wasn't particularly religious but listening to the chaplain helped make the waiting more bearable.

As Jack predicted, the weather went downhill as the day wore on. The sky became overcast. The wind picked up and by afternoon rain lashed the Six Boat. Even the harbor was a little kicked up and the Six Boat rocked at her moorings. It was a long afternoon with everyone staying below deck. Williams kept everyone well fed and the coffee flowed. By dinner time the wind had gone north and picked up to a steady 20 knots, with higher gusts. The trees were swaying in the wind and rain. Lt(jg) Stonecliffe was called to a meeting just after they ate their evening meal.

Stonecliffe came back in about an hour. He came down below with a grim look and called everyone around: "Listen men. This affects us all. The invasion is cancelled for tonight. The weather is too bad. There is a storm coming through that won't allow us to have clear skies or calm seas."

A collective groan rose up from the crew. Engineman Ritt immediately spoke up and asked: "Can we get liberty tonight?"

Stonecliffe shook his head and said: "No. We are restricted to our boats and are not to discuss the change in plans with anyone. You shouldn't feel bad. They aren't going to offload all the troops from the transports. They will be stuck there for another day at least. I understand the heads are already overflowing. Over in Portsmouth the LSTs are bouncing around like corks and the men waiting on those are all sea sick."

Stonecliffe smiled and then continued: "You are in the lap of luxury. Williams here has us eating like kings. You can sleep in your own bunk. And our head is working just fine!"

Overnight the wind and rain didn't let up. In fact, the wind picked up to 25 to 30 knots and was from the north northwest. At daylight on Monday June 5 one of the Coast Guard patrol boats went out into the Channel to check sea conditions. There were heavy swell and a driving wind. The landing craft would be unusable in such conditions. When that word was passed the crews knew they had another long day to pass as they waited out the storm.

Jack thought a lot about Diana. He scolded himself for not making love to her. She was very beautiful and he knew she wanted him. He thought about the evening she showed her breasts under her blouse, without her brassiere. He was older than she was, but that didn't seem to bother her. He doubted anyone that attractive would ever be interested in him again. If he lived through the coming days he would do better and take her to his bed.

Diana went out in the stormy weather on Monday morning, June 5, to again look at the harbor. Nothing had moved. Convinced of her error in her prior message, she sent a new message to German Intelligence saying the invasion fleet had not moved. Then she went to Hawes' to do the bookkeeping and maintain her weekly routine.

Monday June 5th was a long day of waiting and Jack noticed some irritability among crew members. The men of the Six Boat were quiet as they ate their evening meal. There was no word as to when they would go to France. The windy conditions continued, but to Jack it seemed to be lessening. The rain had stopped. Well into the evening Stonecliffe was called to another meeting. He came back a little before 10 pm. He was smiling. His message this time was simple: "We go tonight!"

Jack thought they would never get Poole harbor emptied and ships on their way to France in a timely manner. But they did. Jack was impressed. The thirty Rescue Flotilla boats going to the British beaches left and headed off to the east. Then the remaining Coast Guard patrol boats headed to the American beaches came out and stood off the harbor entrance. They waited while the troop transports and supply ships exited and began forming up into a convoy and heading south towards France. Then destroyers and Coast Guard patrol boats took their screening positions. As they got further out in the English Channel other ships and escorts joined until they had an armada of massive size. There were thousands of ships spread out in formation and heading across the English Channel. The ships for the American beaches formed the Western Task Force. The ships for the British beaches formed the Eastern Task Force.

The weather was still not the best. The rain was over. The moon was visible most of the time with a broken cloud cover overhead. The wind had dropped to 10 to 15 knots and the waves were running 4 to 6 feet. The wind and waves were coming from the northwest and it made for a following sea. The Six Boat didn't handle well in those conditions and it pitched and rolled. There were no sandwiches and coffee to be had as everything below had to be secured.

The Six Boat was in the Western Task Force. At times Jack and his crew could hear hundreds of aircraft passing overheard heading for France. Jeffery Carpenter was the radar operator and had his set on. They all took turns looking at the small radar screen that was full of returns from the huge number of ships around them. That is when it hit Jack that Stonecliffe was right. This was an historic moment.

The Coast Guard Cutter Spencer was one of the escort vessels in their Task Force. It was a Secretary Class cutter like the Campbell.

As it steamed by they sent a message by flashing light. It said: "Good luck Rescue Flotilla." Quartermaster Russell sent a message back by flashing light saying: "Good luck to Spencer." They had to maintain radio silence until the landings were actually underway.

The patrol boat could be operated from inside the pilothouse or from a control station topside, above and behind the pilot house. This latter gave a full 360 degree view of the horizon. The outside temperature was only in the high 40 (F) degree range, but Stonecliffe kept the operation of the boat outside where he could see everything around him. He did not want to get run down by an errant transport ship that got off course.

When Jack judged them to be about halfway across the English Channel he looked at his watch. They were on schedule and if all stayed quiet they would be in the assembly area as planned. They all had steel helmets and life jackets on over their peacoats. Jack was comfortable, although balancing on the moving deck was making his legs ache. He turned to Stonecliffe and said: "I don't believe we are going to be bombed or torpedoed. This is almost boring."

Stonecliffe replied: "I know what you mean. I think we may have surprised the Germans. I don't think they know we are on our way."

Jack said: "With no enemy contact I'm not sure what we are doing here. Weren't we supposed to rescue troops from sinking transports that had been attacked by German planes or U Boats?"

Stonecliffe shrugged. Then he added: "I think we will be needed. This is going to be a long day. Very long."

Jack smiled at him and said: "I just don't want to give up part of my retirement for nothing."

The moonlight allowed them to make out the outline of the nearby ships even though all vessels were blacked out and not showing any running lights. The vessels were holding formation very well. Jack thought they were doing better than the ships in the convoy he had sailed to England with. When they were much closer to France the Western Task Force split. The ships carrying the American troops to Utah Beach veered west and the ships going to Omaha Beach stayed on the same course. There were no attacks by German planes or U Boats. The ships of the Task Force assigned Omaha Beach, including the Six Boat, arrived off the French coast as scheduled. Fourteen other Coast Guard patrol boats were assigned to Omaha Beach.

Jack was watching the sky. He turned to Stonecliffe: "Have you been watching the sky? We lost the moon and stars as we approached the French coast. We have full overcast."

Stonecliffe said: "I don't think it matters. The paratroops will have landed and the bombing runs finished. It will be daylight soon. These waves are still big enough to give the landing craft trouble though." ·

Before Jack could answer he was cut off by the crash of naval gunfire. It was deafening. The warships in the Task Force were laying a naval bombardment on Omaha Beach. The Six Boat was far enough off shore and behind other vessels that Jack and the crew didn't have a clear view of the beach. However, they could see explosions and smoke rising up in the air as the shells landed. The shelling was tremendous. Battleships, cruisers, light cruisers, destroyers, all with multiple guns, were all firing at once. Smoke and flashes of flame leapt from the muzzles of the naval guns. The crew all came topside and stood with Jack and Stonecliffe. They were in awe of the destructive power they were watching. No one said anything over the roar of the bombardment. But they all thought the same thing. No one could live who was under that kind of shelling.

The area of shoreline designated as Omaha beach was about five miles long. It was divided into seven zones with specific units of the 1st and 29th US Army divisions assigned to each of the seven areas. The troop ships took station behind the warships. Each ship was roughly off the portion of beach the troops it was transporting were going to attack. The fifteen Coast Guard Patrol Boats were spread along this line of troop ships. They were to stand by in case any of the troop ships was hit. The Six Boat was assigned the ships holding the men who would attack the central portion of Omaha Beach.

It was hard to hear over the roar of naval gunfire. Stonecliffe grabbed Jack's arm and pointed to a troop ship dimly visible in the grey early dawn light. He yelled in Jack's ear: "I think that is one assigned to us."

Stonecliffe motored over to the ship and stood by. Other Coast Guard patrol boats were finding their stations. There was no return fire coming from the Germans. Stonecliffe was concerned about floating mines. Supposedly, minesweepers had cleared paths to the beach during the night so the landing craft could safely approach. But you never knew.

Dozens of landing craft were in the water and forming up in an assembly area. They took turns going alongside the troop ships to load and then returned to the assembly area. The soldiers scrambled down cargo nets hung over the side of the ship and dropped into the landing craft below. The drop was tricky as the landing craft rose up and down with the wave action. Jack kept a close eye on them in case anyone went into the water attempting to board.

The landing craft were officially known as LCVPs, or Higgins boats. They were 36 feet long and 11 feet wide. They were made of plywood. Fully loaded they carried 36 soldiers. There was a crew of 4 to operate it. Many of the crews were Coast Guardsmen. The bottom was flat, but the propellors and rudders were recessed into the bottom. The front of the boat was a ramp that could be lowered. The idea was to run the boat right up to the edge of the beach, lower the ramp and let the troops exit. The ramp would then be raised and the craft backed away from the beach to return to the troop ship for more men. Due to the flat bottom, and ramp for a bow, they handled terribly in rough seas.

At the center of the line of transports Jack saw McKeil's ship off loading its troops into waiting landing craft. Jack shook his head in wonder. What a small world it was that they should both be here.

Since the operation was proceeding smoothly there was little for the Coast Guard crews to do. Jack waited uneasily for the naval bombardment to end. That would be the signal for the loaded landing craft to head for the beach. They wanted to go as close to the end of the bombardment as possible to get ashore before the Germans could reoccupy any defensive positions.

Jack noticed it was now daylight. It was a gloomy, chilly, overcast day. He felt sad for the men in the first wave of troops to hit the beach. He feared there would be heavy casualties. The wind was still a good 10 knots and the waves two to four feet. Both the wind and waves would make the landing craft harder to handle. As the landing craft pulled away from the assembly area and headed for the beach the naval bombardment suddenly stopped. The silence took everyone by surprise. There was a sense of safety created by the gunfire. Now it was just up to the men heading towards the shore.

Jack asked Stonecliffe: "Are you going to follow the landing craft?"

He answered: "Our orders are to stay with the transports."

Jack said: "I understand, but those men may need us."

Just as Jack said that one of the landing craft ahead of them, and about halfway to the beach, got in trouble. A wave had caught it on its starboard quarter and pushed it sideways. Instead of turning to port and putting the waves directly behind it the coxswain tried to hold her steady. The net result of that was to get the craft fully sideways to the waves. It was in close enough that the waves were beginning to break. Another breaking comber caught the craft while it was still sideways to the oncoming waves. The landing craft tipped up on its side. All the soldiers onboard were thrown to one side and then into the water.

Stonecliffe turned to Jack and said: "Well, that makes the choice of whether to stay with the landing craft easy." He ordered the Six Boat to full ahead and steered for the foundering landing craft that was now dead in the water. As he did so he yelled to Jack; "Get those life rafts you brought along over the side. We'll need those to bring the men aboard."

Jack and McCauley went to the foredeck, untied the rafts and took them aft. One was placed in the water on each side of the boat and tied off. The 83 foot patrol boat had too much freeboard to allow survivors to be easily pulled directly up out of the water. Getting them in a raft and then transferring them to the deck was easier. Spencer and Bollinger took the raft on the port side. McCauley and Turner took the one on the starboard side. As Stonecliffe brought the boat alongside the over turned landing craft Bollinger and Turner got into their respective rafts and started pulling soldiers in and helping them to the deck.

There were survivors everywhere. Some were clinging to the hull of the landing craft. Most were thrashing about in the water trying to get their equipment off so they could float. Some had life jackets, some didn't. Spencer noticed that when a man went under, he didn't resurface.

Jack looked around at the other landing craft. They seemed to be handling the waves better and were now well ahead of the scene Jack and his crew were facing. Jack noticed the northwest wind and waves seemed to be pushing the landing craft to the east and they were maneuvering, trying not to bunch up.

As Jack looked toward the shore he saw a surreal scene. The sky was overcast and the water reflected the grey clouds. There was smoke in the air from the bombardment. The beach itself was wide and full of big steel beams welded into the shape of large "X"'s. They were planted in the sand to impale landing craft trying to come in at high tide. There was a line of bluffs at the back of the beach that rose quite sharply. The bluff was a darker grey than the leaden sky above it. The waves broke with a rush and there were small whitecaps on their crests as they rushed towards shore. Jack could make out an opening in the bluff line and a narrow road coming down to the beach. It was flanked by concrete gun emplacements that didn't look like they were damaged by the naval gun fire. All in all, it looked forbidding.

Jack couldn't study the shore long. He had to help with the men they were taking on board. The deck was filling up with soaking wet soldiers who were shaking from the cold air and water. Russell had brought some blankest to put around them, but they were far too few for the number of men.

Spenser helped the coxswain of the over turned landing craft up onto the deck. He too was shaking. Jack started to help him up and moved him forward to find a place to sit him down. Before Jack could do so the coxswain fell to the deck on all fours and started pounding it with his fists. He was crying and mumbling: "I didn't mean to do it. I just didn't think it would do that. Not so quickly. God dammit I didn't think it would do that."

Jack pulled him up and said: "It's alright son. We know it was an accident. These Higgins Boats aren't meant for these kinds of waves. Anyone could have that happen, and others will, if the Channel doesn't calm down." Then Jack took him forward and sat him down behind the mast.

One of the soldiers just brought on board saw the coxswain across the deck. He had lost his weapon and his pack but still had his bayonet. He pulled it out and lurched towards the coxswain saying: "You dirty son of a bitch. God damn you for drowning my friends. You fucker"

Jack saw what was happening and made a flying tackle catching the soldier at the waist and throwing him back to the deck. The soldier dropped the bayonet and it bounced off the deck and over the

146

side. Jack got him on his back and put his knee in his chest. Jack pulled his .45 caliber pistol and stuck it in the soldier's face. Jack growled: "Listen you dumb bastard, you are on my boat now and you will behave yourself. Either that or I throw your sorry ass back in the Channel."

The look in the soldier's face was pure hate. But Jack wouldn't let him up. Spencer came and stood over them. He smiled and said: "Need any help Chief?"

Jack didn't answer. Spencer pulled out his rigging knife and said: "Let me carve on him for a while."

The soldier realizing he needed to submit said: "I'm alright now. Get your knee off me." Jack studied the soldier's face. It lost its wild look of rage. Jack let him up and pointed for him to sit on the opposite side of the boat from the coxswain.

Jack turned to Spencer and said: "Let's get the four landing craft crew members down below and away from these soldiers or we are going to have more of this."

The rescue effort was about complete. Stonecliffe could see three bodies floating nearby and wanted to pick them up as well. The rescue had resulted in the wind and waves pushing them closer to shore. As Jack pulled the last living soldier onto the deck he looked up and noticed they were much closer to the beach. At that moment the other landing craft were arriving at the water's edge and dropping their ramps and unloading troops. To Jack's way of thinking all hell then broke loose.

The Germans had reoccupied all their firing positions after the naval bombardment ended. There were German troops on the top of the bluff firing down. The concrete gun emplacements were also reoccupied. They had a fields of fire, straight ahead and down the beach in both directions. Thus, American soldiers had to face deadly oncoming and enfilade machine gun fire. The beach exploded from heavy mortar shells raining down. There was a light artillery piece down the beach in a concrete bunker which threw shells into groups of soldiers trying to seek cover behind the beach obstacles. Jack watched men trying to advance across the beach be hit and drop like targets in a shooting gallery. A mortar shell hit a landing craft as it was lowering its ramp destroying the front half of the craft and blowing men and body parts into the air. Mayhem. Nothing but bloody mayhem.

147

The Six Boat was becoming close enough to shore to start attracting the attention of German gunners. One machine gun in particular targeted them. Most of the rounds fell short but some struck the hull. Dead and wounded men lay in the shallow water at the edge of the beach. The German small arms fire splashed like raindrops in a pond. Many cried for help, for medics, for their pain to end. Stonecliffe wanted to help them but couldn't maneuver the boat in that close due to the shallow water. The German fire was intense. Stonecliffe knew his first obligation was to the living survivors he had on board. They were now nearly fully loaded with rescued soldiers.

Jack ran forward and stood next to Stonecliffe. He yelled: "We have to get the hell out of here and get these men to safety. We can't take any more on board. Dead or alive."

Stonecliffe nodded and said: "In the briefings we were told there would be a medical ship in the middle of the assault fleet. Let's see if we can find it."

With that the Six Boat went full ahead away from the beach. It soon passed through the line of warships and into the area filled with troop transports and supply ships. Stonecliffe spotted a ship with large red crosses painted on its side. He ordered them to go alongside and off load the soldiers they had rescued. The medical ship had a boom over the side to lower platforms to be filled with the weak and injured so they didn't have to climb back up cargo nets. Getting the soldiers from the Six Boat onto the medical ship was a methodical and somewhat time consuming operation. Most of the men they dropped off were suffering from hypothermia, shock and minor injuries. In all they picked up twenty-seven survivors. The rest of the men on that landing craft were missing and presumed drowned.

By the time they had fully unloaded the survivors the second wave was getting organized with landing craft coming back from the beach to load troops. Jack noted other landing craft were already being loaded. As the landing craft filled with men they pulled away from the transports and headed to the assembly areas to await the completion of loading. Stonecliffe was unsure of what to do, so the Six Boat stood by the troop transports per their original orders.

Radioman Vincent came up from below and advised: "Mr. Stonecliffe, Chief, I just got a message from command. We have new orders. They want us to follow the landing craft in as they head for the beach. Also, they are warning about floating mines being spotted."

Stonecliffe said: "Thank you, Vincent."

Stonecliffe turned to Jack with a grim look: "This ought to be fun. Better have McCauley uncover and load our machine gun."

Jack nodded his agreement then pointed to two soldiers that had fallen overboard trying to board their landing craft. Stonecliffe also saw them and maneuvered over to them. Spencer brought them on board. They came alongside the landing craft and put them back aboard it. Stonecliffe then took a station among the troop transports to watch for any others who might go overboard in the loading process.

The Three Boat came alongside on its way to the assembly area. Stonecliffe and its commanding officer talked briefly. Jack overheard the worry expressed by the other crew about going back to the beach. They said the first wave had floundered and it was a toss up whether the beach could be taken.

Jack had lost track of time. It wasn't yet mid-morning. The sky was still overcast but the wind and waves were lessening. After it looked like the landing craft loading was complete, Stonecliffe ordered the Six boat over to the assembly area. Two other Coast Guard patrol boats joined them. It wasn't long before this group headed towards the beach. The Coast Guard patrol boats kept a respectable distance behind, but were close enough to move in quickly if needed. They passed through the line of warships and headed towards the beach.

The view was the same as earlier, grey sky, grey land and grey water. There was the sound of firing coming from the beach, but it was not as strong as when the first wave hit. As they got closer Jack could see the only cover for the soldiers was tight up against the base of the bluff. The men who had gotten across the beach were grouped along the base of the bluff. Most of the American soldiers were not firing, but were hunkered down at the base of the bluff. The exit road off the beach was not open, but still guarded by German held concrete bunkers.

As the landing craft in front of them arrived at the edge of the beach, and started to unload, the German fire once again became intense. A lot of the soldiers never made it out of the landing craft as their bows were sprayed with machine gun fire as the ramps were dropped.

McCauley manned the Six Boat's 50 caliber machine gun and started firing. Jack didn't think the fire was effective because they were too far out to clearly identify targets, but it made everyone feel like they were in the fight.

Mortars started raining down on the beach and the water's edge. A landing craft, having dropped its troops, was backing away and was hit by a mortar and swung sideways. Then it started forward and away from shore. It was hit with gun fire and then stopped. Stonecliffe ordered them towards it and slowed as they approached it to avoid hitting bottom. They got alongside and took the wounded coxswain off. The rest of the crew was dead. The enemy firing was so intense Stonecliffe pulled away thinking the bodies couldn't be removed until the beach was taken. The water near the beach was red with blood. Jack took the wounded coxswain below and Williams bandaged a nasty head wound.

Most of the steel beach obstacles were visible because they had landed at low tide. But some were out in the water and a landing craft got in trouble when it got hung up on one. It hadn't dropped its troops and the plywood boat was being raked with German machine gun fire. The artillery piece in the bunker down the beach was taking shots at it. Soldiers were screaming and dying. Many tore off their packs and jumped over the side.

Jack knew what Stonecliffe was going to do. He thought this is the moment my life ends. Stonecliffe cautiously closed on the stricken landing craft and stopped. The bow touched bottom but they weren't aground. He had Jack, Spencer, Turner and Bollinger all helping get men out of the water. Jack yelled at McCauley: "Give us some covering fire!" The 50 caliber started banging away. Stonecliffe repositioned the boat so the bow was against the stern of the landing craft. Soldiers started crawling over the stern and onto the bow, some being hit in the process. Then an artillery shell landed in the water near the Six Boat. It dumped part of a huge column of water on the boat and shrapnel flew through the air. At the same time a line of machine gun bullets laced their way across the port side, superstructure and mast splintering wood and sending men diving for the deck.

Jack wasn't hit, but others were. McCauley fell to the deck grabbing his leg. Stonecliffe was hit in the forearm. Ritt and Flaherty came out of the engine room and said there were small leaks plus the exhaust manifold on one engine had been hit and cracked. Spencer was alright but Bollinger had a round go through his helmet and cut his scalp. Russell stayed on the helm and held the boat in place to take the last of the troops that could move on their own off the landing craft. Then they backed away and headed for the medical ship. Those not hit helped bandage and comfort those who were regardless whether they were soldier or sailor.

The Six Boat made it back alongside the medical ship and off loaded the troops that were wounded. McCauley was put aboard as well. The rest of the Six Boat crew that was hurt insisted they were well enough to perform their duties. Since Stonecliffe applied this same standard to himself he let everyone stay aboard except McCauley. Stonecliffe favored his injured and heavily bandaged arm to keep the bleeding from starting again. Russell was unhurt and would continue to do the wheeling.

After leaving the medical ship they took the few soldiers that were without equipment, but not injured, back to the troop ship they came on. They heard brief naval gunfire to the west. They were later told a German E-Boat had actually tried to attack the fleet gathered off Utah Beach. It had been chased and sunk by an American destroyer.

The Six Boat headed back to the beach. Jack heard the sound of aircraft. Two German fighters, flying low above the sand and water, were strafing the beach. They were so close Jack could make out the facial features of the pilots. Harry Turner ran for the 50 caliber machine gun which was still loaded and ready for firing. But the planes came and went in a flash and he could not get his sights on them. A moment later two Royal Air Force Spitfires came streaking across the beach hot on the tails of the German fighters. The planes disappeared down the beach. That was the only appearance of the Luftwaffe that morning.

The U S Army had also outfitted thirty Sherman tanks with flotation collars. They were launched from LSTs just off shore. One of those was churning its way toward the beach near the Six Boat. The Coast Guardsmen watched it be overwhelmed by the waves and sink. Stonecliffe immediately ordered the patrol boat to the area of the sinking. The tank sank in deep enough water it wasn't visible. There were air bubbles coming up. Jack spotted two crew men floating nearby and they picked them up. The rest of the tank crew never got out.

The Six Boat stayed off the beach, but by now many of the landing craft were returning having put their troops ashore. One was having engine trouble and asked for a tow to the assembly area. Stonecliffe agreed to help. Ritt complained as he didn't have full power on the damaged engine, but they took the craft under tow anyway. They talked with its coxswain. He said: "The second wave isn't doing much better than the first and the men are just bunching up at the base of the bluff trying to stay alive."

Stonecliffe ordered them back out towards the Channel. They put the two men from the tank on one of the LSTs and then tied off the disabled landing craft to the same vessel. Then the Six Boat went over and idled just outside the assembly area. They waited for the third wave of landing craft to form up and head for the beach. They knew that for the invasion to succeed this wave had to take the beach. Omaha was in the center of the invasion beaches and failure here would allow the Germans to isolate and destroy the invasion forces on either side.

The Six Boat was hailed by flashing light from a destroyer escort in the line of warships. Stonecliffe ordered Russell to go alongside. The Captain of the destroyer escort came out on his bridge wing and looked the patrol boat over. The Six Boat showed the effects of the morning effort. There were bullet and shrapnel holes, one engine was running rough, a pilot house window was broken, and there were blood stains on the deck.

The destroyer Captain was young. He exchanged salutes with Stonecliffe. Then he said: "Looks like you have seen some action. Are you seaworthy enough for another run to the beach?"

Stonecliffe said: "Yes sir. We'll go in behind this next wave of troops."

The Captain said: "Good. I need you, if you are seaworthy?" I want to run in toward the beach at an angle, then run parallel to it. I can train my forward 5 inch gun on the concrete bunkers, including the one with the artillery in it. I want to stay 500 or 600 yards offshore. I want to do it right before the third wave goes in. I want you to go ahead of me to keep me from running aground or hitting any mines or underwater obstacles."

Stonecliffe thought about this for a moment. He turned to Jack: "Sounds awfully dangerous to me. But we can spot any sand bars or obstacles and wave him off."

Jack was resigned to their situation. He answered: "I guess they figure the Six Boat is more expendable than a destroyer escort." Jack paused. Then he added: "That beach has to be taken and we have to keep going back to it until it is. That destroyer could make a big difference. We might as well try and end this now rather than later."

Stonecliffe briefly went aboard the destroyer to coordinate the run. The Flotilla Commander confirmed the plan. Command knew the first and second wave had floundered and desperate measures were necessary. After a short while Stonecliffe then came back to the Six Boat and explained it all to Jack and Russell. They would have to run as fast as their engines would allow and stay at least 200 to 300 yards ahead of the destroyer. If the waters started to shoal, or they saw a mine or underwater obstruction they would fire a flare and turn seaward. Otherwise, they would just run down the length of the beach.

As he talked with Jack, Stonecliffe changed his bandage. His arm had started bleeding again.

The destroyer and the Six Boat got in position to make their run. Using signal flags the destroyer let Stonecliffe know they were ready. The Six Boat went full ahead, its bad engine missing under the strain. But they led the way and headed toward the beach keeping the shoreline off the port bow. Turner manned their machine gun and started firing as they drew near to shore. Both ships made a hard turn to parallel the beach. The 5 inch gun on the destroyer began to fire as well as some of its secondary batteries. It immediately became evident to the soldiers trapped at the base of the bluff what the targets were and they let out a cheer.

Carpenter, who was the Six Boat's radar and sonar operator was also watching the depth. He let Stonecliffe know changes in the water depth. Spencer was laying on his stomach on the bow watching the water immediately ahead for obstacles or sand bars. They were drawing some light small arms fire from the Germans, but it wasn't very effective.

The run was successful. They went the full length of the beach and the destroyer's fire took out the German artillery piece and damaged other bunkers. The two vessels headed back out into the Channel. As they separated the destroyer sent the Six Boat a message by flashing light: "Well done Coast Guard."

As they motored off the beach waiting for the landing craft in the third wave, Jack pointed at the damaged artillery bunker and said to Stonecliffe: "Serves those bastards right! That was the gun that almost took us out." But Stonecliffe had passed out and was unconscious on the deck. Jack yelled at Bollinger: "Get him below. We need to get him medical help."

Jack realized he was now in command. He ordered Russell to turn and head for the area where the medical ship was anchored. But as they headed back out toward the fleet he could see the bow waves of dozens of landing craft coming toward them. The landing craft were heading for the beach with the third wave of troops on board. Jack said to no one in particular: "This is it. The third wave has to get the job done."

CHAPTER ELEVEN
HIGH TIDE

Diana slept fitfully on Monday night. She wondered about the invasion. When would it start? Would it be successful? Would Jack be killed? Should she send another radio message? Where was Gromek? Finally, it was morning. She got out of bed and stood in front of the mirror. She looked at the dark circles under her eyes. Diana thought how much she had aged since the war began. She was nude and ran her hands over her breasts. She had no sense of her own sexuality.

Slowly, Diana dressed. Looking out the window she saw the bad weather had passed but it was a grey morning. The overcast sky fit her mood. Diana looked at the calendar. Tuesday June 6. She needed to go to Hawes' and see how Francis Hawes was making out. There would be some bookkeeping to be done even though she was there yesterday. Before she went there, she decided to go down to the harbor.

When the harbor came into view Diana was stunned. It was empty. All the ships had left. She went down to the quay to look for the Coast Guard patrol boats. They were all gone. Diana sat down on a bench to think. She looked towards the English Channel. She thought there must be a terrible battle going on in France. Who was winning? There was no point in sending another radio message. It would only state the obvious--that the invasion had started.

Diana left the quay and headed to Hawes'. It was just after 9 am. Diana hoped there wouldn't be much to do and she could go back to her flat and lie down before she had to go to the Lion and Cross. She arrived and went into her little office and started looking at some paper work left on her desk requiring entries in the general ledger.

Francis Hawes immediately discovered her and stood in the doorway of the office saying: "Isn't it exciting! The invasion I mean! I hope we can finally see victory this year."

155

Diana tried to look pleased. Then she said: "What have you heard about the fighting?"

Francis said: "Nothing official yet. The coastal ports like ours knew it was on late last night when the ships all started leaving. The wireless broadcasts say General Eisenhower will make an announcement later this morning on behalf of the Allied Command."

Diana said: "I pray for all the men involved."

Francis said: "As do I." Then a more serious look came over her face. She stepped fully into Diana's office and lowered her voice. She continued: "The local police are here about Frank's death. There is someone with them from the military. They want to talk to some of the employees, including you. I don't know what to make of it. Frank didn't have an enemy in the world. The bus hit him by accident. Anyway, they will let you know when they want you."

Diana felt her heart rate shoot up and pulse quicken. She tried to remain calm and said: "Why would they want to talk with me? I don't know anything. I only heard about it from the bar keep at the Lion and Cross."

Francis could sense this news disturbed Diana and didn't want her upset. Diana had been very loyal to her since Frank died. Francis replied: "Don't worry my dear. I have told them how good you are to have around and how much help you have been. I'm sure this is all due to wartime and is just a formality."

Diana nodded her understanding and said: "Just have them come find me when they are ready. I have to leave before lunch time as I'm at the Lion and Cross this afternoon."

Francis left and Diana sat there for a few minutes while the anxiety built in her. Then she tried to make some bookkeeping entries, but was too distracted. She felt wetness under her arms. She tried to think of what they would ask?? If the topic was Frank's desire for sex, she would just deny everything—other than some mild excusable office flirtation.

After close to an hour one of the route salesmen stuck his head in her door and said: "They are ready for you now."

Diana asked: "What do they want to know?"

He answered: "We aren't allowed to talk about it." Then he waved his hand as if to brush away the whole topic and went on down the hall.

The police officials were using Frank's old office. There were two men waiting for her. One was seated behind the desk and wore the uniform of the local police. The other man was standing and had on a British Army uniform which Diana recognized as belonging to an airborne regiment.

Diana went in and closing the door behind her asked: "May I sit down?"

The local police official was older, had white hair and rimless glasses. He said: "Of course, and pointed to a chair in front of the desk.

The army officer wore the rank of major and remained standing. He had a red beret that lay on the desk. He had thinning light brown hair. He was clean shaven and needed reading glasses. He had a cane that he used occasionally. A broken leg in a training jump had ended his airborne days and put him in intelligence. His face was lined but still could be youthful when he smiled. As Diana sat he was thumbing through a file.

The police official started: "Miss Winter, we are here about the untimely death of your employer, Frank Hawes. I'm Inspector Marshal from the local constabulary. Major Howard here is assigned to military intelligence." Both men noticed Diana's attractive figure and very pretty face. Howard thought she looked pale and drawn despite her beauty.

Inspector Marshal continued: "We understand you worked for Mr. Hawes for a number of years?"

Diana simply answered: "Yes."

Major Howard sat down and took over: "Happy relationship?"

Again, Diana simply said: "Yes."

Howard then asked: "What do you know about Frank Hawes death?"

Diana was a little relieved that this was the topic. She responded and said: "Nothing other than what I heard from the other employees or read in the newspaper."

Howard said: "And what is that?"

Diana answered: "He was waiting in a group of people for a bus. Someone behind him tripped or fell resulting in Frank, Mr. Hawes, falling in front of an oncoming bus."

Howard said: "A bit out of the ordinary isn't it? I mean, people do get preoccupied with their problems and sometimes step into traffic without looking. But here a man falls and pushes Hawley at just the right moment so he is hit by a bus. Then the man who pushed him disappears. Odd, don't you agree?"

Diana said: "I don't know?"

Howard said: "Where did you work before Hawes'?"

Diana was worried. She said: "I had a similar job with an importing company in the north of England. I don't remember its name. Near Liverpool. They are no longer in business. That is why I came here."

Howard said: "Yes, you seem to have omitted that on your application for work here as well. Do you have a British passport?"

Diana said: "Yes. I was born in England and went to school here."

Howard said: "Yes, I see you listed your schooling on your work application."

There was a pause while Howard looked at her employment file. Then he looked directly at her and said: "Would you be surprised to hear some of the other employees thought you and Frank Hawes were romantically involved?"

Diana was worried now. She had just lied about where she was born and her prior employment. Now they wanted to know about the sexual contact with Frank. Diana held steady eye contact with Howard. Then she answered: "Yes, I would be surprised to hear that. Frank Hawes and I were not romantically involved, I thought of him as a father figure, or older brother."

Howard asked: "No meetings after work in this office for romantic interludes?"

Diana felt a drop of perspiration fall from her underarm. Then, somewhat fiercely, she said: "None."

Howard looked pensive. Then he asked: "The other staff here says you aren't going out with anyone on a regular basis. Why is an attractive woman like yourself without any male companionship?"

Diana decided she wasn't playing this game. With finality she said: "I don't know."

Howard asked: "Where does your extended family live?"

Diana said: "I have no family. I'm all alone. I live by myself here in Poole."

There was another pause. Then Howard produced a piece of paper and showed it to Diana. Inwardly, Diana froze. She tried not to let the fear show in her face. Howard asked: "Do you know what this is?"

Diana took the sheet of paper. It was the list of German codes Hawes had taken from her dresser drawer. Diana continued looking Howard directly in the eye and said: "No."

Howard took the paper back. Then he said: "It appears to be a list of German codes for encrypting messages. Can you explain how this got in your employment folder?"

Diana looked down, then up at Howard. She answered evenly: "I'm sorry, I don't know. I've never seen my employment file."

Again, there was a pause. Howard put the codes back in a folder on the desk. He looked directly at Diana and studied her face for what seemed to her, the longest time. Then Howard looked at Inspector Marshal and said: "I have nothing further."

Marshal looked at Diana and said: "That will be all. If we need something more we will be in touch. Do not discuss our session here today with anyone. At least not until this investigation is cleared."

Diana stood and said: "I won't." She then politely shook each of their hands and went to the door.

As she reached to open the door Howard said "Good Day" to her in perfect German.

Diana paused, and for a moment almost turned and thanked him in German. But she caught herself. Then she said to Howard: "I'm sorry. Are you saying something to me?"

Howard smiled and said: "No Miss Winter. You may go."

After Diana left the two men sat together to review the interview. Marshal started out by saying: "I hope I haven't wasted your time. But when Francis Hawes brought the sheet of paper with the codes on it to our attention during a follow up interview, I thought I ought to call in you boys in military intelligence."

Howard was thinking about the interview. He answered: "No, I'm glad you did. Something isn't right here. Is Francis Hawes sure the codes were in Diana Winter's folder?"

Marshall said: "Yes. And we can't seem to find much background on her before she arrives in Poole."

Howard said: "I'm going to have a look at her travel records, passport application and school records. We may even look at her finances. Her prior employers would have been contributing to her old age pension. The government should have a record of them. It just strikes me she is hiding something-or just very nervous about being questioned."

Marshal said: "You intelligence types can find out more, faster than I can. So have at it. I'm going to have my men keep an eye on her. If I learn anything I'll let you know."

Howard said: "Just before the invasion we picked up two unidentified radio transmissions from the general area near her flat. The signal was too brief to get a decent fix. But it is interesting that she lives nearby."

The men got up to leave. Marshal asked: "Do you think she was sleeping with Hawes?"

Howard smiled. Then he said: "I doubt it. If she was, he was the luckiest man in Poole."

Diana walked back to her office. She was too upset to do much work. She was glad no one spoke to her. Diana quickly finished what she had been working on and then left quietly without saying a word to anyone.

Diana went back to her flat. As she came up the stairs she noted no one was in the bath. She hadn't bathed this morning and had perspired heavily. She went into her flat, got a robe, towel and toilet items and went down to the bath. She locked the door behind her, undressed, and drew a tub of hot water. As she slid into the tub the warmth eased her tension. It allowed Diana to think. The only redeeming aspect of the morning was the fact the authorities didn't have enough on her to arrest her. But that would change when they looked more closely at her. They wouldn't find any employment records for the 1930s and early 1940s when she was in Germany with her father. If they checked with her schools they would learn she was born in Germany. Finally, there would be no record of a passport application.

Diana wanted to talk to Gromek, but knew if she did it could be a death sentence. He would have to report the interview to his superiors and she knew he would be ordered to eliminate her to protect the rest of the network. Even if she hid the Howard meeting, they might find she was no longer useful and order her death anyway.

Diana was depressed when she first got out of bed and now she bordered on complete mental free fall. She thought about Jack. He had been good for her. Despite the fact they had only shared some passionate kisses, he had momentarily awakened her sexuality. That struck her as odd. There were attractive soldiers and sailors in the Lion and Cross that tried to get her into bed quite regularly. But Jack didn't. He was respectful. Kind. He treated her better than any man she ever knew. She suspected he knew, as she did, that in the middle of this war no normal romance that led to marriage and children could exist. Diana prayed Jack was alive and was determined to be his lover if he returned.

Diana wondered how she could keep herself alive or out of prison. Turning herself in and offering to spy on her colleagues for the British was out of the question. She was not a traitor. Besides, she was just a small isolated member of the network and knew very little. She could be of no value to the British if she was honest with them.

Diana recognized she still held a forged British passport that would get her into most countries. She had enough money in the bank to purchase a steamship ticket. Diana remembered her conversations with Jack where he talked about life in Michigan's Upper Peninsula and his affection for the Tidewater of Virginia. Perhaps she could leave all this behind and go to America? Maybe Captain McKeil would be sailing back to the States to pick up more troops? She might be able to get passage on his ship. Whatever, it seemed to be her only hope and time was of the essence.

Jack brought the Six Boat alongside the medical ship. Stonecliffe was in and out of consciousness. Carl Williams had taken over first aid duties and turned the galley and berthing area into a first aid station. He had tightened the dressing on Stonecliffe's arm and that had stopped the bleeding. He was pale and sweating. Jack went down to help get Stonecliffe up on deck. He looked at Williams and said: "What do you think?"

Williams said: "I don't know. Probably severe blood loss and shock."

The medical ship lowered a platform to lay Stonecliffe on. Jack rode up to the deck of the medical ship with him. He told Russell to stand by until he could talk with a doctor. Russell took the Six Boat a short distance away and waited for word. There were two corpsmen and a doctor doing triage on deck. They looked carefully at Stonecliffe. The doctor gave orders to take him below. Jack immediately approached the doctor and asked; "Is he going to be alright? He is my commanding officer and I don't want to lose him."

The doctor saw the worried look on Jack's face. He said: "I suspect so. We'll stabilize him and get him back to a hospital in Portsmouth. We are going to start getting a lot of casualties from the beach. I don't have time to talk."

Jack nodded his understanding and went to the ships rail. He waved his arm to bring the Six Boat back alongside. When Jack was back aboard and the Six Boat pulling away from the medical ship Jack told the crew Stonecliffe's status. Jack ordered Vincent to send a message to Command saying Stonecliffe had been wounded and transferred and that he was assuming command. Then he said to Russell: "You are the senior rated man aboard after me. You are the executive officer for the time being."

Russell smiled at Jack. He said: "What are your orders skipper?"

Jack smiled back and said: "We are going to visit the beach again. Let's catch up to the landing craft now going in."

Engineman Ritt was standing nearby and waiting to talk with Jack. Jack asked: "What is it?"

Ritt looked grim. He said: "I have to shut down that bad engine. There are several problems. I think it is losing compression. The only way I can fix it is to tie this boat up and tear the engine down."

Jack said: "Keep it running until it quits. We need whatever power we have to go in behind this third wave. I know you want to do what would normally be called for, but nothing is normal this morning."

Ritt wanted to argue but Jack cut him off. Then he turned to Russell and said: "You stay on the helm. Give her whatever power we have and head for the beach."

As they approached the beach Jack saw that many of the landing craft were already unloading their troops. The sounds of battle increased. To Jack the enemy fire didn't look as fierce, but men were still being hit all along the beach as they headed for the base of the bluff. Mortars still came down from the German positions exploding and killing soldiers. Machine guns still opened up on the landing craft as their ramps dropped and soldiers tried to rush out, only to be cut down.

Waves of blood red water washed against the shore and the dead were everywhere, their bodies being gently moved back and forth at the waters edge. Many were without limbs or died in grotesque positions. The bodies that were face up often had open staring eyes.

Jack saw a mortar land in front of the open ramp of a landing craft. Jack thought most of the men had already got off, but wasn't sure. The landing craft backed away from shore and then stopped. The ramp was down and heavily damaged by the mortar. The craft was flooding and listing heavily. Russell got the bow of the Six Boat up to it. Jack went forward and looked for survivors. The coxswain was dead and must have died as he was trying to back the boat away from shore. Jack looked into the boat itself and saw masses of flesh mixed with pieces of green uniform. Whoever had still been aboard when the mortar hit was now mangled, unrecognizable flesh. Jack thought he was going to be sick. He motioned for Russell to back away.

Spencer came up and said: "Let me go aboard and check the survivors."

Jack turned on him angrily and said: "No. Do you hear me. No. I don't even want you to look. And don't ever ask me what I saw. Let it sink so God may have all their souls and they don't have to float there like that."

Spencer was taken aback. In all their time together Chief Trevenen had never raised his voice at him. He said: "Sure Chief. I'm sorry."

Just then they started to attract fire from the Germans so Russell quickly turned them and got them back out in the Channel. For the moment they weren't needed, so the Six Boat just idled waiting for a call for assistance. They watched the battle ashore. The attack seemed futile and Jack began to think about how they would get the surviving soldiers off the beach.

Jack looked at Russell and said: "The third wave flooded the beach with men. Surely it should be enough to take the heights and get off that damn beach."

Russell didn't respond. He just watched the fighting and prayed it wasn't all for nothing.

After what seemed a lifetime, in a somewhat coordinated effort, the American soldiers rushed the bluff and exit roads together. Jack could see demolition charges going off, sending explosions up into the air as the Americans blasted apart concrete and barbed wire defenses. Then to the relief of the crew of the Six Boat, the infantry was moving off the beach and going inland.

Jack looked at his watch. It seemed like forever since they had first arrived off the French coast. But it was only late morning. As the assault waves of American soldiers moved inland Jack saw the next phase of the invasion taking shape. The fighting on the beach was over. Landing craft were heading to the beach empty to pick up wounded soldiers. LSTs that had been standing by in the invasion fleet churned towards shore. Like the Higgins boats their bows touched the shore and then opened to unload jeeps, trucks, tanks, ammunition, and more troops and supplies. The plan was obvious. The US Army would continue flooding the coast with men and material to assure its toe hold on France.

One of the Higgins boats full of wounded and heading out to a medical ship was having engine problems. Jack could hear it missing. The Six Boat took it in tow and got it out to the medical ship. Based on the waves of wounded coming off the beach Jack was sure hundreds of men needed medical care.

After this tow, the Six Boat again just stood by and watched the unfolding scene ashore. The overcast was breaking up and Jack thought by afternoon there would be some sunshine. The wind and waves had largely subsided and Williams got some coffee and sandwiches going. Jack found his tremors were back in his hands. His legs ached and felt weak from standing for so many hours. He went below and sat in the captain's chair in the pilot house. The coffee and sandwich were welcomed. Jack was very hungry. It struck Jack that in the intensity of the fighting he hadn't had time to feel any emotions. Not fear, not dread, not even gratitude for being alive and unhurt. He had been too busy doing his part to keep them all alive. As he began to relax slightly, Jack felt as though the worst was over. The Six Boat had survived.

Captain McKeil stood on the bridge of his ship. He too had watched the drama unfolding ashore. His ship was empty now, all the troops he had carried had gone ashore in the first and second waves. He thought it was useless slaughter until the last moment when the 29th Division was finally able to fight its way off the beach. He wondered how the fighting was going inland. The LSTs were moving in to pour more support ashore. His orders were to stay anchored until released to go back to England for more troops and supplies. McKeil figured they wanted the troop ships to stick around until command was sure the invasion was a success and they didn't need to take the assault troops back off the beach.

McKeil was proud of himself. He hadn't taken a drink since Monday. He decided things were stable enough he could go below to his cabin and get a little liquid relief. He still had some scotch left. After a drink or two he would get the cook to bring him some lunch. It could still be a long day and night ahead for him and his crew.

McKeil was just settled in his cabin when there was pounding on his cabin door. McKeil opened the door. It was one of his able seamen. The seaman was excited and spoke rapidly: "Captain, come quick, there is a mine floating just off our port quarter. It doesn't seem to be anchored to the bottom. The Mate says its drifting down on us."

McKeil went up to the bridge as quickly as he could. The Mate was there with a set of binoculars to his eyes watching the mine. Quite gruffly McKeil said: "What the hell is going on. I was just about to have my lunch."

The Mate said: "I think it is a German mine that got cut loose by the mine sweepers early this morning and then came out with the tide. With the tide at the stand it is just drifting around. I think the wind and coastal currents are bringing it towards us."

The mine was close enough to the ship McKeil didn't need binoculars to see it. It was drifting towards the stern. It looked like a huge soccer ball with spikes sticking out of it. The ends of the spikes held detonators that would detonate the explosives inside if they hit the hull of a ship. Mckeil went out on the bridge wing to get a better view. The Mate followed. McKeil's ship had a machine gun emplacement built on the top of each side of the bridge as anti-aircraft protection. They were manned even though they hadn't had anything to do.

McKeil yelled up to the machine gunner on his side and said: "Get some fire on that mine before it gets any closer. Blow the god damn thing up."

The problem was the machine gun was mounted to fire upwards at enemy aircraft, not downward close aboard the side of the ship. Try as he might the gunner could not hit it. McKeil and the Mate leaned far out over the bridge wing rail to follow the movement of the mine. As they did so the mine disappeared from sight behind the counter of the stern. McKeil braced himself for an explosion. None came.

McKeil ran down to the main deck on the port side and again leaned over the rail to look aft and see the mine. It was visible now. About ten feet off the side of the ship and slowly moving forward. McKeil desperately thought of what they might use to fend it off. He took another look over the side when the mine struck the side of the ship.

There was an ear shattering explosion, a flash of flame, and black smoke. The ship was rocked and lifted upwards. A huge column of water arose. A hole was blown in the side of the ship and the flooding from it was immediate and severe. The fire and collision alarms went off. The crew ran to their emergency stations. The Chief Engineer had been in his cabin and came to the bridge. He had expected to see McKeil but only the Mate was present.

The Chief Engineer asked: "Where is McKeil?"

The Mate said: "I don't know. I think he may have been killed in the blast." The Chief Engineer immediately left to sound the ship and start trying to control the flooding.

The Six Boat had just been idling waiting for an assistance call when the blast was heard. Jack ran back up on deck. Spencer came up to him and said: "What the hell was that? Was that a torpedo?"

Jack said: "There is no way a sub got in here undetected. That could be a mine. Either that or some of the Army munitions went up accidently. Let's get over that way and see if we are needed." The Six Boat headed through the fleet to where the sound of the blast came from.

McKeil's ship came into view. It had a list to port and the top of a large hole in the port side was visible above the waterline. There was a life boat swung out on the port side but no one was abandoning ship. Jack figured they were all below trying to seal off the flooded compartments.

Spencer said: "We've seen this story before. That is McKeil's ship."

Jack said: "Let's go toward the port side and see if we can raise anyone on the bridge."

Spencer said: "I just hope she doesn't roll over on us while we are alongside."

Bollinger was on the bow of the Six Boat. As they closed on the stricken ship he pointed to starboard. Between the Six Boat and the ship a head was bobbing among the small waves. Jack said: "Let's try and grab him."

McKeil wasn't killed in the blast. He was blown overboard. His face and hair were badly burned. He had no hearing. He only had limited vision in one eye. His chest and left arm gave him great pain. He had hit the water with considerable force and sank. He had no life jacket on. Realizing he was drowning he had pulled himself to the surface. There were bits of debris floating nearby and with his right arm he grabbed a piece of wood. It gave him just enough buoyancy to keep his head above the water. With what little vision he had left he saw a boat coming towards him, but he was too injured to wave or call out.

Jack went forward to the bow with Bollinger. Jack held a boat hook he would use to try and grab the man floating nearby. Russell stopped the Six Boat. Jack saw it was McKeil. It was evident he was very badly injured Jack could see the burns on his face and scalp. Most of his hair had been burned off.

Jack said: "Captain, it's Chief Trevenen. We have you." Jack waved the end of the boat hook in front of McKeil. It was easily within his reach. But he made no move to let go of the wood keeping his head up and grab the boat hook. Bollinger took off his helmet started to take off his boots to go over the side and grab McKeil.

Jack waved the boat hook in front of McKeil again and yelled: "Take it man, take it!"

McKeil stared Jack directly in the eye, then he let go of the wood he was holding. He disappeared under the water.

Bollinger shouted: "I'll go in after him!"

Jack shook his head and said: "No. He is gone. You couldn't save him."

Despite their difficult relationship watching McKeil disappear into the sea hit Jack hard. Spencer yelled to Jack: "Someone is waving at us from the bridge."

Jack didn't answer for a moment. He just stared at the water where McKeil had been. Then he seemed to come back to reality and said to Spencer: "Let's go over and see what he wants."

As they came under the bridge wing Jack yelled up: "What's your status?"

The Mate was still on the bridge. He answered: "A floating mine hit us. Our Chief Engineer thinks he has the flooding under control. Our engine room is flooded and we can't make steam. We have called for a tug. Can you stand by in case we need you?"

Jack answered: "Yes. I'm sorry to report we tried to pick up your Captain, but he was too far gone and has drowned."

The Mate nodded his understanding. He added: "I saw you try to get him. The Captain was blown overboard when the mine went off."

Jack was noticing the list was increasing. The crew might think they have the flooding under control, but Jack wasn't taking any chances. Like Spencer he didn't want this ship to roll over on them. The Six Boat pulled away and took station at a safe distance. Soon they were joined by another Coast Guard patrol boat and a destroyer escort. The ship settled lower in the water, but wasn't destined to sink, at least not today. It would have a new use as part of a secret project known as the "Mulberry" harbors.

Diana finished her bath and then laid down for the rest of the afternoon. She didn't want to think anymore, but couldn't stop going over and over her circumstances in her mind. Eventually she fell asleep. She awoke with a start. Diana wondered how long she had slept? What day was it? What time? Her clock told her it was about 4 pm and she reasoned it was still Tuesday. She needed to dress and go down to the Lion and Cross.

On the way to the pub Diana took the time to look over the harbor. It was still empty. She walked down the quay and saw the Coast Guard patrol boats also hadn't returned. Diana stood and looked out the harbor entrance at the English Channel. It appeared quite calm. The sun was breaking through and the air warming. It would be a nice spring evening. She couldn't imagine the death and destruction that must be happening on the other side.

Diana went in the Lion and Cross and went to the little office to see what bills needed to be paid. The pub had a good early crowd. Much better than usual for a weekday. There were even some American and British servicemen.

The cook stuck his head in the door and said: "Did you hear General Eisenhower's speech on the wireless?"

Diana said: "No, I've been busy."

The cook said: "The General says the invasion is a success. We have had people in here all afternoon toasting the troops-and each other."

Diana looked rather down and said: "That's good."

The cook noticed her demeanor and asked: "Is everything alright? Are you worried about those Coasties from the patrol boats?"

Diana looked up and brightened a little asking: "Have you heard anything about them?"

The cook said: "No. They pulled out about dark last night. My guess is they may be in France for quite a while. The crew from the Six Boat was good to have around. Very good people. I hope that cook, Carl Williams comes back. We had a bit of fun cooking together."

Diana nodded her agreement then said: "I hope they all come back."

The cook pointed to the kitchen and waved as he headed back to fill an order.

Diana couldn't be more conflicted. The news the invasion was successful didn't surprise her, but still it left her sad. She thought of all the dead German soldiers who probably died for nothing. This war couldn't be won. Her messages warning of the invasion were useless. Things were down on a much more personal level now. She didn't want Jack's life to be wasted along with all the others. She wanted Jack to live, to return to her. Diana prayed out loud: "Please God, let him come back to me."

CHAPTER TWELVE
SIREN'S SONG

The afternoon off Omaha Beach seemed endless to Jack. The process of getting more men, equipment and supplies ashore continued. With the beach having been taken and no enemy fire coming down on them, the support effort became almost routine. The crew of the Six Boat could frequently hear gunfire coming from the fighting inland. Every now and then, some of the warships anchored off the coast would provide naval gunfire to support the fighting inland. The crew of the Six Boat remained impressed with the size and power of the naval guns. It looked to them that the goal of flooding the coast with men and equipment was working.

The beach continued to have men and equipment coming off LSTs. The Higgins boats continued their trips back and forth. Barrage balloons were floating over the sand, although there wasn't a German plane in sight. British and American fighters frequently flew low over them, heading inland. Allied bombers could be seen periodically, flying high above them heading south into France. Jack wouldn't know it until years later, but 150,000 men had been in the assault waves that went ashore at the combined beaches on D-Day, June 6. Thousands had been killed and thousands more wounded. But the secret of when and where the invasion would take place had been kept. The Allied surprise was complete.

There was a constant stream of Higgins boats bringing the wounded and dead out to the medical ships. Jack wondered how Stonecliffe and McCauley were doing. Jack noticed more ships were arriving from England. He wondered if the medical ship he put Stonecliffe on was headed to Portsmouth.

The action for the Six Boat slowed in the afternoon. They had an occasional tow. Twice they responded to men who had fallen overboard and safely rescued them. The engine trouble continued. One engine was down completely and the other running rough. Still, Engineman Ritt kept them going. Jack thought the afternoon seemed longer due to the adrenalin rush of the initial attack having worn off. They were all tired. None of them had slept well for two days. They were a quiet group of men as they watched the drama of the invasion unfold before them.

Late in the afternoon the weather had improved. There was mixed sun and clouds. The wind had gone down and the temperature had warmed. Jack was topside thinking it was finely feeling like a June day. Vincent came up from below and said: "Message, Chief. It's from Commander Stewart, the Rescue Flotilla Commander. He wants us to rendezvous with him. He's on the Twenty Boat. He wants to meet off Point du Hoc in an hour."

Jack responded: "Tell him that's affirmative. We'll be there."

Point du Hoc was between Omaha and Utah Beaches and had been the site of a US Army Ranger assault earlier in the day. The Rangers had scaled steep rock cliffs to silence an artillery position. After fighting their way to the top with many casualties, they found the guns had been removed! It was a logical place for the two Coast Guard patrol boats to meet while allowing the Flotilla Commander to remain close to both beaches.

An hour later Russell was maneuvering alongside the Twenty Boat. Jack had taken off his steel helmet and watch cap. He had on his peaked cap and had straightened his uniform. His foul weather jacket showed the blood stains and dirt from his hard morning.

The Six Boat showed the effects of combat. Its decks were blood stained. On the way to the rendezvous, they had picked up the bodies of two dead American soldiers that were floating near each other. They were under a canvas on the after deck. The windows on one side of the pilot house were shot out. Assorted bullet and shrapnel holes could be seen. The two life rafts they carried to assist in getting survivors aboard were gone. The machine gun had been stowed after jamming. The idling engine was running rough.

Commander Stewart stood on deck within hearing range. Jack saluted him smartly and the salute was returned. The Commander asked: "What's your condition?"

Jacked answered: "We are still operational. We only have one engine, but my engineman says he can keep it going. They are trying to get the other engine restarted. We are taking on a little water, but the bilge pumps can handle it. The hull is basically sound. I think one of the rounds we took put a leak in our potable water tank. We have no armament other than our side arms. We need fuel."

The Commander nodded his understanding. Then he asked: "What the status of your wounded?"

Jack said: "Lieutenant Stonecliffe and Gunner's Mate McCauley are on one of the medical ships. It was still anchored off Omaha Beach last time I saw it. McCauley had a nasty leg wound. Mr. Stonecliffe was suffering from blood loss and shock after he was hit in the arm."

The Commander said: "Senior Chief Trevenen, you are the senior enlisted in our flotilla. Are you comfortable keeping command of the Six Boat until we know more about Mr. Stonecliffe's recovery?"

Jack said: "Yes, sir."

The Commander said: "Good. I'll have a replacement for Stonecliffe if his recovery keeps him away from his duties for any length of time. You can get fuel from the a tank ship refueling the Higgins boats working Utah Beach. It is just to our west and is showing a red flag."

Jack said: "I'll find it."

The Commander added: "After you fuel I want you to meet the Five Boat off Omaha. Your two boats will escort medical and other ships back to Portsmouth. You'll leave here at 1700. Then you can head for Poole Harbor and stand down for repairs. Get the list of parts and equipment you need up to the supply clerk tomorrow morning," Jack said: "Yes, sir." Then he asked: "Sir, how is the fight going?"

The Commander smiled and answered: "It was close for a while but we have them on the run. Our flotilla has performed well. Dozens of men rescued. The British beaches weren't as hot as Omaha but I hear they are running into heavy resistance inland. Utah wasn't as bad as Omaha for us. I followed you and the other Coast Guard boats off Omaha. I know you had a bad time but did superb work under fire. You will be recognized for it."

Jack felt a rush of emotion at the praise. His voice was a little husky as he said: "Thank you, sir."

As the two boats pulled away from each other Commander Stewart looked at the damaged Six Boat. He shook his head slightly, in wonder. The matchbox fleet had truly done its duty today. He just hoped the Six Boat made it safely back to Poole. He'd hate to lose its crew.

The Six Boat met the Five Boat as planned and they took their small convoy back across the English Channel. Jack wasn't sure what their mission was in escorting the ships. A destroyer escort accompanied them. He presumed they were to perform rescue services in the event one of the ships became a casualty. Jack felt safe from German attack so he made temporary watch sections to rotate the crew and allow them each some rest. They could only seat seven in the galley so they dogged the watch and Williams got a hot meal up.

Jack spent most of the trip in the pilot house sitting in the captain's chair. His hand tremor had been bad at dinner, but the weakness in his legs was passing the more he rested them. He hoped Stonecliffe was alright. He didn't want a new commanding officer. You never knew what that brought.

He thought about Diana. He wasn't sure what time they would get to Poole, but he wanted to see her as soon as he could. The boat would take two or three days to repair. He wouldn't have to worry about readiness or getting underway on short notice. There would be liberty time for all. Her flat was only a short distance from the harbor. He hoped to be a frequent visitor.

Darkness caused Jack to check the positions of the ships and their progress toward the coast of England more often. But all remained quiet and orderly until they were close to Portsmouth. Their single engine started to miss badly and they had to radio the destroyer advising they would have to drop out due to engine trouble. The destroyer commander offered to let the Five Boat drop out as well to provide them with assistance. Jack declined the offer saying they would head straight for Poole Harbor as best they could.

Engineman Ritt and Jimmy Flaherty eventually shut the one good engine down for close to an hour while they worked on it. The Six Boat just drifted in the darkness on a gentle swell. To Jack it was calming. Then Jack heard the engine start up and it sounded much better. The Five Boat called them. It had just broken off from the convoy and was heading for Poole. Jack gave them his position and the Five Boat came up on them. The two patrol boats and their weary crews headed for home.

As they were entering Poole harbor Jimmy Spencer looked at Jack. He had aged in the last 24 hours. The lines in his face stood out. He looked pale and thin. Almost frail. Spencer said: "Chief, I think you had better go find your brunette tonight. We can keep an eye on the Six Boat. You need a good night's sleep and you won't get it in that cramped berth below."

Russell was standing nearby and said: "I agree. I'll be aboard. If I need you in a hurry I know where to find you. I'll start on the repair list first thing tomorrow."

Jack wanted to protest, but was too tired. Instead, he just quietly said: "I appreciate it. A night's sleep ashore will be good for me."

After the Six Boat tied up at the quay, Jack went below and found a clean pair of pants to wear. He was too tired to fully change clothes or try and shave. He just headed for Diana's flat. About half way there he almost lost his nerve and thought about going back to the boat. It was long after midnight. He was too tired to be good company. What if Diana wouldn't want him there? But his footsteps kept carrying him to her, as though it was his mission.

Jack went into Diana's building and up the stairs. He tapped lightly on her door and waited. There was no response. He knocked on the door a second time, feeling anxious she might not be there. He leaned against the door jamb and waited, eyes closed. Then the door opened. Diana stood there holding her robe closed. It took her a moment to recognize Jack. She had never expected to see him there tonight.

Diana gasped and said: "My God, Jack darling, what are you doing here? Are you alright? Come in and let me look at you."

Jack stumbled through the door and sat down wearily on a chair by the dining table. He took his jacket and hat off. Diana knelt in front of him and took his face in her hands so she could look right at him. She had noticed blood stains on his foul weather jacket when he was in the hall.

Diana said: "Jack, look at me. Are you hurt? Are you bleeding? Do you need a doctor?"

Jack reached out, took her in his arms and pulled her upward towards him. He held her close. He could feel her warmth. She smelled so good. He said quietly: "I'm fine. I just need a good night's sleep. And to hold you. The blood on my jacket is from helping other wounded men. I wasn't hit."

Diana held him tightly and said: "Thank God you are alright. I was so worried. You are going to stay here tonight."

Jack smiled a little sheepishly and said: "That's what I hoped to do."

Diana stood up and crossed the room and straightened the bed clothes. The bed was hardly big enough for two but would have to do. She looked at Jack and said: "Come over and sit on the edge of the bed and let's get your shoes and socks off."

Jack came over to the bed and sat on the edge. Diana knelt down and untied his shoes. Jack fell backwards across the bed, eyes closed. It scared Diana at first, thinking Jack may have passed out. But then his regular breathing told her he had just fallen asleep. She could see the past days had taken a toll on him. He looked older. The worry lines in his face had deepened. Diana thought he may have even lost some weight. She undressed him. Jack barely awoke while she was taking off his clothes. Diana studied his nude form. He had a good body, fit and muscular. His penis was flaccid, but of enviable size. Finally, she swung his legs up on to the bed and covered him. She took off her robe and slid her nude form in next to him. Diana held him in her arms and they both slept warm and still.

Jack awoke with a start and instantly sat up believing he had heard the General Quarters alarm. He had been dreaming he was back on the Campbell. Jack noticed it was daylight. For a moment he didn't know where he was. Then he remembered—he had gone to Diana's. He turned his head and saw Diana sleeping next to him. She was only partially under the bed clothes and he could see her firm breasts. Jack reached down and felt his groin. He was nude too. He wondered if they had made love, but then thought they couldn't have. Jack had been too worn out.

Jack reached over and gently touched Diana's breast, then her nipple. She stirred. Jack moved his face to her breasts and began to kiss them. Diana awoke fully and turned on her side facing Jack. She looked serious. Diana asked: "How do you feel this morning?"

Jack said: "Better than I did last night. I needed to sleep. What time is it?"

Diana looked past him to the clock on the night stand and said: "It's still early."

Jack moved his face back to Diana's breasts and started to kiss them again. Diana gently pushed him away and said: "We will have plenty of time to do that. I will take good care of you. But right now you need a bath and I haven't shaved my legs. I wasn't expecting company. Let me see if the bath is open and draw us a hot tub."

Diana got out of bed. She purposely lingered nude beside the bed so Jack could have a long view. Then she pulled on her robe and went out to draw a bath. Jack marveled at her hour glass figure and black triangle of silken hair between her thighs. He wanted to kiss her endlessly.

Diana came back and said: "We are all set. Pull on your pants and go down and get in the tub. I'll be along in a minute. So Jack went down the hall and closing the door behind him, pulled off his trousers and got in the hot water. It felt wonderful. Diana appeared shortly with towels and toilet articles. She locked the door behind her. She took off her robe and got into the end of the tub opposite Jack. It was and old tub. Rather large and with legs. There was plenty of room for both of them. Jack started to reach for the soap to wash. He knew he smelled strong from all the nervous perspiration in prior days. He was surprised Diana let him in her bed.

Diana took the soap from Jack and started washing him. Neither spoke. Jack just closed his eyes and enjoyed her touching him. He came to full erection before Diana even began to gently stroke his member. Jack groaned a little and felt he was close to coming. Diana sensed it too and stopped touching him. She leaned over, kissed him on the mouth and then whispered: "We'll finish that back in the flat."

Then Jack washed her. He couldn't resist her breasts and had to stop and take her nipples in his mouth and gently suck on them. They were hard. He did one then the other. Diana was aroused. Diana put her hand down and touched her vagina. Her inner lips were opening. She knew she would be wet for Jack when he entered her.

Diana whispered in Jack's ear; "Darling, let me do my legs."

Jack sat back in the tub as Diana raised a leg straight up and quickly ran a razor over it. Then she did the other. Jack couldn't help but study her beautiful thighs as she shaved.

Diana stood up, reached her hand down to pull Jack up and kissed him deeply. Then she stepped out and handed Jack a towel. They both dried off, covered themselves, and then went back to the flat. Neither could wait to have the other. They were both nude in a moment. They stood and locked in an embrace. They kissed deeply again. Jack had a large erection that pressed against Diana's groin. Diana knelt down and took him in her mouth. Jack groaned with pleasure. Diana brought him to the edge but wouldn't let him come. Instead, she lay him on his back on the bed and mounted him. Her vagina was just above Jack's erection. She reached under herself, took his member in her hand, and guided it into her tight wet quim. It was her turn to groan with pleasure. She had never known joy like this.

Diana, breathing hard, rode Jack, and rode him until the rush of her own orgasm hit her. She cried out: "Oh God Jack, Oh God, I'm there, I'm there. Don't stop thrusting. Oh, darling. Oh, darling."

Feeling Diana's rush of sexuality, Jack could no longer control himself. With two deep thrusts, he burst forth. He came violently, with every cell in his body telling him he was alive, and could still give life. Diana could feel him in her and tightened her vagina to hold Jack in. They couldn't get enough of each other.

Gradually they calmed. Diana lay on top of Jack, her breasts against his chest. Jack stayed in her until he became soft and slid out. Then they moved to be side by side facing each other. They were quiet. They touched and kissed. Jack dozed. When he awoke Diana's kisses went down Jacks body until she was at his penis. He was beginning to stiffen. Once again she took him in her mouth. Jack responded by growing larger. Jack held her shoulders and drew her upwards and then rolled her over on her back. Diana spread her legs wide and Jack entered her. She wrapped her legs around Jack's lower back. They moved in unison, not as fierce as the first time, but their union was complete. Their bodies mingled and became one.

Afterwards they rested in each others arms, legs still entwined. They touched and kissed. Jack thought he would never know such joy again. Finally, Jack said: "As much as I would like to, I can't stay here all day and hold you in my arms. I have to get back to the boat."

Diana said: "I know dear. Are you going to be alright? I mean, you looked like you were on your last legs when you came in here last night."

Jack said: "That's because I was. But you brought me back to life."

Diana asked: "Was it bad over there — I mean, during the invasion?"

Jack looked away. Then he turned back to her and said: "It was bad."

Diana asked: "Are the reports we hear true? Are the American and British troops winning?"

Jack said: "I don't know about winning, but they are ashore and moving inland. I had no idea of the size of the invasion until we got to the French coast and watched it all happen. There were thousands of ships, tens of thousands of men, unimaginable amounts of equipment and supplies. My boat had two men wounded. One was our Gunners Mate and the other out Lieutenant, Mr. Stonecliffe. I hope they are both alright. I don't want Stonecliffe replaced by another officer. He was just the right person for our duties and our crew."

They were silent for a few moments. Then Diana said: "Jack, I'm tired of war. So very tired. I can't remember a time when there wasn't a war. If I wanted to go to the United States, how would I do that?"

Jack thought for a moment. Then he said: "I don't know? I suppose you would have to go up to London and visit the American Embassy and see what they say."

Diana asked: "Do you think Captain McKeil could take me back on his ship, I mean, when it returns to the States?"

Jack said: "McKeil is dead. Besides, you would still need the proper paperwork."

Diana was completely taken aback. She sat straight up and looked at Jack, saying: "My God, what happened to him?"

Jack said: "A floating mine hit his ship. He was injured in the blast and blown over the side. My boat tried to rescue him, but he was too far gone." Jack was silent. In his mind he began to relive his rescue attempt. He was waving the boat hook in front of the drowning McKeil. He saw again the burned face and staring eyes. That vision was overtaken by one of dead bodies washing back and forth at the edge of the beach in blood red water. Jack closed his eyes and covered his face with his hands to make it all go away.

Diana saw the emotional turmoil in Jack and took him in her arms. She said: "It's alright, dear. We don't have to talk about it anymore."

After another long silence Diana said: "Let's get you up. I can get you some eggs and toast. Then we'll send you off to your men. I'm sure they need you."

Jack hated to leave Diana's bed. He needed a shave so he borrowed her razor. It worked better on her beautiful legs than his beard. He had a couple of pretty good nicks. After breakfast together, and a deep kiss, Jack left. He didn't know when he would see her again so he made no promises. He noticed his hand tremor was gone.

Jack exited Diana's building, crossed the street, and headed down a side street towards the harbor. Jack was amazed at the normalcy of it. There was no war here. No death or dying. He and Diana had eaten breakfast and talked about the weather, their respective plans for the day, shopping. A normal couple starting their day. Jack knew his patrols would take him back to France. It was like he would be commuting to war. He dreaded it.

Jack continued toward the harbor. It was early enough few people were on the street. The businesses hadn't opened. In the morning quiet he also reflected on Catherine. His wife had been dead thirty years. Surely, she wouldn't mind his caring for another woman. While Diana filled his thoughts, he still missed Catherine.

As Jack walked he stopped thinking about Catherine and Diana and started thinking about how they would get the Six Boat operational. Just ahead of him a local police car stopped at the curb. A tall man in civilian clothes got out. He started walking towards Jack. As he passed, they each exchanged a "Good Morning". Jack kept going. He didn't look back to see the man go up the street and take a position in a doorway where he could observe Diana's flat.

When Jack got back to the harbor, he could see other Coast Guard patrol boats had come in. One was getting underway to head to the fuel dock. Jack went on board the Six Boat and went below. He could hear work being done in the engine room. Russell was sitting at the table in the galley drinking coffee.

Jack asked: "Any problems last night?"

Russell said: "Not a one. We were all tired and except for a watch we all slept sound. You look a hundred per cent better than when you went ashore. You had better put in for a new foul weather jacket. That one looks like it has had it."

Jack nodded his agreement. Then he said: "I need to put on some clean clothes as well. What's up with the repairs."

180

Russell answered: "Flaherty is back aft tearing down the engine that quit on us. Ritt is up at the Flotilla offices learning what we need to do to requisition parts. Spencer is ashore trying to find some civilian materials to plug bullet holes and get some new glass for the pilot house windows. Turner has the .50 caliber apart to see if he can get it operational again."

Jack noticed the Twenty Boat was tied up behind them. Jack asked: "Seen anything of the Flotilla Commander?"

Russell said: "No. But his Yeoman stopped by and asked you to come up to the Flotilla offices about 11:00 for a meeting. He also dropped off a letter appointing you as our Acting Commanding Officer. That will allow you to sign requisition requests."

Jack then asked: "Heard any word about McCauley or Mr. Stonecliffe?"

Russell said: "Nothing."

Jack had a troubled look come over his face. He said: "I'd hate to lose Stonecliffe. At this point I don't want to get a new Commanding Officer." Jack paused, then continued: "What's up with the other boats. They still doing escort duty?"

Russell said: "I'm not sure. More of them keep arriving. I'm assuming we'll get assigned some kind of patrol duties. There are ships going over to France all the time with equipment, men and supplies. Our job can't be over."

Jack said: "I'll bet the meeting at 11:00 will tell us what our assignment will be. Let's turn too and get the boat in as good a shape as we can, as soon as possible."

Jack went off to the 11:00 meeting as ordered. Most of the other patrol boat commanding officers were there. Jack was the only enlisted person present. He wondered how long they would leave him as an acting commanding officer. The briefing laid out their patrol and escort duties in the coming days. It seemed routine to Jack, after what they had been through. There was a massive effort to resupply the army in France—and expand its size. Ships and small convoys with war material continuously crossed the English Channel. While the patrol boats would be rotated between assignments, there wouldn't be much liberty.

To Jack's amazement, he learned of the construction of two massive artificial harbors. Some of the construction materials had already started arriving in France. There would be tugs, barges, construction crews and pier components going to France daily. The goal was to get them open as quickly as possible. Coast Guard patrol boats would stay on station at the construction sites throughout the project. The artificial harbors, called Mulberrys, would be in use until Le Harve, Cherbourg and finally Antwerp were captured and their port facilities repaired.

When the briefing was breaking up Commander Stewart said: "Senior Chief Trevenen, I need a word with you before you leave."

Jack waited until the others had left and then asked Stewart: "Sir, have you had any news about Mr. Stonecliffe, or my wounded Gunners Mate."

Stewart said: "Yes, that's what I wanted to tell you. Mr. Stonecliffe is coming back to us before the end of the week. I want you to remain in command until then. Your Gunners Mate was not so lucky. He has a bad leg wound and will be going back to the States. Stonecliffe and he are in the same hospital and Stonecliffe can fill you in upon his return. How are the repairs coming?"

Jack said: "We are in the process of getting parts and other materials to make the necessary repairs. I'd say two to three days to get us operational. I'll know more tonight."

Stewart said: "Good. Keep me informed. Can you get by with your Third Class Gunners Mate for the time being? Getting a replacement for McCauley will take some time."

Jack said: "We'll manage, sir."

Stewart turned to leave the room, but as he did he said: "Let me know if you have any trouble procuring parts."

Jack went back to the boat and had a meeting with the other crew members. He passed on his understanding of their patrol assignments in the coming weeks. They would be assisting cross Channel shipping and patrolling the French coast. Then he told them of the two "Mulberry" artificial harbors. One would be built at Omaha Beach, and the other at Gold Beach in the British sector. Part of their duties would be to assist with any marine casualties, towing or men overboard during the construction of the Omaha Beach harbor.

Spencer groaned: "Not Omaha Beach. I'd hoped we'd never see that nightmare place again."

Jack said: "Settle down. No one will be shooting at us this time. It should be fairly decent duty. These harbors are huge. The break walls are made up of scuttled ships and huge cement caissons that were built in various English ports and are being towed over. It sounds like the break walls are close to a mile offshore. There are four pierheads inside the break walls with docks on them. They are connected to the beach by six miles of flexible floating roadways held up by pontoons. The two middle pierheads are connected to each other by a long dock. Multiple cargo ships can tie up and unload cargo at once. The docks built on the pierheads are being built on steel spuds sunk into the ocean floor. The dock can move up and down on these spuds to account for the tides."

Vincent said: "Are you sure about this? It doesn't seem possible to build such a thing."

Jack said: "It is amazing. You know what they say, compared to war all other human endeavor pales."

Ritt asked: "Did anyone say anything about how long we keep this up? These boats can't take a pounding everyday and keep going forever."

Jack said: "We are here for the duration as far as I know. The artificial harbors will stay in use until the major ports are captured and put in working order. But the resupply effort across the English Channel will last until the end of the war. The patrol schedules keep us busy so there won't be a lot of liberty. Let's get this boat in good order and enjoy the next couple evenings as they may be the only liberty for a while. Mr. Stonecliffe gets back shortly and I want us squared away by then."

The crew settled in to repairing the patrol boat and good progress was made. Jack now had full responsibility for all the paper work. The requisitioning went smoothly, at least for the engine parts. The Coast Guard had foreseen that need and sent a wealth of replacement parts for the engines with the Flotilla. Jack paid out of his own pocket for the glass to fix the pilot house windows. Spencer had to get that from a civilian source--the local ironmonger.

There were after action reports that needed to be typed and given to command. Jack was able to reconstruct June 6, D-Day, in a fairly unemotional manner. The report took him most of a day and he had flash backs a few times as he tried to write about the rescues. The flashbacks were upsetting and caused him to perspire. By the time he was done with the report his hand tremors were back. In all, he believed they were responsible for saving seventy-one men at Omaha Beach. Vincent typed up his draft. Jack showed it to Russell for his comments. Like Jack, he didn't want to relive the day, and said nothing after reading it.

By the end of Thursday, the second day of repairs, the boat looked like it did before the invasion. The pilot house glass had been replaced. Any bullet or shrapnel holes had been patched and painted. The blood stains had been largely removed. There would be a residual stain in places that would remind everyone of "Bloody Omaha". One engine was running smoothly and Ritt was closing in on the second. Commander Stewart was coming down for an inspection in the late morning on Friday. Jack pushed everyone to get the boat ready. He knew they were under scrutiny and were needed to be operational as soon as possible.

Jack gave the crew liberty in the evenings. For the most part they went to the Lion and Cross. Jack had not seen Diana since he left her flat. He didn't want to set a bad example for the crew by spending each night ashore with his lover. He wanted to be near the boat if there was an emergency or a recall. He also had to admit to himself that he was conflicted about the relationship. Diana had been kind and supportive. She was a wonderful lover. But Jack wasn't sure this was the time or place to start a relationship that he wouldn't want to end. The damn war consumed people.

Diana was on her way to work at the Lion and Cross late Thursday afternoon. She decided to go down to the quay and see if Jack's boat was in. Jack had just put down liberty for the crew. But Jack, Spencer and Bollinger were still aboard getting ready for the next morning. Diana walked over to the boat and was immediately spotted by Spencer.

Spencer called to Jack: "Chief, you need to come topside. You have a guest."

Jack came out of the pilot house. Diana asked: "Can I come aboard?"

Jack was surprised and a little flustered, but said: "Yes. There isn't much to see. Just a working patrol boat."

Jack walked Diana through the pilot house and galley and then back topside to the steering station. Diana was impressed with how small and compact the boat really was. She thought how brave these men must be to go out in bad weather in such a small vessel. Diana noticed some of the bullet holes that had been patched. She was frightened for Jack.

Jack asked Spencer: "Can you keep an eye on things for a little while. I want to walk Diana to the Lion and Cross."

Spencer said: "Sure Chief, take your time."

As they walked back to the pub Jack said: "I'm still the Acting Commanding Officer and I doubt I'll get away to be with you. When Stonecliffe gets back I may have more freedom, but we should be operational by then and out on patrol. So I don't know when we can spend a day, or night, together. I want you to know you are very good for me. I think of you and want you beside me."

As they walked Diana listened and it made her sad. She wanted to escape into Jack's arms. But the war wouldn't allow it. Diana looked at Jack with sad eyes and said: "I understand. We both have responsibilities. I am going to go up to London next week and visit your Embassy to see how I get a visa for America."

Jack smiled and said: "Let me know what happens. I hope you get there, if that is what you want. I wouldn't recommend the Upper Peninsula of Michigan, at least not without me by your side. Too much snow. I think you'd be better suited for Virginia."

That brought a smile to Diana's face. They were at the pub. Jack embraced her. Diana whispered: "Be careful darling. Let me know when you can get away so we can be together."

Jack went back to overseeing the readiness of the patrol boat for inspection. He stayed aboard that night, although seeing Diana awoke his sexual desires and he almost left and went to her. But his sense of duty won out and he spent a restless night aboard in his cramped bunk.

Friday saw Stonecliffe arrive. Jack thought he looked fit and rested. His wounded arm remained in a sling, however. He greeted each member of the crew warmly. Looking around the boat, he complimented them on the work they had done to repair the damage. Ritt proudly started both engines and they ran smoothly. Commander Stewart arrived shortly thereafter and inspected everything, thoroughly. He had no major complaints. He also complimented Jack and the crew. Commander Stewart was invited for lunch. He and Mr. Stonecliffe, along with the enlisted men enjoyed a special seafood feast Williams had been planning for this day.

After lunch Jack and Stonecliffe finally had a moment alone. Jack asked: "How are you, really?"

Stonecliffe said: "I'm fine. Technically I'm on light duty for a few more days, but with this crew and our assignments I don't see a problem. I'll have to be careful. I don't need the sling all the time, and I have full range of motion."

Jack said: "I'm glad to hear it. I didn't want to lose you. We are a happy crew and a new commanding officer could change that. What about McCauley?"

Stonecliffe had a sad look come over his face. He answered:" The leg wound got infected and initially the doctors were worried he might lose the leg. That worry seems to have passed and he is scheduled out on a hospital ship to the States along with other D-Day wounded. We'll have to get along with just Harry Turner for a while. I don't see that as an issue, do you?"

Jack said: "No. Harry can handle our light armament. I can tighten the watches a little to make up for being a man short."

Stonecliffe asked: "How was it after I lost consciousness? We were having a rough time of it before then."

Jack gave Stonecliffe a vacant look and then simply shook his head and said: "It didn't get any better until the troops finally got off the beach. Even then there was the dead and dying to contend with. The Higgins boats were constantly coming and going and sometimes needed help. It is a day we all want to forget."

Stonecliffe asked: "What about your health?"

Jack said: "I was pretty well gone by the time we got back to Poole. The younger guys were doing better. I get bad dreams that will sometimes wake me. I see all those dead soldiers staring at me, as though we somehow failed to rescue them." Jack paused and considered whether to share his next thought, but decided to do so. "I spent the first night back at Diana's flat."

Stonecliffe knew it was hard for Jack to admit these things. He paused then said: "I think our part of the war settles down after a month or so and the patrols become routine. The Germans are on the run and I don't think they are going to give us much business in the Channel. You might get liberty to go to Cornwall for a weekend. Diana might like that."

Jack just smiled.

Stonecliffe added: "Let's visit the fuel dock and then take the Six Boat out for a short run just to make sure all is working as it should. But before we do that let me tell you what a fine job you did assuming command and bringing the boat and crew in safely."

Jack solemnly shook Stonecliffe's hand. Jack was without words.

At dawn on June 10 the Six Boat headed back to Omaha Beach to take station near the construction of the artificial harbor. The weather was more spring like. The trip over was almost pleasant. Jack was anxious. He wasn't sure how he or the other men would react to seeing the place of so much death and destruction.

When they arrived the invasion beach had changed. It had grown into a small port. The beach and the bluff line were there, but the beach was lined with LST's offloading men and vehicles. The roads off the beach had been opened up. Trucks, men and equipment were continuously moving off the beach. The barrage balloons still flew. Support ships stood off shore. It was a beehive of activity.

The crew of the Six Boat was impressed with the work that had already been accomplished on the artificial harbor. The break wall was almost done. One pierhead was open. Jack noticed McKeil's ship had not been towed back to England. It had sat off Omaha Beach half flooded. Then it was towed to a location to form part of the break wall, and scuttled. Several other ships had been similarly used.

The sight of the scuttled ships caused Jack to flashback. He was still troubled by McKeil's death. He felt guilty for not saving him. McKeil had been at sea all his life. He bore its inevitable scars; drunkenness, contemptuousness, selfishness, self-delusion. But Jack thought he died with dignity. He knew it was time to go. He simply let go of the wood he was clinging to, and slid under the sea. He never said a word or changed his expression. Jack thought it fitting both McKeil and his ship rested together.

CHAPTER THIRTEEN
HOMEPORT

More than a week had passed since Diana had been interviewed about Hawes' death. She had heard nothing from the authorities. Each morning she had left her flat she expected to be arrested, but nothing happened. She began to think the police might not check up on her past.

Diana had also not made any contact with her network, or sent any reports or messages. She felt if she was under suspicion she should not do anything that might draw attention to herself. Truthfully, there wasn't much to report. Poole remained an embarkation point for men and material going to France. But it was nothing extraordinary. She could have passed on some information about army units, or ship movements. However, Diana was convinced this information would really make no difference. She saw the war as lost and she was of no importance.

Diana had taken a day off from both her jobs and rode silently in a train headed to London. The passenger car was crowed--standing room only. It was only through the courtesy of a young British Army corporal that she had a seat. He had given her his seat. He had stood in the compartment for a while trying to make conversation with her, but gave up after her clipped responses. He left to go have a smoke. Diana was preoccupied with the idea she might be able to go to the United States. The American Embassy was her destination.

Getting from the railway station to the Embassy took longer than she expected. The walk was much longer than she realized and she ended up using a taxi. The Embassy was busy and a receptionist directed her to the second floor where she entered an office that had a sign on the door reading VISAS. Other people were ahead of her waiting their turn in line. Diana noted they were mostly women.

There was a counter with a young man behind it. He was nicely dressed in a suit. He was clean shaven and his hair nicely cut. Diana could hear the conversations with the women ahead of her. Based on what she could hear Diana learned most of them were marrying American servicemen and wanted to go to the States.

After a long wait it was Diana's turn. She took out her British passport and said: "I would like to know what I need to do to get to the United States, to stay there and live there. I'm very employable. I have bookkeeping and accounting skills."

The young clerk was going to give her a form to fill out but thought it might not be necessary. He asked: "Are you a British citizen?"

Diana said: "Yes."

The man continued: "Any family or dependents in the United States? Or about to marry a US citizen?"

Diana said: "No."

The man said: "We have work visas for special occupations, but not yours. Travel visas for short visits are possible, but you want to stay. With the war on things are difficult. Your situation doesn't fit our requirements. I would suggest you check back with us in a few months. Look on the bright side. You won't have to risk a dangerous crossing of the Atlantic Ocean. The U Boats are still sinking ships."

Diana's heart sank. She knew she had no way out of her circumstances. It was as though she had been handed her death warrant. Diana's eyes became a little teary. She put her passport in her hand bag and took a deep breath. Then she looked at the clerk and said: "Thank you."

As Diana turned away the Clerk said: "I'm sorry miss, I really am. But you are better off in England at the moment."

Diana didn't get back to Poole until late. She lay on her bed thinking about Jack. Could she ask him to marry her? Marriage would get her a visa to the United States. No, Jack wouldn't do it. Even if he considered it she would have to tell him everything and that would end the relationship. Besides, marriage would attract attention to her. Either British or German Intelligence might come after her. She thought she might leave the country through Ireland, the same way she had come to England. But there was still a problem with a visa to get to another country. She had no one to forge documents. Besides, where would she go?

Diana was sure McKeil would have taken her aboard his ship, without any questions. Now that door was closed. She doubted if she had time to develop a relationship with another ship captain.

Diana just closed her eyes and longed for sleep. She relived her lovemaking with Jack. That seemed to calm her. She reconciled herself to waiting for the next turn of events. She finally slept.

As the following days passed Diana watched for Jack in the Lion and Cross, but he didn't come in. More than once Diana went down to the quay and looked for Jack's boat, but it was always gone. She missed him and assumed he was alright since no one in the pub had talked of anyone being killed or wounded. Many other patrol boat crews came in.

Late one afternoon Diana was in the Lion and Cross helping to wash glasses behind the bar. She looked up and saw Gromek standing alone at the far end. Diana's heart leapt. She slowly but deliberately walked toward him.

Gromek smiled his toothy grin and said: "Cousin Anna misses you."

Diana poured a drink for Gromek and then said: "And I miss her. I haven't seen you for quite some time. Are you well?"

Gromek said: "Yes, I'm fine. Perhaps you still visit the park mornings?"

Diana knew he wanted a meet. A park bench struck her as safe. Diana said: "I'll be in the park tomorrow before nine. I can go there before work."

Gromek smiled at her. Diana left him to go back to washing glasses. Gromek finished his drink and left.

The next morning Gromek sat on a park bench. Diana walked up and sat down. Gromek didn't look at her. He just said quietly: "No one has heard from you in over two weeks. We thought you may have been arrested."

Diana had thought about what she would say all night. She wasn't going to lie. She was still loyal. Diana answered: "Shortly after Hawes died the police came and interviewed the employees at his business. That included me. There was a Major present from British Intelligence. He had the codes Hawes took from my flat and must have kept in his office. I thought it best to stay out of sight and not contact anyone. Besides, nothing of any great importance has happened here since the invasion."

Gromek paused. This news troubled him. Then he asked: "What did you tell them?"

Diana answered: "I told them nothing. I said all I knew was from the newspapers or office gossip. They seemed satisfied and have not been back. If they check my full background there may be problems."

Gromek asked: "Did they say anything about me?"

Diana said: "Not specifically. From the questions they asked it seemed as though they thought Hawes' death might not be an accident. My impression is they do not know who was involved, or why."

Gromek was silent for a few minutes while he digested this news. Diana could be under surveillance and now he might be exposed by meeting her. He had a flash of anger against Diana he carefully controlled. Gromek stood up and without looking at Diana said: "We will be in touch." Then he strolled off.

Diana sat for several minutes. Then she got up and started slowly walking to Hawes' to do her morning bookkeeping. Diana was worried.

The policeman assigned to surveil Diana noted the time of the meeting in his notebook.

The Six Boat was underway everyday it seemed. Jack was more relaxed and many of the patrols were not stressful with summer weather and gentle seas. Jack especially liked patrols along the English coast. The rocky cliffs and green fields above them were beautiful. The escort of the tugs and barges bringing construction materials from England to France for the artificial harbors was tedious. Sometimes they didn't do more than 3 or 4 knots due to the heavy loads on the barges. Many days were spent in France at the site of the construction of the artificial harbor. They stood by to assist in emergencies, that to Jack's relief, were few. Occasionally, there was a construction worker who fell in to the water, or a man overboard from one of the ships. Sometimes they had to provide a tow. They did limited patrols on the French coast watching for enemy movement.

Stonecliffe improved rapidly and discarded his sling. The rest of the crew seemed content and Williams made sure they were eating well. They had not had much liberty, but the artificial harbor at Omaha Beach was finished in record time and was fully functional the first week after D-Day. That resulted in less demands on the patrol schedules and Jack looked forward to seeing Diana. It looked like they would be back in Poole for three days on June 19. Before that they had to go to Portsmouth and assist the Coast Guard units in that area. They also had to keep an eye on shipping heading to the artificial harbor at Gold Beach in the British sector. The crew got evening liberty in Portsmouth and found one or two pubs where they could make themselves at home.

On the morning of June19 the Six Boat was proceeding west along the French coast from the artificial harbor at Gold Beach. It was heading to the artificial harbor at Omaha Beach. From there they would escort a small convoy back to Poole. Everyone looked forward to three days rest. As they motored along both Jack and Russell noticed the weather looking sour. The barometer was dropping and a heavy cloud deck was moving in from the north northeast. The weather reports the day before had predicted some wind and rain, but nothing too serious.

Jack went below and saw Stonecliffe in the galley getting some coffee. Jack said: "I think we are in for some weather. I'm not familiar with these waters, but both Russell and I sense a storm coming."

Stonecliffe didn't look too worried. He said: "The weather forecast doesn't seem to say we are in for anything too terrible."

Jack answered: "I know, but we may need to batten down fairly quickly. Let's pass the word there is a storm coming and get everything stowed properly."

Stonecliffe nodded his approval. He ordered some more speed as he wanted to get to Omaha Beach ahead of any weather.

By the time they arrived off Omaha Beach and its artificial harbor, the weather had gone to hell. The sky was dark grey. The wind had picked up and lashed the patrol boat with heavy rain. There was a four or five foot sea running and visibility was poor. The deteriorating weather kept the ships at the pierheads from unloading as the floating dock was rising and falling. The floating roadways were also rising and falling. Stonecliffe radioed command that the Six Boat would stand by until the storm passed.

But as the afternoon wore on the wind increased and the seas were even higher. Many of the waves swept over the break walls.

The ships inside the break wall moved off the dock face and tried to anchor. After a short while the ships didn't like not having any sea room. One or two were dragging their anchors. They moved outside the break wall to ride the storm out in the open Channel.

There were small craft and Higgins Boats in the harbor that broke loose. The Six Boat could do little as there was no place to take them even if they got a line on them. They just washed up on the beach. A dock worker was swept by a wave into the sea. With a nice bit of boat handling the Six Boat was able to pull him from the water.

There was an Army truck stopped on a piece of the floating roadway about halfway to shore. The roadway was bouncing up and down as the pontoons on each end of it rose and fell with the ever higher waves that swept under them. The driver was out of the truck and trying to keep his balance on the pitching roadway. He was waving his hands frantically at the Six Boat.

Stonecliffe and Jack were both topside for better visibility. They were drenched and the rain stung as it struck their faces. The water ran off their oilskins in rivers. Russell had the helm. Jack looked at Stonecliffe and yelled in his ear to be heard over the sound of the wind: "I think we can get that driver. We can't get near that tossing roadway, but we could throw him a line and pull him aboard."

Stonecliffe yelled back: "I don't think we have enough water at the bottom of the wave trough in that close. I don't want to put us on the beach."

Jack said: "Are you willing to leave him?"

Stonecliffe waited a moment then yelled: "Alright, we'll try. But first tell Ritt I want all the power he's got if we have to back away suddenly from the roadway. We'll have to go in, quickly turn upwind, and then throw him a line. These break walls don't give us much protection from the surf."

Jack nodded and went below to tell Ritt the maneuver. Then he and Stonecliffe told Russell the plan. He nodded he understood.

Russell took the Six Boat parallel to the roadway and then turned to head in toward the stranded truck. Spencer got a rope and monkey fist to throw to the driver. Jack said: "I'll go forward and throw it, put a life line on me."

Spencer said: "Sorry Chief, that's my job. You old timers might get yourself drowned."

Jack paused, then said: "Alright, but be careful. That foredeck is slippery. Let me put a life line on you."

Russell turned and brought them into the wind neat as you please. The patrol boat was being pushed by wind and wave, but Russell used the engines to hold the boat steady for a moment. Spencer made a perfect throw. The driver picked up the line but couldn't bring himself to leap into the water. Jack and Spencer waved for him to come to the boat. Russell couldn't hold the position without the patrol boat breaching. He had to power away. The driver let go of the line and Spencer brought it aboard.

Spencer yelled in Jack's ear: "That son of a bitch is going to get us drowned."

Jack said: "He is just scared. We'll make another try. Get ready."

The Six Boat went in for another similar try. This time the driver got the idea he was going to be left to drown if he didn't jump into the water and let them pull him over. Tying the rope around his waist he leapt. When he surfaced Spencer already had him halfway to the boat. Jack and Spencer pulled him alongside and then lying on the deck were able to pull him up from the water. As Russell turned and pulled away Stonecliffe felt the boat, forward, touch the sand bottom under them.

The Six Boat went to anchor in the lee of the remnants of the break wall. The concrete caissons that formed the break wall near them weren't moving. They had protection from the driving wind and waves of the full blown nor'easter. All that night the storm raged and the wind moaned. No one slept. They had two anchors out. They constantly took a round of bearings to make sure they weren't being driven on to the lee shore. Ritt inspected the bilges but didn't see any flooding or structural damage from the grounding.

The two men they rescued stayed on board. The boat was bouncing too much to allow Williams to make a hot meal. He was able, after a fashion, to make some coffee and sandwiches. They all waited for daylight thinking about their lost liberty back in Poole.

The following dawn revealed heavy damage to the artificial harbor. The break wall was swept away in places. The pierheads were damaged. Some of the spuds in the ocean floor that held up the dock were standing at an angle. One of the docks was partially submerged. Some of the anchors holding the pontoons in place had been dragged or the anchor lines had broken. Thus, some of the pontoons were swept away and the sections of roadway they held up were sunk. All in all, it was a dismal sight.

The storm continued all that day. Stonecliffe radioed he was staying at anchor. Later they learned from radio traffic two Coast Guard patrol boats had foundered in the storm, but the crews were safe. Jack and his crew spent another long night waiting for the weather to clear.

Finally, on June 21 the storm abated. They got the two men they rescued ashore. The damage to the artificial harbor had continued throughout the storm. As the Six Boat slowly motored out of the harbor to head for Poole, it was obvious the harbor was wrecked and could not be used.

The Channel crossing was far from smooth and they could not make good time. There was still a good sea running and at times the seas were confused making it hard to know how to best handle the patrol boat.

At one point Jack looks at Stonecliffe and said: "I don't know what the plans are for us but these boats can't take this much wear indefinitely. This is two bad storms in June! I can hardly wait to see what the fall and winter bring."

It was almost dark as the Six Boat approached Poole Harbor. Vincent was sick and in his bunk. Carpenter was covering the radio. Stonecliffe was topside. Carpenter came up and said: "We got a message for you, Mr. Stonecliffe. Commander Stewart wants to see you as soon as we tie up."

Stonecliffe said: "Thanks." He turned to Jack who was standing nearby and asked: "I wonder what this is all about?"

Jack shrugged and said: "It is probably a new patrol assignment. I'm sure they think we had our liberty at Omaha Beach while riding out the storm."

They entered the harbor and tied up in their usual spot at the quay. Stonecliffe changed into his dress uniform to go and meet the Flotilla Commander. He said to Jack: "While I'm ashore fuel and provision the boat. See if Vincent wants to see a doctor. I want to be ready to get underway in case this is a quick turn around, and they are sending us right back out."

Jack smiled and said: "Aye, aye sir. Tell them we want to patrol the Cornish coast. There are lots of little seaports along there where we would like some liberty!"

Stonecliffe smiled back. Jack waved as Stonecliffe quickly went up the street and disappeared around a corner.

Jack got the boat ready for patrol as ordered. The crew was not happy. They wanted to stay tied up, get some hot food and a good night's sleep. An hour or two at the Lion and Cross wouldn't hurt either.

Stonecliffe was back in about an hour. He had a worried look on his face. He went below and announced they were not getting underway, and would stand down for 36 hours. Other than the men who had the duty, the liberty lamp was lit. Needless to say, the boat cleared out as most of the men headed for the Lion and Cross. Jack was tired, but wanted to see Diana. He changed into a clean uniform and decided he was going ashore. He hoped Diana wasn't working late.

Stonecliffe stopped Jack and said: "I need to talk to you. Let's go topside, back by the stern, out of everyone's hearing."

They went back aft and Jack asked: "What's going on?"

Stonecliffe looked troubled. He took a moment to compose his thoughts before he spoke. Then in a quiet voice he said: "There is no good way to say this. The Commander informed me Diana Winter is a German spy. He wouldn't tell me what they had on her, but they are going to arrest her soon. You are to say nothing to anyone and stay away from her. That is an order from the Flotilla Commander."

Jack was stunned. After a long pause he said: "That is not possible. It couldn't be. I'd have recognized her as a German operative. She never even wanted to talk about the war. Like the rest of us, she is just weary of it and wants it all to end."

Stonecliffe said: "She wants it to end alright, she just has a different view than you and I as to who should win." Stonecliffe paused. Neither said anything. Then Stonecliffe added: "Jack, you could be in trouble here. The authorities know you two liked each other. It makes it appear as though you might be helping her, either innocently, or purposefully. I don't think they know you slept with her. I didn't volunteer that. They didn't ask me about it directly. But if I'm asked I have to tell the truth."

Jack was beginning to get angry. He raised his voice slightly and looking directly at Stonecliffe he asked: "Do you think I gave away secrets? Hid the identity of a German agent? All so I could get a great piece of ass?"

Stonecliffe said: "Of course not. I argued on your behalf when I was told all this. The best thing you have going for you is the fact you don't have any secret information to reveal. You are only a chief petty officer tasked with keeping this boat running. You are a damn good boat driver and leader of men. You have a spotless record. Your bravery in the past few weeks is recognized by all. But a woman like that can taint you."

Jack was clearly agitated. He hadn't realized how much he had looked forward to being with her. He said in an argumentative and loud tone: "The hell with all of this. It's complete bullshit. It is just the over active imagination of some junior officer in the intelligence business. I was going to see Diana tonight, and still am."

Stonecliffe said firmly: "Senior Chief, if you do I'll call the shore patrol and have you arrested. You are restricted to this boat. If you do as you are ordered this will all play out and no one will be accusing you as having a role in any of it. You need to accept the reality of the situation and the fact you can do nothing about it."

Inwardly, Jack collapsed. He hated the Coast Guard, the war, his life. He almost took a swing at Stonecliffe to vent his anger, frustration and sense of loss. But looking into Stonecliffe's' youthful face, he knew he couldn't strike him. Instead, he just abruptly turned, went below, took off his uniform and lay on his bunk. There he stayed all night. Staring at the bottom of the bunk above his.

The next day the crew of the Six Boat knew something had happened to disrupt their happy boat. Neither Stonecliffe nor Jack spoke. If either gave an order it was spit out in a brief clipped manner that invited no discussion. The two stayed away from each other and everyone else. The crew was glad they didn't have to go back out on patrol until the next day. Everyone hoped things would improve by then and stayed busy with various chores around the boat.

Later in the afternoon, Jack was sitting on a bench on the quay, next to the Six Boat. He was splicing a line. Spencer came up to him and said: "Anything I can do for you Chief?"

Initially, Jack ignored him, but then said: "You have liberty tonight. Go to the Lion and Cross. If Diana is working ask her to meet me outside the back door about 10 pm."

Spencer said: "I know she is working. I saw her briefly last night. She asked about you. She'll be glad to see you. I'll be sure to give her the message."

Jack said: "Thanks. But don't tell anyone I asked you to do this."

Spenser, smiling, said: "Sure Chief. I'm the soul of discretion."

Major Howard and Inspector Marshal had lots to do around the time of the invasion and Diana Winter had fallen to the bottom of each man's work load. But the records searches were now complete and Howard had all the information. Diana, or whatever her true name was, was not born in England, and her passport was a forgery. She had no work record before Hawes. Major Howard had sent a man around to where her employment application said she went to school. The report said she had never been a student there, at least not by the name Winter.

Inspector Marshal had sent a copy of his surveillance report over to Howard. It showed Diana was a somewhat solitary person. A good employee who kept to herself. A plain clothes officer had spent a little time in the Lion and Cross trying to pick up some gossip about her but didn't learn much. She socialized a little with an enlisted man off one of the American patrol boats that tied up in the harbor. Howard chuckled. She wouldn't learn much from him.

Inspector Marshal had talked to the American Flotilla Commander. The Commander was certain the enlisted man, a Chief Petty Officer, was loyal. He had an excellent service record. Howard thought he would interview the American sailor after he picked up Diana and interrogated her.

Major Howard was intrigued with the part of the report referencing the meeting Diana had with the man in the park. Could this be a German national named Ernst Wehling who was known to be in England? Howard was aware of a German agent who seemed to move around the West Country of England. He went by various names. Howard couldn't identify him as Wehling prior to this, but now he has a good description. Whoever this agent was, Howard could place him near one murder and one disappearance. Did he have anything to do with Hawes' so called accident?

The end of the report had the important finding. A plain clothes policeman had looked around Diana's flat while she was at work. It was neat and clean, but plain and not particularly well furnished. There was nothing incriminating. He had left. The officer then looked in the hall to see if there were additional storage areas for the flats in the building. He saw a door at the end of the hall. It led into the attic. He investigated and saw a case tucked away in one corner. He opened the case and found a short wave radio. He carefully put it back in place before leaving.

Howard now knew who sent the radio messages from that area to German Intelligence right before the invasion. He also knew why the German encryption codes were in her employment folder. Diana was possibly the reason Hawes was killed. The information he had in hand was more than enough to arrest Diana. He would ring up Inspector Marshal and arrange it for tonight, after she left work.

As 10:00 pm neared it was almost dark. The crew of the Six Boat was mostly ashore. Vincent was still not feeling his best so he took the night watch with Flaherty until midnight. They were sitting in the pilot house listening to music on a broadcast channel of the boat's radio. Stonecliffe had gone ashore and left word that if he was needed he would be at the officer's quarters that had been created in the small hotel up the street. Tomorrow they would go back out on patrol.

Jack was still aboard. He was thinking about what he would say to Diana. It was getting close to the time she got off work. He hoped Spencer had told her he would meet her outside the back door of the pub about 10 o'clock. Jack changed into a clean set of work khakis. Since D-Day he had taken to wearing his .45 caliber semi- automatic pistol in a shoulder holster rather than on his hip. It was less cumbersome-or noticeable. He checked to make sure the pistol was loaded and put the safety on. He put it in the holster under his left arm. He covered the gun and holster with a work jacket. He pulled on his peaked cap and went forward. He stopped to talk to Vincent.

Jack said: "I'm going ashore. If you are looking for me, try the Lion and Cross."

Vincent was surprised Jack was going on liberty. The scuttlebutt was he was restricted to the boat. Plus, Stonecliffe was ashore. He asked: "Chief, Mr. Stonecliffe has gone ashore. Doesn't he want one of you on the boat at all times in case we need to recall everyone and get underway?"

Jack said rather gruffly: "We are making an exception tonight. You know where we both are." With that Jack went topsides and left the patrol boat. Vincent went on deck and watched him leave, but lost sight of him in the darkness.

Diana was also watching the clock. Spencer had talked with her earlier in the evening and told her Jack would meet her out back after she got off work. They were busy tonight but she was going to leave at 10 o'clock regardless. Several merchant ships with war material had arrived from the United States. Diana had started to strike up conversations with some of the sailors. If one of the ships was going back to America she wanted to make a friend who might get her aboard, without the proper travel papers.

Diana finally told the bar keep she was leaving and headed for the back door. It was finally a warm evening and she didn't need a coat. Diana stepped out into the darkness of the side street behind the bar. She didn't see anyone so decided to wait for Jack outside. She lit a cigarette and drew deeply on the tobacco. Diana didn't know if Jack would want her tonight. But if he did, she too was anxious for more lovemaking. She had been thinking all day about how good he felt inside her.

Out of the corner of her eye Diana caught the movement of a man stepping out of the shadows. It surprised her. It wasn't Jack. The man walked up to her and she saw it was Gromek. Diana breathed a sigh of relief. She said: "You surprised me. I wasn't expecting you." Then she saw he had a pistol in his hand and it was pointed at her. She gasped and dropped the lit cigarette. Her hand came up to her throat in shock. Fear spread over her. Diana couldn't move or speak. She just stared at the dark outline of the pistol dreading the inevitable.

Gromek spoke: "You will come with me. To the building across the street, where we can talk in private. I don't want to kill you. But if you don't obey me you will die right where you stand."

Gromek motioned with the pistol for her to cross the street. There was a vacant building that had never been repaired after having sustained bomb damage earlier in the war. Diana nodded her assent and walked deliberately across the street and through an open door. Gromek pushed her into an interior room and closed the door behind them. He turned an electric torch on and stood it on the floor. Diana turned to face him. The light cast ugly shadows over both their faces.

Gromek cursed at Diana in German and then hit the side of her face with the pistol. Diana felt the sharp pain of the blow and fell to the ground. Diana was stunned. She pushed herself up on her side. Gromek kicked her in the kidneys, repeatedly. Diana cried out. Gromek turned her face up, kneeled over her, and began punching her face. Her mouth and nose were bleeding freely. Gromek stood. Diana tried to crawl away. He reached down and tore the back of her dress open and ripped the back of her brassiere in two.

Diana clutched the front of her dress and spitting blood said: "You won't like me like this. I will never let you enter me."

Gromek looked at her with scorn, then he said: "I wouldn't soil myself on a traitor like you." Then he tore off the top of her dress. She clutched at her brasserie tryng to cover herself, but Gromek pulled it away. Diana thought she was going to pass out. Gromek realized that too. He wanted her conscious. Gromek stepped back and waited for her to come around.

Jack had gone to the rear of the Lion and Cross. He didn't find Diana there. He waited a few minutes and then went inside and asked for her. The barkeep told him she had gone home for the night. Jack thought that was odd. Maybe she didn't get his message. Jack decided to head for her flat to see if she was there.

After several minutes Diana tried to sit up. She still lay on the floor, but was able to push herself up and hold herself up with one arm. She tried to cover her breasts with the other arm. She looked at Gromek and said: "Why are you doing this to me. I have done nothing wrong."

Gromek said: "We know you have been talking to British Intelligence. You admitted that to me. You are sleeping with the American sailor. He is in contact with their intelligence services. You are going to become their asset and spy on us. You were seen going into the American Embassy in London. Don't deny it. What I have done to you so far is just the beginning of our little visit. You must tell me everything about your disloyalty. That is the only way to save yourself."

Through the fog of her pain Diana realized she must have been followed to London. She didn't want to admit she was just trying to leave the country. He would kill her for that. But was it better than letting him think she had become a double agent? Her thoughts weren't clear and took time to come to her.

Gromek was getting impatient. Gromek pulled Diana to her feet. He raised his pistol and struck her face again. He smiled and said: "I have broken your cheek bone. Your beauty is marred forever."

Diana fell back to the floor. She mumbled: "I am not a traitor. I am not disloyal. I only wanted to leave. To get away from war."

Jack had almost arrived at Diana's flat. He could see the building ahead, but her light wasn't on. There was no point in going on, so he turned and headed back to the pub. As he neared the back entry he stood quietly in the dark and waited, hoping Diana might arrive. He heard something in the building across the street. A muffled cry. Jack walked across the street and saw an open entryway. The building was dark but there was a small light in one of the interior rooms. Jack pulled his pistol from its holster, took off the safety and walked into the darkened building.

Gromek was growing weary of trying to get Diana to talk. He took no pleasure in beating women. He completely torn off her dress and then her panties, but he had no sexual interest in her. He thought the degradation might cause her to talk. But it didn't. He was authorized to kill her. He thought it was time. Diana was lying face down on the floor bleeding. Gromek pulled her to her feet and pushed her back against the wall. Diana no longer tried to cover her nakedness. Her arms hung down and she was barely conscious. Her face and breasts were covered in blood. Gromek put the pistol barrel under her chin and said: "Last chance to talk, or you die."

At that moment Jack stepped through the doorway and saw the back of a man who was holding Diana's naked and bleeding body up against the opposite wall. The man held a gun to her. With steel in his voice Jack said: "No one is going to be doing any dying around here, unless it's you."

Gromek stood very still but turned his head enough to see Jack and his pistol. He turned his face back to Diana, smiled and said: "So you are not a traitor, eh? Why else would your American be here?" Then he pushed Diana away. She clung to the wall trying not to pass out.

203

Jack said: "I want you to drop the gun and turn around slowly."

Gromek didn't move for several moments. Then he spun around lightening quick and lowered his pistol at Jack. Jack hesitated wanting to make sure Diana wasn't in his line of fire. A shot rang out. The bullet hit Gromek in the chest throwing him backwards and causing his blood and tissue to spatter toward Jack. Gromek hit the wall behind him and then slid lifeless to the floor. Jack didn't know what happened. He hadn't fired. Gromek had moved too quickly. He turned and looked at the open doorway behind him. Major Howard stood there with a smoking pistol in his hand.

CHAPTER FOURTEEN
TIDAL POOLS

Jack was sitting in an interrogation room in the local police station. He had been brought here by Major Howard, who had also disarmed him. He was handcuffed. The handcuffs were attached to a metal fitting on the top of the table in front of him. The table was also bolted to the floor. Jack sat on a straight backed wooden chair which was very uncomfortable and made his back and legs ache. The room had no windows and was painted an institutional grey. Jack had lost track of time but thought it must be getting towards dawn.

Jack's head also ached, and he couldn't stop thinking about Diana falling naked and bleeding to the floor. Major Howard's pistol shot came back to him, as real as the moment it happened.

Jack's head was sunk on his chest and a tear formed in the corner of his eye, when the door opened and Major Howard came in. Jack immediately looked up. Howard was using his cane. Howard was having a long night as well.

Howard smiled at Jack and undid the handcuffs. It was hard to tell if his smile was kindly or admonitory. A policeman came in with two mugs of tea, sat them on the table, and left. Howard sat down in a chair on the opposite side of the table from Jack. He said: "Sorry about the detention. We had a few things to sort out. We've not been introduced but I'm Major Howard. At the moment I'm attached to British Intelligence."

Jack took a drink of his tea. The warm liquid tasted good. Then he said: "I wasn't aware I had broken any laws."

Howard said: "The Poole police take a dim view of people walking around their streets at night with pistols under their arms."

Jack asked: "How is Diana?"

Howard answered: "She is in hospital, semi-conscious, and under guard. The doctor thinks she will recover. She may not look the same, but espionage is a risky undertaking. By the way, her real name is Angela Hofsteder. I haven't had a real crack at interrogating her yet, but I did get that out of her."

Jack realized any hope he had that Diana wasn't really a German agent was dying. His heart sank even further. He sat quietly for a few moments. He held tightly to the mug of tea with both hands. Then he said to Howard: "Thanks for saving my life. That was a nice shot. How long had you been there?"

Howard said: "We got there a short while ahead of you. We stayed out of sight to learn more about each of your roles in all this. Your name came up in our surveillance reports. You'll be glad to know I don't believe you are working for German Intelligence or even innocently helping the woman you know as Diana Winter. I had thought that all along, but hearing Diana accused of being a double agent and working for you convinced me. A man with your service record doesn't become a turn coat. Especially after being so courageous on D-Day, saving all those soldiers and sailors." Howard paused. He looked a little sheepish then said: "Besides, you have no access to classified information. Anything she could have learned from you she could have learned by observing the harbor, or chatting up any one of dozens of patrons in the Lion and Cross."

Jack asked: "So why am I still here?"

Howard said: "I need to know why you showed up when you did. Had you and Diana agreed to meet?"

Jack said: "Mostly it was coincidental. My commanding officer had restricted me to my patrol boat and told me to stay away from Diana. He said she was under suspicion for spying. I wanted to see her and find out the truth of the matter. I sent word for her to meet me outside the back door to the Lion and Cross when she got done working. When she didn't show I went looking for her. The rest you know."

Howard said: "So you disobeyed orders?"

Jack said: "Yes."

Howard had no particular reaction to that admission. Then he asked: "Do you love her?"

Jack thought carefully, then said: "I was very fond of her. If our lives had been more normal we might have grown to love each other. In my view the relationship hadn't gone that far. The war kept us apart."

Howard leaned forward intently. He asked "I need to know more about your time with Diana, what you observed about her activities? Who did she meet, talk to or talk about?"

Jack took Howard through the brief relationship. He made no reference to the night he slept with Diana. Jack did not want to violate their intimacy. He owed her that. Howard realized the time Jack and Diana spent socializing was minimal. In short, Jack created a picture of a reclusive woman who made no reference to her past and seemed to have no close friends. Jack made clear she was honestly weary of the war and wanted to go to America, thus her trip to the American Embassy.

Howard asked a couple of questions to clarify Jack's remarks. Nothing Jack said surprised him. The picture Jack created fit the pattern of German agents working in England. They kept a low profile and didn't let anyone get close to them who might want to know about their personal history. What was different here was Diana's desire to end her services to German Intelligence. Had she fallen for Trevenen? She was naïve to think she could walk away. That was her death warrant.

Howard asked: "Did Diana ever talk with you about this man Hawes, or his wholesale tobacco business?"

Jack said: "No. I know she worked there, but that is all."

There was a pause while Howard made some notes. Then Jack said: "May I ask you a couple of questions?"

Howard said: "Yes, but depending on what you want to know I may not be at liberty to answer."

Jack nodded that he understood then asked: "What do you believe her role was as an enemy agent?"

Howard said: "Diana was simply the eyes and ears for German Intelligence in Poole. I haven't talked to her yet, but I'm sure she would report comings and goings of ships, troop movements, coastal defenses, that sort of thing. She wouldn't be high up in the German spy network, but agents such as her can develop valuable information."

Jack said: "I have to ask. Are you sure about these allegations?"

With an air of finality, Howard said: "We have her shortwave radio and encryption codes. Tonight we matched her fingerprints to the radio."

Jack sat silently.

Howard made a few more notes. Then Jack said: "Who was the man you shot? Why was he beating Diana?"

Howard said: "I don't know all the details, but I believe he was a German agent by the name of Ernst Wehling. I suspect the Germans thought she was defecting; maybe due to her time with you, the visit to the American Embassy, something else she did or said. Wehling must have been watching her too. He may have killed Hawes, although the motive is not clear. It may be tied back to Diana. By the way, let me give you another piece of advice. When you pull a pistol, don't hesitate to use it."

Jack, again, just sat silently.

Howard left the room briefly and then returned. He said: "At the moment I'm willing to give you your freedom. Unfortunately, your command isn't. They are making some noises about court martialing you. There are some members of your shore patrol who are here to take you to the American brig. I recommend you go along quietly. I'll give them your pistol."

Jack rose, and put on his hat. Two US Navy petty officers with shore patrol arm bands came in and said: "Senior Chief Trevenen, we have orders to take you into custody due to your unauthorized absence from your patrol boat. Come along with us."

Jack went quietly. He nodded at Howard as he left the room and said: "Thanks again for stepping in and saving my life."

Howard smiled and said: "Just doing my duty. You may need some help with your command. I'll be in touch."

With that, the shore patrol put Jack's arms behind his back, hand cuffed him and escorted him out the front door of the building. It was daylight. As the shore patrol walked him down the street, shame and humiliation overwhelmed him.

Jack sat on a steel cot in a cell in the US Navy brig just outside Poole. It was an old two story building with windows in the front. The Master-at-Arms had his offices on the first floor. After some brief paperwork Jack was taken to the second floor. There was a row of cells along the back wall. The cells had solid walls between each one. The front of each cell was made of steel bars with a swinging door, also made of steel bars. The back of the cell was the outside wall and had no windows. Jack could look out through the bars at the front of his cell and see a window on the opposite side of the corridor. It too had bars, but at least it let in a little natural light. There was a bucket in the corner of the cell for relieving yourself.

The two shore patrols who arrested him also put him in his cell. Jack asked for his Commanding Officer to be called. When this was ignored he asked to see a lawyer and demanded to know specifically what he was being charged with. This request was ignored at well. One of the shore patrolmen laughed at him and said: "If you know any lawyers, tell us their name and we will call them."

After the shore patrols left Jack sat alone with his thoughts trying to figure out what to do. A voice from one of the other cells asked: "Are you Navy?"

Jack said: "No, Coast Guard."

The voice said: "Me too."

Jack asked: "What are you in for?"

The voice answered: "Unauthorized absence."

Jack said: "What's your name?"

The voice answered: "Seaman Jacobs. I'm a Gunners Mate striker."

Jack asked: "Why were you UA?"

Jacobs said: "I was part of a Coast Guard gunnery crew put aboard a merchant ship to man a three inch fifty. The ship had the craziest captain. After our convoy got attacked by U Boats south of Ireland he decides we'd be safer on our own. He just up and leaves the convoy. The Convoy Commander couldn't get him to come back. The escorts were busy so they ignored us and away we went. We pulled into Poole all alone. Do you know how lousy the odds are for a ship alone? We made it, but I said I'd never sail with the son of a bitch again. So I walked off. That's why I'm here. That and a little disagreement with the shore patrol when they picked me up. Why are you here."

Jack said: "That's a long story we'll save for another time."

Jacobs said: "What's you rate?"

Jack said: "I'm a Senior Chief Boatswain's Mate."

Jacobs let out a low whistle then said: "Jesus, I thought Chiefs walked on water. The ones I knew told the officers what to do. You must be in a lot of trouble."

Jack said: "That remains to be seen."

At that point the two men became silent, lost in their own thoughts. Jack thought the sailor's story far fetched, and it certainly gave him no comfort. Jack had never been in trouble with the law and he was very worried. Not knowing what he was charged with, and not being able to do anything about it left him feeling helpless. He hadn't eaten or slept and physically he felt weak. His hand tremor was back. At times he felt nauseated. Then he thought of Diana. She must be in pain. Major Howard's comment she would never look the same haunted him.

At one point he was served a weak broth and a piece of stale white bread. Jack couldn't eat. He tried to sleep but he couldn't turn off his mind. It kept racing through the events that landed him here. Jack thought back to 1913. That was his first year in the service. It was a tough year too. But this was worse. Anxiety rose in Jack as he wondered if he would be imprisoned, or given a dishonorable discharge. Jack thought that couldn't happen. I haven't done anything that bad, have I?

By looking through the window Jack could tell it was evening. He heard doors opening and closing. Then Stonecliffe and a guard appeared in the corridor and walked towards his cell. Jack was embarrassed to have Stonecliffe find him like this. But he was glad to see him. Perhaps now he would learn more about what was planned for him.

Stonecliffe was saddened to see Jack behind bars. He thought Jack looked old and tired. The guard opened the cell door. Stonecliffe stepped in and the guard locked the door behind him. Stonecliffe asked: "Chief, how are you?"

Jack tried to grin and said: "I've been better. Can you find out why I'm here? I haven't been told what I'm charged with. The Brits had me all night and then the shore patrol brought me over here."

Stonecliffe said: "At the moment you aren't charged with anything. It took all day to get this mess settled. Initially, Commander Stewart wanted to Court Martial you for disobeying orders, breaking restriction and consorting with the enemy. But I argued against that. Major Howard cleared you of any involvement in Diana's espionage activities. As your CO I didn't want you charged with a court martial offense. Plus, there is a public relations aspect to your arrest."

Jack looked confused. Hearing he had no pending charges was a great relief. But he had to ask: "What do you mean--a public relations aspect?"

"You are a bit of a thorny problem. Based on our actions on D-Day the Commander put the boat in for a Coast Guard Commendation Medal. He also recommended you for a separate commendation for taking over after I was wounded and completing the mission. Coast Guard Public Affairs put out a press release touting our 'heroic exploits'. Stewart would look foolish if he turned around and charged you."

Stonecliffe shook his head and then continued: "The Naval Command got involved, as did Major Howard. Howard was very supportive of you and your cooperation. Other than ignoring my orders to stay aboard, there is really nothing that a court martial would convict you for. Your actions couldn't be construed as desertion. Your unauthorized absence can be handled at a Captains Mast which is a lot better for you. It also keeps the Coast Guard from getting a black eye in the press. Commander Stewart left you here while all this was being decided to make a point."

Jack felt relief wash over him. He asked: "We can leave here? Now?"

Stonecliffe said: "Yes, but there is more. You are relieved from duty on the Six Boat. There are more Coasties than patrol boats since two foundered in the storm. You are being replaced by a Chief Boatswain Mate from one of those. The Six Boat will also get a Gunners mate from one of them. You are assigned to the Flotilla admin staff. Stewart only has two Yeomen, and has a lot of new tasks. The loss of the patrol boats will produce two investigations, he has to take you to Mast, plus all the regular work. That should take a month or two to work through. Then you are being shipped back to the States and will be retired."

It took a few moments for Jack to take this all in. Going back home and getting to retire was a dream any sailor in Jack's position would normally welcome. But Jack felt like he was being throw away after decades of loyal service. And why, because he left his boat to go three blocks to talk to a woman who he thought innocent. If Diana had just been an ordinary waitress, Jack doubted if anything would have happened, other than Stonecliffe telling him not to do it again.

Stonecliffe watched as his words took a toll on Jack. The two men's roles had reversed. Jack had been the older of the two, the more experienced. Stonecliffe always consulted him on decisions of any importance. If Stonecliffe gave the crew an order the men would all look to Jack to see if he approved. Now it was Stonecliffe who was the stronger of the two. The one in charge.

Jack said: "Thanks for standing up for me with the Commander. We were always loyal to each other."

Stonecliffe said: "I know you are loyal. In fact, that's what caused all this. You tried to be loyal to Diana."

Stonecliffe called for the guard to let them out. He helped Jack up. He said to Jack: "You are being released in my custody. I thought it easier on you if you didn't have to come back to the boat tonight. The admin staff are billeted in the upstairs of a house near the Flotilla office. There is a bunk there for you. Spencer will bring your sea bag over. Just report to the Flotilla office at 7 am. Can you do that?"

Jack tried to stand up straight and said: "Yes, sir. Thank you."

The two of them left the building. Stonecliffe had a jeep and drove Jack to the house where he would be staying. They rode in silence.

Within a few days, Commander Stewart took Jack to non-judicial punishment, commonly called a Captain's Mast. He fined Jack one month's pay. He also restricted him to the Flotilla office, and the house where he slept, until transportation to the States was arranged. The whole proceeding didn't take a half an hour. Stonecliffe came as his representative. There was just the three of them present. Jack sensed the punishment had been decided upon well in advance.

When they were finished Stewart said: "Senior Chief, your rank and your retirement benefits are not affected by this proceeding. I take no pleasure in punishing you. However, I can't ignore the senior enlisted member of the flotilla fraternizing with a German agent. There is a war on. Stewart paused, then less sternly he added: "Your work here in the office the past few days is exemplary. Keep it up. You are dismissed."

So it ended. Jack became reconciled to his departure from England. The two Yeomen he worked with were good men but they were his only company. Jack couldn't go down to the quay and see the crew of the Six Boat due to being restricted. But they all came up to see him one evening. Stonecliffe and the two new men stayed aboard. The men were very supportive of him and teased him about getting to retire. Spencer particularly wanted him to stay in touch. He thought there might be business opportunities for them together after the war. Their new Chief was alright but it just wasn't the same without Jack. They had all been together for a long time, and the events of D-Day sealed that bond.

Most of the evenings Jack was alone. There was a small garden behind the house where he stayed and he could go out there and smoke his pipe. He often just lay on his bed reading, or thinking. He often thought of the moments he spent making love with Diana. He remembered Howard asking him if he loved her. He remembered his carefully phrased response that would not admit that level of affection. But now, he had to admit he was in love with her—or at least in love with what she represented. A young, vibrant, sensual woman who wanted him.

Getting Jack home was easier said than done since he didn't fit any typical transportation category. In the end he was given orders to board a civilian cargo ship leaving from Poole and joining a convoy heading back to New York. The sailing date was set in September. From New York he would go to Cleveland and the Ninth Coast Guard District offices to be discharged from active duty and retired. Jack thought about Diana. He was sure she wished she was heading for New York as well. Jack wondered what happened to her. They never would have met if there hadn't been a war. Jack wondered if they had met in another time and place whether she would have cared for him?

About a week before he was to leave Major Howard came to the Flotilla office to see him. Jack was surprised by the visit. Howard asked Stewart if he could borrow Jack for a while and naturally, Stewart agreed. It was sunny. The two strolled down to the quay. Howard didn't need his cane. Most of the Coast Guard patrol boats were out, but a few were tied up. The Six Boat was out.

Howard said: "The job you men performed is about done with the war moving east and the French ports open. I wouldn't be surprised if some of your fellow Guardsman will be following you home soon."

Jack said: "How did you know I had orders back to the States?"

Howard said: "I've been keeping track of you. I thought I might need you for Angela Hofsteder's trial. In fact, that is why I came today. To let you know this little episode is ended. You can go home with no worries. We never did decide exactly what happened to Hawes. But all the bad actors are accounted for so it really doesn't matter."

That comment gave Jack a start. He hadn't realized he was still part of an active investigation. He thought of Diana. He asked: "What happened to Diana after you arrested her."

Howard said: "She got out of hospital and was, of course, imprisoned. She was assigned a barrister on her behalf. We offered her a greatly reduced sentence for her cooperation. But she wouldn't talk. Not one word. The fact her fellow countrymen were willing to beat and murder her seemed to make no difference. Loyal to the end."

Jack said: "Maybe she thought she had to prove something, to herself."

Howard said: "She paid a big price. Angela, Diana as you know her, will spend the next thirty years in prison."

Jack gasped at the sentence.

Howard said: "She is lucky, she might have been executed. But her barrister convinced her to plead guilty to avoid the worst of the punishments."

Jack had to ask: "How does she look?"

Howard answered: "Her facial bones were broken and her classic beauty is marred."

Jack was silent. He looked across the harbor and briefly studied the merchant ships at anchor. The tide was coming in. The sea gulls cried overhead. Then the two men turned and walked back to the Flotilla office. They stopped outside. Jack said: "Thanks for all you did. I don't know how to repay you."

Howard shook Jack's hand and said: "No need to repay me. I'm happy to help a good Cornishman any day."

The two parted. Jack thought, I won't see him again. Suddenly he felt an overwhelming sense of loneliness and homesickness. It seemed to smother him. He'd had enough of the idiocy of war. Enough of soldiers and sailors dying in combat. Jack wanted to be home, with his own friends, amidst places that were familiar. He wanted to forget all that now surrounded him; to determine his own purpose in life.

Jack thought of Diana, sitting on a hillside on a warm afternoon watching the sunlight dance off the deep blue waters of the English Channel. Then he thought of her being caged, held like an animal, in the darkness of prison.

Madness, all madness.

1954

CHAPTER FIFTEEN

EPILOGUE

After Jack retired from the Coast Guard in the fall of 1944, he went back to the Keweenaw Peninsula. It had been his boyhood home. But he felt lost. The peacetime Coast Guard had been his real home. He missed the companionship of his fellow sailors. He had no sense of direction anymore. He questioned what role he still had in life. Combat had left its scars.

The copper mines in the area were all doing well due to the war. Great Lakes shipping was busy. Jobs were plentiful. But Jack just decided to live on his retirement pay for a while. He visited his old friends at the Portage Ship Canal Coast Guard Station. Chief Mike Duggan was still there. The Coast Guard had put a training center for new recruits on the station grounds two years earlier. Other Guardsmen were responsible for its operation, but Duggan still thought it was a "pain in the ass." It was all part of the Coast Guard growing by tenfold to meet the needs of the war.

When the winter of 1944-45 arrived Jack still wasn't working. The weather kept him from going outside, given the heavy snows. Mostly, he visited with Duggan. Sometimes he stopped at a local bar, but he wasn't much of a drinker. It reminded him of the Lion and Cross. He often thought about the crew of the Six Boat. At night, in bed, he would think about Diana and remember how good it felt to be inside her. His girlfriend from before the war, Dorothy, had married while Jack was away and now had two very young children.

Jack had buried his wife Catherine at Vermilion. When the weather broke, he borrowed a car and drove the two hundred miles to visit the grave. She was buried on the top of the first lakeward dune facing Lake Superior. The station at Vermilion was still manned and the crew cared for the little cemetery where Catherine and others were buried. Jack was flooded with memories. Despite the friendly welcome from the station crew, Jack was left feeling sad and very lonely. He stayed at the grave for almost an hour telling Catherine of all that had happened to him.

Upon his return, Duggan brought him the news that Coast Guard Rescue Flotilla One was disbanded in December, 1944. Their search and rescue mission had been completed. About thirty of the patrol boats in the match box fleet came home for further duty in American waters. The remaining patrol boats were given to the Royal Navy. The crews were assigned to other Coast Guard overseas assets or returned to the United States. Thus, Rescue Flotilla One became a footnote in history.

Jack eventually went sailing on a Great Lakes freighter hauling bulk cargoes. At one point his ship was unloading coal in the Saginaw River and needed assistance from a tug to depart. It was a pleasant day and Jack happened to be on deck as the tug nosed in to push his ship's bow towards the channel. He noticed a familiar face in the wheel house of the tug. It was Jimmy Spencer. Jack made a point of making inquiries and later that year Jack paid Spencer a visit in Bay City, Michigan.

Spencer gave him a warm welcome and they traded histories of their doings since each had last seen the other. Spencer had been sent back to the States after the Recue Flotilla had been disbanded. The crew all went to different assignments. He went to the Coast Guard icebreaker Mackinaw homeported in Cheboygan, Michigan. This was fine with him as he was from Michigan. After the war ended Spencer was discharged and went to work for an uncle who owned a tug boat. Shortly thereafter, the uncle retired and Spencer ended up buying the tug.

Spencer had plans to expand the company and acquire more vessels. He would need to hire good men. He offered Jack a job on the spot. Jack accepted. That was 1947. They had been together since then.

The plans Spencer expressed to Jack in 1947 had become a reality. The company had grown and had three tug boats and other work vessels that sailed all the Upper Great Lakes. The company offices were in Bay City, Michigan on the Saginaw River. When not underway, the tugs all tied up there as well.

Jack could hardly believe it was 1954. He sat at his desk in the company offices and looked out the window at a rainy morning. Jack was over 60 now and was slowing down. He had a Coast Guard license and could wheel any of their vessels, but only took the local runs. He couldn't take hours standing on a steel deck. Mostly, he took care of scheduling and overseeing the paperwork for each job. He was glad Spencer still considered him a benefit to the business. Spencer and the other staff were good friends to him.

Jack had gone completely grey, although he still had all his hair. He was still physically fit, but had put on weight. The lines in his face were deeper. Jack rented a small house in Essexville, near the mouth of the Saginaw River and Lake Huron. He bought a used car to commute to work. He had taken up fishing on Saginaw Bay and become quite good at it. Spencer kidded him and told him he could open up a charter fishing business in his retirement. It was a quiet life, and often lonely, but Jack managed to keep busy.

This particular morning Jack held an invitation in his hand. He read it, and then turned to Spencer who was also in the office and said: "Have you seen this invitation? It is for a ten year reunion of Rescue Flotilla sailors. It is going to be held in France, near the invasion beaches."

Spencer was in his mid-thirties and still had his boyish good looks. He was married with a young son. He turned towards Jack and said: "Yes, I saw it. I have no desire to see those places again. It will only remind me of agony and death. We were lucky. By all rights we should have taken more casualties to the Six Boat crew than we did. I still think about the men who died that morning."

Jack held the invitation in his hand. A tremor became noticeable. Jack had a flashback to Omaha Beach and the men dying in the water in the first assault wave. When he first retired he had these more often. He also had bad dreams. He would see the staring eyes of the dead soldiers as their bodies floated face up in the shallow water near the beach. Thankfully, these had also grown less numerous with time.

Jack said: "Stonecliffe is active in keeping the Rescue Flotilla members in touch. I heard he went to work for a chemical company in New Jersey and is one of their top executives."

Spencer smiled and said: "You should have stayed closer to him and you'd be nearing a second retirement from a big company on the East Coast instead of being a tug boat operator."

Jack smiled and said: "I'm doing just fine thank you. I wouldn't change a thing about my life. Besides, I think Stonecliffe had enough of me after he pulled me out of that Navy brig near Poole."

Spencer turned to go out and as he left he said: "Send whoever sent us the invitation our regrets and tell them we won't be able to attend."

In September of that same year Jack had a visitor stop by his house one Saturday afternoon. It was a perfect late summer day. Warm and sunny but with a hint of fall haziness in the air. The trees were just starting to show some color. Jack was washing his car in his driveway when a taxi from town pulled up. A woman got out and walked towards Jack. The taxi waited, engine running. Jack didn't recognize the woman. She walked up to him, extended her hand, and with a very English accent said: "Senior Chief Trevenen, do you remember me?"

The accent took Jack back in time. He wondered, could this be Diana? Diana was in prison. This woman had short hair that was completely grey. She had no figure. One cheek was slightly fuller than the other. Her eyes looked tired and her complexion was showing age. Jack said: "I'm sorry, I'm not sure who you are?" Jack didn't take her hand.

The woman lowered her hand and said: "My name is Angela Hofsteder. You knew me as Diana Winter. I know I have changed, and perhaps you don't care to see me. My taxi is waiting and I can go."

Jack was more than surprised. It left him without words for a moment. Then he said: "How did you get here?"

Diana said: "May I stay for a short while? Answering your question will take some time."

Jack said: "Of course, send your taxi on its way. We can always get another, or I can take you back into town."

Diana went to pay the taxi. Jack went inside and started the kettle boiling to make some hot tea for them. As he made the tea Jack thought carefully about this turn of events. Jack wasn't sure he wanted to see this woman. She had caused him a lot of trouble. Yet he wasn't angry with her. Perhaps he just didn't want her to see him—an aging sailor in a pair of dungarees and a white t-shirt washing an old car. But curiosity got the better of him. He wanted to know how she got there.

Jack heard the taxi pull away. After the tea was ready the two then went to sit on Jack's small front porch. You could see the river from there. It was quiet. Relaxing.

Diana said: "Thank you for talking with me. I'm sure you never expected to see me again." Hesitatingly, in a small voice she asked: "Did you learn I was a German agent during the time you knew me in Poole?"

Jack said: "Yes, I learned that. I tried to save you when you were being attacked by one of your fellow agents. Do you remember my pointing my pistol at him?"

Diana answered: "Vaguely. The beating gave me a concussion and my memory isn't the best. I was arrested and imprisoned after that. To avoid being executed I pled guilty. I never agreed to cooperate and tell the British authorities anything I knew about the German spy network. I was sentenced to thirty years. I think they thought that would change my mind about talking, but it didn't. Prison was a nightmare. Dirty, dark, damp and at times freezing cold. My face had been injured in the beating and the care for that was ignored. For many months it was hard for me to eat."

Diana paused. Jack could tell it was hard for her to tell the story. He sat without saying a word waiting to see if she would continue.

Diana sighed, then started again: "The other women in the prison hated me for being a German agent. At times I was segregated from the rest of the population for my own safety. At other times I became the lover of one or more of them to stay alive." Diana paused. Then she said: "I'm not a lesbian. Not anymore."

Jack could see the anguish in her. He said: "You don't have to tell me all this. It's over now."

Diana said: "Yes, I do. I want you to know. While I was in prison the world changed. West Germany became an ally of the British and Americans. The Russians were now the enemy. The war time prison sentences against many Germans seemed excessive or un-necessary. If nothing else it was costing money to keep people like me behind bars. After five and a half years my sentence was commuted and I was deported to West Germany. The economy there had recovered from the war years and I got a good job with an American manufacturing company in West Germany. Because I could speak English, German and a little French I became an executive assistant to the vice president. I often told him of my desire to go to America. When he transferred back to the company offices in Philadelphia he arranged for a work visa for me and I have been living and working there for almost two years."

Jack was stunned. He looked at Diana and understood the pain she had experienced. He thought about what Major Howard had told him all those years ago: "Espionage is a risky undertaking." He asked: "Why was the other German agent trying to kill you?"

Diana said: "My employer at the tobacco wholesaler, Frank Hawes, had been trying to blackmail me into sex. He found a copy of my encryption codes for radio messages in my things and kept them in the office. I reported that to the network. I think they had him killed. Maybe by the man who beat me. When I reported that I had been interviewed by the police and British Intelligence after Hawes' death, I think they decided I was a liability and worthless to them. That is why I wanted to go to America, to escape."

Jack sat for a few moments. Then Diana added: "I never slept with Hawes. He was a despicable man."

Jack didn't respond to that. Then he asked; "Why didn't you cooperate with the authorities after you were caught?"

Diana said: "I needed to be loyal. I felt I had failed somehow and I wanted, in the end, to be a good agent, a good German. It was all I had left."

Jack asked: "How did you find me?"

Diana smiled and said: "It was actually easy. Do you remember Carl Williams, the cook on your patrol boat? He opened a very successful restaurant in Philadelphia after the war. He has since opened one or two others in the area. I happened to see a newspaper article about his success. When I decided to try and find you, I remembered the article and called him. Apparently, there is a roster of Rescue Flotilla crew members for reunion purposes. He had a copy and gave me your business address. I'm on holiday and had time to come to Michigan. I stopped by your office and they gave me directions here."

Jack shook his head in amazement. He said: "Carl Williams, a successful restaurant owner. It seems everyone has done better than me. I don't know why you would want to see an old sailor like me again?"

Diana looked across the river. Then she turned to Jack and said: "You can't repeat anything I have told you. I don't want to dredge up the past, or cause any more pain, for anyone. I just wanted someone to know the story of what happened to me. I wanted someone who cared about me to know. That was you. I think you were the only man I ever loved. I was married once. A German pilot who was killed early on in the war. But he never treated me with the kindness you did. He never awakened my feelings the way you did."

Jack was a little embarrassed. He said: "Diana, we can't go back in time. Even if we could I have nothing to offer you." Jack then told his story of learning about her role as a spy, trying to save her from being shot, and then being arrested himself. All of which concluded in his removal from sea duty and eventual retirement.

Diana was saddened by Jack's story. She felt responsible, and a little guilty for causing Jack to be disciplined. She said: "I'm sorry dear Jack. Truly. I never meant to hurt you. I never involved you in any of my work, or repeated anything you might have said. I know you must have been humiliated and hurt by being relieved of your command."

They were both silent. Then Jack said: "Let's just let it all stay in the past. Try and enjoy the moment. Will you have time on your holiday to see any of Michigan? The Upper Peninsula has the most beautiful scenery. Very different than around here. Remember how I used to tease you about all the snow?"

Diana smiled. Then she said: "I have to return to Philadelphia. Jack, I have a cancer. I have a doctor's visit coming up. But I think it is really quite hopeless. I wasn't sure how much longer I would be able to travel like this, so I decided I had better come."

Jack didn't know what to say. Then he asked: "Do you have family who can be with you through your illness?"

Diana said sadly: "I have no family. My father was my only family. He lived in Dresden during the war. He died in the inferno created the night the Royal Air Force fire bombed the city."

Jack was quiet while he thought about what he could say to comfort her.

Then Diana added: "You say you have nothing to offer, but that is untrue. You gave me the riches of an honest and caring person who put me ahead of themselves. And I think you did love me, just a little, or you wouldn't have tried to save me that awful night when our lives changed forever."

They both sat quietly for a long time, enjoying the view. Diana had looked forward to this meeting for many months. Now it was here she felt disappointed, empty. The expectation had been greater than the reality.

Finally, Diana stood and said: "Perhaps you could drive me back to my hotel?"

Jack stood and said: "Certainly."

Before they left the porch Jack took her in his arms and held her for the longest time. Then they walked to his car and drove in silence to the hotel. When they arrived Jack got out and opened the door for her. He looked at her and quietly said: "When medieval cartographers drew a map of the world it was shown as flat. At the edge of the world they wrote 'Beware, Dragons Beyond this Point.' Both of us once went to the edge of the world. We saw the dragons, and for a time lived among them. But that is long past. Neither of us has anything to regret or seek forgiveness for."

Diana paused. She looked deeply into Jack's eyes and said: "Thank you."

They parted, but with a sense of closure. They never spoke again.

BIOGRAPHY

STEPHEN J. TRESIDDER is the third generation of his extended family to have lived or worked in Michigan's Upper Peninsula. The early generations were Cornish miners who knew the Keweenaw Peninsula well. Mr. Tresidder was a U S Coast Guard officer and served on the Great Lakes. He practiced law in Northern Michigan for many years. During that time he had an active trial practice which took him to several Upper Peninsula courts. He also served as a mediator. He was an adjunct faculty member at North Central Michigan College. He is retired and resides in the Harbor Springs, Michigan area. He devotes his time to photography and writing.